"A smashing debut m⟨...⟩ charming characters, and a plot that kept me guessing. Georgia Kelly is an adorable heroine whose clever wit and humor made me laugh out loud!"

—Jenn McKinlay, *New York Times* bestselling author of *Vanilla Beaned*

"Georgia Kelly is a plucky heroine whose love of stained glass, kittens, and her grandfather will draw you in and keep you turning pages. *Ill-Gotten Panes* is filled with small-town characters, intelligent cops, and a heroine who feels like a dear friend."

—Nancy J. Parra, author of *Newlywed Dead*

"Georgia makes an appealing lead character . . . Cozy fans may want to watch how this series develops."

—Booklist

"[A] sweet debut . . . This cozy will snag those intrigued by the stained-glass side of the story and a gorgeous cover (can't go wrong with Tiffany)."           —Library Journal

"A carefully plotted book, with enough suspects and possible motives to keep readers guessing throughout the book . . . This page-turner ended exactly as I had hoped it would, and I will be eagerly awaiting the next installment."

—MyShelf.com

"The mystery is a good one, with all bits and pieces coming together at the end, like a stained-glass design . . . I was glad to learn more about stained glass, how Georgia selects the glass, plans the design, and blends the colors."

—Kings River Life Magazine

*Berkley Prime Crime titles by Jennifer McAndrews*

**ILL-GOTTEN PANES**
**DEATH UNDER GLASS**
**A SHATTERING CRIME**

# A SHATTERING CRIME

## Jennifer
## McAndrews

BERKLEY PRIME CRIME, NEW YORK

**An imprint of Penguin Random House LLC**
**375 Hudson Street, New York, New York 10014**

A SHATTERING CRIME

A Berkley Prime Crime Book / published by arrangement with the author

ISBN: 978-0-425-26797-4

PUBLISHING HISTORY
Berkley Prime Crime mass-market edition / June 2016

PRINTED IN THE UNITED STATES OF AMERICA

10  9  8  7  6  5  4  3  2  1

Cover art by Stephan Gardner (Lott Reps).
Cover design by George Long.
Interior text design by Kelly Lipovich.

Penguin
Random
House

*For Tracy*

*For Christine*

# ACKNOWLEDGMENTS

I've thanked a lot of people along this journey, but this time around, I'm keeping it simple.

As always, my thanks to the team at Berkley Prime Crime for all they have done to bring Georgia Kelly and the little town of Wenwood to the world. Thanks to my family near and far, and to the writing and mystery community for their support, comraderies, and martinis. But mostly, my thanks to the readers—to those who worried about Georgia and Grandy and saw their town in the streets of Wenwood, and to those who took my words and put them in the hands of their friends and said, "Read this. You'll like it." I wish you joy.

1

The morning of the groundbreaking ceremony for the new Riverside Promenade—"a shopping and dining destination for friends and families"—I made the mistake of taking the weather forecast at face value. With this being my first autumn in Wenwood since a childhood visit in which my mother routinely over-dressed me in anticipation of subzero temps, my cute suede waist jacket was an easy mistake to make. Sure, I'd checked the news and watched the weatherman on Channel 6 predict we were in for a seasonably cool and breezy day with plenty of sunshine. I did not realize seasonably cool could mean flirting with the freezing mark and it was only breezy if you were hiding within or beside something that blocked the gusts of biting wind. There was indeed sunshine aplenty, and I was happy to have brought along my sunglasses "just in case," but there was no warmth to be found in the abundant rays.

This all means I stood jaw clenched to prevent teeth chattering, hands jammed in pockets of a coat more fashionable than functional, and knees braced close beside each other to keep my warmth to myself. The wind coming in off the river repeatedly stole my breath as it blew by, and I almost, but not quite, regretted the decision to attend the groundbreaking ceremony. Almost because of the aforementioned cold, and not quite because it had gotten me out of the house and allowed me the rare pleasure of spending time with Tony Himmel during the week and in daylight. A big change from our habitual evenings and Sundays.

Unlike me, Tony seemed to thrive in sunshine and outdoors regardless of the temperature and now stood content as you please in a plaid flannel over a faded UNC sweatshirt. He had needed little convincing to take a few minutes out of his day overseeing construction at the nearby marina to meet me at the groundbreaking. I made it a point to remind myself over and over that he had been willing to walk away from the job for a bit because of his fondness for being outside, and I placed very little import on his willingness to walk away because I asked him to. Believing I was not a priority for him was much easier on me. Once burned and all that.

Scary emotions aside, Tony stood close behind me and a little to the right, my shoulder aligned with his chin, amid several dozen residents all waiting to celebrate the first shovel full of dirt. A crisp, white party tent, its peaks reaching into the azure sky, had been pitched nearer to the water's edge than where the crowd had gathered for the ceremony. All attendees would be invited inside following the groundbreaking for some hot beverages and fancy pastries supplied by Rozelle's Bakery.

While Tony turned to talk business with a man to his right, I scanned the crowd for a sign of Rozelle's tight gray curls, which I imagined I would find peeking out from beneath a sensibly warm hat. Several women in attendance at the ceremony fit that loose description but there was no sign of Rozelle. Maybe I wasn't the only one who thought it was too cold to be standing on the riverfront.

"I love your earrings," a woman to my left said. She was smartly dressed, with matching hat and gloves, and a scarf tucked up beneath her chin. Me? None of those things, because I hadn't realized the forecast was given in secret code.

I had no need to reach up and check what earrings I was wearing. They were narrow drops of colored glass, fashioned into a waterfall cascade. "Thanks," I said, which was when I realized my lips had gone numb. And it was only October.

"Do they . . . Are they noisy?" She squinted a little and leaned closer.

"When they're not plastered to my cheek by the wind, yes. They sound like a fairy chime." I stamped my foot, encouraging the blood to return to my toes, but all that happened was the impact of the hard ground shuddering through my ankle and up my shin.

"Oh, fairy chime. I love it," she said on a breath. "Where did you get them, if I can ask?"

I cracked a smile. "Sweets and Stones, right in the village."

"The new shop? I'll have to check it out."

"She—" Tony began. A well-placed elbow to his midsection kept him from finishing.

"Try their mint chocolate drops, too. They're fabulous," I said.

The woman smiled and looked away from me as a group of men made their way from their roadside limo to the site designated for the groundbreaking. The men wore suits and hard hats and the kind of smiles politicians spend years mastering. Two I recognized as members of the town council. The others I presumed to be the commercial landowner types.

In a voice meant for only me to hear, Tony asked, "Why didn't you tell her?"

I gave him a combination shrug and head shake. I had no explanation for why I didn't want to admit to the curious woman that the creator of the earrings I wore was me. Me, some jeweler's wire, and the leftover slivers and bits of years' worth of stained glass projects. I should have been eager to tell her, or anyone, that the fairy chime earrings were my creation, talk up their beauty and versatility and surprising durability. But when it came to "tooting your own horn," as my grandfather would say, I was tootless.

"You need to learn to take credit for your work," Tony said.

"I'll add that to my to-do list."

I watched, along with several dozen residents of Wenwood, as the head honchos from the development company and the esteemed members of our town council reached the square of blue all-weather carpet it had been someone's sorry job to drag out onto the stretch of dirt and scrub grass and anchor with time-worn cement blocks. An aide stood nearby, a pair of shovels tied with red ribbons leaning up against his hip. And beside it all, an excavator waited to tear into the earth, teeth in the air ready to bite.

It wasn't until one of the suited men stepped forward, clearly preparing to speak, that the edge of the gathered crowd broke away. From the folds of their jackets they revealed previously concealed posters and overlarge signs. One of the men raised a poster above his head and led the group in a protest chant.

"Save our shoreline!"

Clearly prepared for such an outburst, the suited ringleader brandished a bullhorn and began to speak over the protestors. Every fourth word reached me; the rest whirled away with the wind or were buried by the protesters. I leaned back, turned to catch Tony's ear. "You've done these things before. What are they saying up there?"

"Nothing interesting," he said. "New beginnings, great stuff ahead, a bunch of insincere thanks." He stood so close behind me I felt him shrug.

"Insincere?" I asked, mindful of keeping my voice down, not knowing to whom the wind might carry my words.

"These guys . . ." he sighed. "They were never going to take no for an answer."

As surely as if his response had included encouragement to look at the evidence, I slid my gaze a little farther along the road and westward to the newly vacant land where all too recently strings of saltbox houses had stood. For decades the little houses were home to brickworkers and their families—the hardworking founding residents of Wenwood. But when the brickworks shut down, it left a void in the local industry. After standing vacant for better than twenty years, the brickworks was undergoing a renovation, the old factory becoming home to a new marina. The promenade was the next step in what so many hoped would rejuvenate Wenwood. Sadly, that rejuvenation was to come with rezoning and a cost. And not everyone was happy to pay the bill.

"Save our shoreline!"

I focused once more on the speaker. His voice buzzed through the bullhorn, words indistinct. With a broad, bleached smile, he handed the bullhorn to the aide, and accepted a shovel in exchange. He took a few steps to his left and joined the suited men to form a loose half circle in which all the men held a shovel, blades hovering inches above the dirt.

The men all froze in place, shovels poised at the ready, smiles carved on their faces, while a smattering of bareheaded men with pro grade cameras snapped pictures.

I shivered a bit, raised my shoulders, and ducked my head to try and block the wind against my ears with the collar of my coat.

"You okay?" Tony asked.

"Freezing," I admitted.

He chuckled and wrapped his arms around me. Pulling me back against his chest, he shifted his stance so his body kept the wind off me. "How's that?"

Warm. Thoughtful. I smiled, wished my lips weren't quite so numb. "I might claim to be cold more often."

"Sounds good to me. It's going to be a long winter ahead."

I shivered again, less from the cold than from the apprehension that skittered up my spine and raised gooseflesh on my skin. Winter was indeed approaching. The closer it got, the nearer the marina project was to completion. Soon enough Tony's presence there wouldn't be required at all. Periodic check-ins would suffice. I didn't want to think about what his next project would be . . . or where.

He ran his hands briskly up and down my arms, the heat friction sending sudden thawing messages along my skin. "Why don't you go and see if they need a hand in the refreshment tent?"

Go into the tent? Out of the wind? Into the warm? The idea tempted me. And my earlier inability to find Rozelle in the crowd made sense at last. She would be nice and toasty inside the party tent, making sure all her cakes and cookies and assorted treats were ready for the crowd to enjoy. Maybe she really could use some help.

Still . . . "Seems kind of, I don't know, disrespectful? What with that guy speaking . . . about . . . something."

He stifled a chuckle.

"Okay, seems somehow wimpy," I amended. "Like I should be made of tougher stuff or something."

He leaned forward a little, his breath whispering warmth against my ear. "I like that you're made of softer stuff."

"And I'm supposed to leave you after that proclamation?" I asked.

He laughed then, and a blast of cool air raced up my back as he shifted away from me. "Go inside. Get some coffee before the rush. I'll fill you in on all the details afterward."

Yielding to wisdom and temptation, I slipped to the back of the gathered crowd and, shoving my hands deeper into the pockets of my pitifully lightweight jacket, headed for the party tent.

I gave a wide berth to the gaggle of protesters, shrinking inwardly from the glare their ringleader gave me. If he wanted me to join his cause, he'd do better to comb the crumbs from his mountain-man beard and invest in a coat whose elbows and pockets hadn't been patched with *Batman*-themed duct tape.

A blast of wind pushed me sideways and blew away the latest protest chant. Ahead, the coated canvas walls of the party tent bowed inward in turns as the wind curled from one side to the next. Beyond, small swells and white caps lifted on the opaque blue-green river.

Quick as I could, head bowed for some sort of aero-dynamic aid, I ducked through the gap in the coated canvas that served as a door and stepped into the brightly decorated tent. Rectangular tables draped with plastic covers in autumn hues of orange, red, and yellow filled the bulk of the area, and the fragrance of coffee scented the air.

With the sudden absence of wind, Rozelle's voice seemed unusually loud to my frozen eardrums. "No no no no," she said. "Not that box. That's my box. The other boxes, those are for today."

She tugged a plain white cake box from the hands of one of her regular bakery helpers, dressed today in the white blouse, black slacks, and black vest of a member of a caterer's wait staff. The dark-haired girl spun away from Rozelle, ponytail swinging and eyes raised to the overhead canopy of the tent, and slowly lifted a box from a nearby stack.

"And don't mix the chocolate chip with the oatmeal raisin," Rozelle called. "That'll just make people cranky, and then they push the raisin ones out of the way to get to the chocolate chip ones. Makes a mess of everything."

The helper had wandered away before Rozelle finished speaking, but I got the sense Rozelle was only talking to herself anyway.

"Need any help?" I asked as I dodged between tables and through pockets of warmth. At the center of the space and in each of the corners, outdoor heaters, coils glowing amber, kept the chill of the riverfront from disrupting the cozy atmosphere.

Rozelle glanced in my direction. Momentary confusion clouded her round face before recognition spurred a smile. "Georgia," she said. "What are you doing here?"

She leaned sideways a bit, as though trying to peer behind me. "Is Pete with you?"

First of all, despite his age, Grandy still had almost a foot on me, so there was no way I could block Rozelle's view of him. Second, Grandy had said only a damn fool would be idiot enough to go stand out in the cold to watch someone pretend to dig a hole. But I didn't think Rozelle needed to hear that.

"He's home." I unzipped my jacket to let more of the warmth reach me. "My mom and her husband are arriving for a visit sometime tonight, so he's, you know, getting things ready and . . ."

Grandy wasn't exactly dusting in the corners and laying out the guest towels. He had more of a "you invited yourself, you clean up for yourself" policy. But along with Rozelle not needing to know Grandy's opinion regarding those of us attending the groundbreaking, she also didn't need to know that Grandy wasn't about to roll out the red carpet for his only daughter and his latest son-in-law.

Dropping the cake box on the nearest table, Rozelle lifted a hand and gave a halfhearted wave. "Don't worry about it. I understand. No matter how old they are, they're still your kids." She pulled a small pair of scissors from the pocket of the bright blue vest she wore and clipped the string on the cake box in such a manner that the string fell neatly away from all corners. "I made some special cheese Danish for one of the men today," she said, lifting the lid on the box. "You should bring some home for Pete."

I held up a hand. "That's okay, Rozelle. You know he needs to keep his sugar intake low."

"Of course I know that," she said. "These are sugar free.

They're also nut free and gluten free. But they taste nice. You'll bring some back." She slapped the lid closed. "After. If there's any left over. You want to help?"

When I assured her that I did, she called over her eye-rolling assistant and introduced her as Nicole.

"Georgia's going to put out the cookies so give her that box," Rozelle directed. "You make sure the coffee's ready to go."

Nicole—smooth-skinned, bright-eyed, sweet smile— nodded and handed me the box of cookies she held. "Chocolate chips separate from oatmeal raisin," she said, her voice a breathless high pitch. "Put some on the platters on each of the tables."

After a moment spent removing my jacket and draping it over the back of one of the nearby folding chairs, I got to work doing exactly as Nicole had directed. Empty platters graced the center of each table, and I laid out cookies on each. I was happy to be out of the cold, happy to be finished with my part-time job for the rest of the day, and happy most of all to have scored easy and early access to an urn of hot coffee. By the time the sounds of the groundbreaking ceremony gave way to applause, signaling its end, I was already seated with a cup of coffee for me and one waiting for Tony.

Attendees shuffled in slowly, as though not quite certain how to act without a table assignment. They drifted in twos and threes to empty seats or queued up for hot beverages and the special cakes and pastries on offer. A few waved as they passed me by, but Tom shouted his hello as always. "Georgia!" he said at his customary decibel. "Georgia! I'm glad you're here."

I waggled my fingers in greeting while he pulled out a chair across the table from me. "I'm surprised to see you away from the luncheonette. How are you going to get your crossword done without Grace's help?"

He shrugged out of a navy blue quilted jacket and draped it over the back of the chair. Grinning, he shook a finger at me. "Now, now, the day is young." He dropped into the chair, and another older gentleman ambled up to the table and stood behind the chair next to him. "I want you to meet my friend Terry," he said, tipping his head to the right.

"Oh, you're Terry." I smiled and offered a hand to shake. "Tom mentioned you were coming back for a visit. I'm Georgia Kelly."

Terry took my hand in both of his. "Glad to meet you, Georgia."

"This is the young lady I was telling you about." Tom rested his elbows on the table and leaned in. "She's a natural."

"A natural?" I repeated. I hesitated to ask what I was a natural at.

Tom nodded. "Police never would have figured out who killed poor Andy without her help."

Terry lowered himself into the vacant chair, eyebrows raised in appraisal. "Oh, you're that Georgia."

To the best of my knowledge, I was the only Georgia in Wenwood. But I've been wrong about things like that before.

"And she's the one," Tom said, "who worked out who killed Ned Gallo. Smart girl."

I shifted uncomfortably against the hard folding chair. I hadn't moved to Wenwood to take up life as Nancy Drew Girl Detective. It just sort of worked out that way. And it wasn't exactly what I was hoping to build a reputation on.

While Tom embellished the extent of my involvement in crime solving, I searched the tent for some sign of Tony. By the lack of people coming through the tent entrance, it seemed most of the folks who had been outside had made their way in. Even the group that had been protesting had helped themselves to coffee while they bent the ear of one of the men from the town council. Rozelle stood calmly beside their bearded ringleader, white cake box hanging from one hand while her other hand rested on the ringleader's shoulder. She shook her head at something he said before giving his shoulder one final squeeze and moving away.

"Have you ever thought about getting involved officially in police work?"

Terry's question brought my attention back to the two men. I smiled, but only a little. "I'm really not cut out for, um, public service."

"What is it that you do now?" he asked.

I drank down a little coffee before explaining my life situation. "I do custom stained glass work," I said. "Some window pieces for homes and some decorative pieces I sell through Aggie's Gifts and Antiques in Wenwood and now Sweets and Stones. I also work three days a week at a lawyer's office and . . ."

I kind of didn't want to admit to the last. How lame

was it that at thirty-two years old I was still working part-time in my grandfather's dine-in movie theater? Sure, it was only waiting tables two nights a week and the tips came in handy when buying sheets of stained glass, but it wasn't the sort of job a grown woman brags over.

Looking away from what I was somehow sure would be disappointment in Terry's eyes, I finally spied Tony over by the coffee urns, deep in conversation with one of the suited men still wearing a hard hat. By the easy way he stood and the relaxed manner in which he held his coffee cup, Tony was enjoying the conversation. A little twinge of sadness jolted through me like a hiccup. I self-ishly wanted him to stop having business-y chats and come and sit by me. But despite the job at the movie theater, I was in fact a grown woman with a measure of in-dependence and I reminded myself I did not need a man's companionship in order to enjoy a town event. In the same instant, I tried hard to ignore the little voice inside me pointing out that I couldn't exactly call myself independent while I was living in my grandfather's spare room.

Oh, lord. I took another slug of coffee, wishing there was a bit of Irish in it. Why? Why does my mind wander down these paths?

"Lawyer's office and?" Terry prompted.

I opened my mouth, ready to gloss over the movie the-ater thing and instead fall back on the old "looking for a permanent job in accounting," but Terry's gaze shifted away from me, and he turned to look over his shoulder seconds before I registered the change in the rhythm of the conversation around me. What had been a continuous rumble of indistinct words and short bursts of laughter had transformed into a series of gasps and shrieks of distress.

Terry was the first of us to rise, but I pushed to my feet in time enough to witness the leader of the protesters take a deep, sucking breath, shudder once, and topple to the ground.

2

My first-aid skills were nil, but that didn't stop me from jumping out of my chair and rushing toward the fallen protester. I had no idea what I would do when I reached him, but that didn't stop me. Perhaps it's some sort of human instinct, to hurry to the aid of the needy. In any case it seemed to be, given the number of folks who did the very same thing. Tables were pushed aside and chairs toppled as a crowd formed around the protester.

"I'm a nurse." A stocky man with a clean-shaven head elbowed his way through the ring of onlookers. "I'm a nurse, let me through."

Different suggestions were tossed out as to how to best help the man: "Get him on his side," "Try CPR," "Elevate his feet."

Even with my limited knowledge, I knew elevating the man's feet probably wouldn't help. But I didn't have anything better to offer.

"Give me some room here," the nurse said.

"You heard the man," Terry called out. "Everyone go back to where you were. Take a seat." Folks shuffled backward, and the nurse disappeared from view as he lowered himself to the ground.

Someone tugged at my elbow. I turned to find Rozelle gazing up at me. "Georgia, what's going on? What happened?"

"Someone . . . choked, I think," I said. Even as the words left my mouth, I felt the first twinge of doubt. The man had pulled in a breath. Loudly. Choking people didn't breathe—that was the whole problem. "Or a heart attack maybe?"

"Who someone?" Rozelle asked. "Who is it?"

A woman beside me saved me from admitting I didn't know the man's name. "David Rayburn," she said.

Rozelle's hand fluttered at her throat, and heat suffused her cheeks. "David? Oh no. The poor man. So young for a heart attack."

I estimated Rozelle to be in her early seventies. She was spry enough, full of energy, but that didn't mean she didn't still think a man in his fifties was young.

"Did someone call 911?" Terry shouted out.

Answers in the affirmative sounded from several different people. I realized then I'd left my phone inside my purse, and my purse at the table. Craning my neck to see if it was still slung over the back of the chair, I spotted Tom tugging it across the table and Tony moving toward me.

I met him halfway between the cluster of onlookers and the table I had vacated.

"What happened?" he asked. "Someone pass out or something?"

I held tight to the hand he held out to me. "Something like that." I told him what little I knew, including the name of the man who had taken ill. "Do you know him?" I asked.

He considered for a moment before shaking his head. "Doesn't sound familiar." He tipped his head, leaned in a bit to catch my eye and hold my gaze. "What do you say we grab a cup of coffee over at the site? I think things around here are going to be breaking up."

I looked back to where the crowd had gathered and out to the rest of the tent. People were wandering off in twos and threes. Only those standing watch around David Rayburn looked as though they intended to remain.

"Let me get my bag," I said.

Nodding, Tony pulled out his phone and bent his head over its small screen. He had the considerate habit of only checking messages when I was occupied doing something else. I kind of liked that about him.

"Georgia," Tom said when I reached the table. "Have you seen Terry?"

I pointed toward the group of onlookers. "He's over by there, helping out, I think."

"Oh." Tom's brow furrowed and his lower lip jutted out a bit. He held my purse aloft. "You left this," he said.

"Thanks." I leaned across the table to retrieve my bag. "You want me to send Terry back over?"

Tom waved away the suggestion. "He can't go anywhere without me. I drove."

Self-preservation sensors deep inside my brain sounded an alarm. Perhaps Tom was an excellent driver; I didn't know for sure. What I did know was that he wasn't known for having a sharp memory. One wrong turn because he forgot where he was going and it could be next stop Illinois—or whatever westernmost state he reached by the time the gas ran out.

I bundled into my too-thin coat, said my good-byes, and rejoined Tony for the walk across the riverfront. One last look over my shoulder showed me that the folks gathered around David Rayburn had gone very still, and I sent up a silent prayer that the poor man would be all right.

As we stepped out of the tent and into a gust of wind off the river, Tony laid his arm across my shoulders and pulled me in for a quick hug. "You okay?" he asked.

"Why wouldn't I be okay?"

The wind flattened a hank of sun-blond hair against his cheek. I didn't even want to think about the rat's nest my own hair would be in that wind if I hadn't taken the time to restrain it with a tight braid.

He nodded vaguely in the direction of the tent. "I don't have a good feeling about that guy in there."

"I'm trying to think positively." I pushed my hands into the pockets of my jacket and shifted a little closer to him, nearer to his warmth. The walk between the reception tent and the construction site wasn't a long one, a thousand feet, maybe less, but I was acutely aware of the time it was taking us to make the walk. Yes, Tony was the boss. The construction project, the new marina, it was all under his control. To me, that meant he should be able to take a lunch break for as long as lunch took—or for as long as the groundbreaking event lasted. To Tony, that meant leading by example, and putting in more hours than anyone else on the crew. The longer it took us to change locations, the less time we'd have to actually sit in each other's company.

Still, I would take what I could get, and happily sat in the sparsely—and cheaply—furnished trailer that served as the location office and thanked Tony sincerely for the hot cup of coffee he handed me.

"Looks like you were having a nice chat with one of the men who pretended to shovel dirt," I said before sending a little cool breath across the surface of the coffee.

Tony's grin flashed briefly and he leaned back against his desk, crossing his legs at the ankle. "Bennett," he said before continuing in a slow, careful tone. "We've been in touch."

I waited, but he said no more. I risked a sip of the coffee then prompted him. "About?"

His gaze met mine but only for a moment before skittering away. "About who he's thinking of using for this project."

"I thought they already had a construction company lined up. I thought they'd be using the same group that's been leveling the area."

But he shook his head, still slow and careful. "Demolition and construction are as different as they sound."

"So," I began, drawing out the O, choosing my words. "You're looking to have them consider Stone Mountain for the job?" I couldn't say "hoping." Not only did I not know if that was what he hoped, either for himself or for his construction company, but I also didn't want to accidentally make it sound like I myself was eager for his company to get the job—because I wasn't sure how I felt, and didn't want to explore it either. And I certainly didn't want to risk learning our feelings on the matter were, well, about a thousand feet apart.

"Trying to get a feel for whether our bid has a shot," he said. Again his gaze bounced off mine. He gripped the edge of the desk, put his weight into his hands for a moment. "Your mom and her husband on schedule to arrive tonight?"

I blinked, taken aback by the sudden change in topic. "Um, yeah, last I heard." I had told him as much via text message. Why the confirmation?

"They have plans while they're here?" he asked.

"They're just visiting as far as I know. Mom has some old friends she wants to catch up with." I turned my head a bit, looked at him from the corner of my eyes. "Why the sudden interest?"

His grip on the desk tightened, white showing across his knuckles. "What, uh, what would you say if I told you I'd like to meet them?"

"Wait. My . . . my mother?"

Tony nodded. "I'd like to get to know her. And her husband."

"I barely know her husband."

He kept nodding. "And I'd like to spend more time with your grandfather, have a conversation that lasts longer than the latest pop music hit."

I hit the point beyond words and merely gaped at him.

He stood and took a step toward me. "Georgia, I own my own company. I've never been divorced—or married. I pay my taxes, I eat right, and by current standards I believe I might be considered somewhat attractive."

Well, at least he didn't say, "According to my ex-girl-friends, I'm hot."

"So what it is that makes me not the kind of man you want to introduce to your family?"

I took a breath, let it out in a sigh. The simple truth was such a cliché, I knew he would think I was lying. It wasn't him. It was me. How was I supposed to find words to convey that and make him believe it?

I made my voice gentle, patient. "Tony," I said. "You know that I—"

"It's because of my past, isn't it?"

"That's not—"

"It's all right, Georgia. I understand. I understand your reluctance. Parents—or grandparents—are careful about who their daughter dates. And rightly so. But this is only a problem—"

"Right. It's only a problem if I make it one. But I'm not making it one. There's—"

The door swung open and a burly man wearing a scuffed blue hardhat and carrying a clipboard shuffled into the trailer. "Yo, boss," he said. He nodded an acknowledgment to me but otherwise showed no concern for my presence, or what he may have interrupted. "We got a problem with the backflow in the secondary pipe."

"Don't suppose you could handle that on your own, could you, Fred?" Tony asked.

Fred shrugged. "If I could, I wouldn't be standing here jawin' about it."

I got up from my chair, set the coffee on the edge of Tony's desk. "I need to get going anyway," I said. Not that I had anywhere I had to be, but because Fred had unwittingly given me an out and I was only too happy to take it. Pushing up on my toes, I swiped a kiss against Tony's cheek. "I'll talk to you later."

"Georgia," he said in a way that might have stalled me. But there was no conviction in his voice. No "wait" following "Georgia."

I waggled my fingers and hurried out of the trailer. Yes, I'm a chicken. Tony and I had been dating long enough to count by months rather than weeks—but only just. Still, given the duration of our relationship, it made sense that one or both of us would ask that anxiety-inducing question: "Where is this relationship going?" My belief that such a question could raise anxiety made clear my feelings on the matter. I didn't know where we were headed as a couple. I was simultaneously afraid it would all end by the time the marina project wrapped and afraid it would progress to something more, something serious and even the slightest bit committed. And Tony meeting my family definitely skewed toward serious.

Outside the door, the sight of emergency vehicles circling the party tent yanked me away from thoughts of my own meager problems. I might have issues with bringing my boyfriend home to meet my family, but the ambulance was a reminder things could always be worse.

Family could be coming for a visit.

\* \* \*

"Georgia, did you remember to pick up extra toilet paper?"

Grandy walked steadily down the steps from the living room to the space I had adopted as my workshop.

"Georgia?" he prompted.

It wasn't that I hadn't heard the question or needed time to recall the answer. I'd only just begun creating a lead join between two pieces of crimson glass. With soldering iron in one hand and spool of soldering wire in the other, I didn't dare look up and certainly wasn't about to take the hot tip of the iron away from the lead wire. Once I started the process of running hot lead along a join, there was no stopping until I reached the seam end.

"I remembered the toilet paper," I said, setting the soldering iron back on its base. "I guess you didn't remember that you already asked me that."

Letting out a deep sigh, he crossed the few feet from the bottom of the steps to the end of the table where I was working. He set both hands against the surface and leaned in. "When you get to be my age, Miss Smart Ass, see how well you remember inconsequential conversations."

I grinned. "Toilet paper is hardly inconsequential."

He huffed in response, tipped his chin in the direction of the stained glass piece. "What are you working on there?"

Plucking at a corner of the glass, its pieces tacked together with strategic solder joins, I rotated the glass so Grandy could get at least a hint of the light-through-color effect. "Sun catcher on steroids," I said.

"Are those"—his brow rolled and rumpled—"poinsettias?"

"Mm-hmm."

"Christmas? It's too early even for Halloween."

"Not in crafts and retail," I said. "The more of these I can get into Carrie's shop . . ."

As the dog kicked up a ruckus upstairs, I let my words fall away. There was no use trying to compete against Fifi's bark. She may be small for an English bulldog—or so my vet tells me—but she has a bark that would send shivers of fear down a soldier's spine.

Friday, my kitten who was threatening to become an actual cat, let out an alarming yowl from somewhere on the main floor of the house then streaked down the steps like the little blizzard she was and came to a sliding stop beneath my worktable. I knew from past experience that she would crouch there, wide-eyed and motionless, until the dog quieted down and peace once again reigned.

Grandy's eyes lit from somewhere deep in his heart. "They're here." He pushed off from the table and clapped his hands together, rubbing his palms one against the other.

He headed back up the stairs, predictable spring in his step. No matter how old my mom was, this was still his little girl coming home. His gleeful anticipation had grown greater as Mom's arrival drew closer. What tasks he couldn't do himself in preparation, he supervised as I performed, going so far as to direct where I should put

Friday's cat box when I moved it out of my bedroom—
which Mom would be taking over for her visit—and into
the little guest room to which I had been relegated.

Sighing, I clicked the power switch on the soldering
iron base to "Off." Fifi's bark had shifted subtly from
protect to curious and Grandy was shouting hellos out
the door. It was time I, too, headed up the stairs to greet
my mother and her new husband.

"Well, Friday," I said, kneeling down to peer at her
beneath the table. "Wish me luck."

I didn't get a single mew out of her. I pretended her lack
of response had more to do with being afraid of giving up
her position and less to do with not giving a rat's tail how
well Ben and I did or did not get along.

After switching off the radio that always played softly
in the corner while I worked, I ran a hand over the tangle
of corkscrew curls that passed for a hairdo, smoothed
down the wrinkles in my sweatshirt, and headed up the
stairs.

It doesn't take but a few seconds to climb the steps to
the main floor of the house, and I didn't think I'd been
dragging my feet at all. But by the time I reached the living
room, my mother was already through the front door. Fifi
was doing her famous back-end wiggle of joy, tongue lolling half out of her mouth as Mom greeted her with the
same lovey voice that people tended to use around infants.

Of the many things I had been given when I adopted
Fifi from her previous, short-term owner was a book akin
to *Dog Ownership for Dolts*. I studied that manual in
depth for the first two weeks Fifi was in the house whining

at Friday, stealing Grandy's slippers, and carrying her water bowl from room to room. In my reading I learned dogs often were able to recognize members of their owner's family even if they hadn't met them before. This nicely explained Fifi being instantly enamored of my mother.

And okay, even if Fifi lacked that skill or the theory of dogs recognizing family was bunk, I fully understood why she was instantly in love with my mother. My mom had that effect.

"Fifi, come," I said.

Fifi sat.

My mother's gaze met mine, and I shrugged as I walked toward her. "We're working on it," I said.

Mom's arms came around me in a fierce hug. "Georgia. I'm so happy to see you," she said on a breath.

"Glad you're here," I responded.

I leaned back to look at her. While she hadn't changed much since I had last seen her at her justice of the peace wedding, still I marveled at how she seemed to look more like Grandy every time I saw her. Or maybe it was because I was living daily with Grandy that I was finally seeing the resemblance—the same height and proud posture, same brown eyes, same "I see everything" expression intensified by narrow lips and a stern chin. Luckily, what made Grandy a handsome man made my mother an attractive woman—because it would really be a shame if she looked like a handsome man.

"Benjamin," Grandy said. One hand holding the door open, he extended his other to shake hands with Ben as the younger man came through the door.

"Pete." Ben slapped Grandy lightly on the shoulder as if they were buddies from way back.

As Grandy closed and locked the door, Ben joined me and Mom, leaning down to press a kiss to my cheek. "Georgia, sweetheart." And then he skittered sideways a bit and looked down. Fifi stood by his side, nose smashed against his knee, working frantically to pick up every single scent on Ben's khaki slacks. "Well, hello there." Easily as tall as Grandy had been in his prime, Ben had to both bend and crouch for his fingers to reach Fifi's head. He gave her a friendly pat; she continued to sniff.

Mom excused herself to the bathroom with reminders to us that it had been a long drive. She was one step up the stairs and on her way before she turned back. "Georgia, put the kettle on for some tea?"

I peered at Grandy, flicked a glance at Ben. Me going into the kitchen with Mom upstairs would leave the two men alone. There were only two ways that could go: perfectly polite or perfectly disastrous.

With a mental shrug I headed into the kitchen. "Fifi, come," I said sternly. Of course, she left Ben's trousers instantly and trotted right behind me. It would have been nice to think she was showing a glimmer of learning that command, but it was more likely—okay, a certainty— that she was simply coming along because I was going into the kitchen. Fifi was highly food-motivated.

I lifted the red enamel tea kettle from its place at the back of the stove, kept an ear open for conversation from the living room.

"How was the drive?" Grandy asked.

I rolled my eyes, stuck the kettle under the faucet. The crash of water into the kettle drowned out what was no doubt a recitation of road conditions and traffic patterns from the bridges to the thruway, with a side note on the exorbitant price of tolls. Fifi padded into the kitchen and lay down in her favorite place beneath my customary chair, big eyes watching every move I made pulling down cups and saucers and otherwise assembling a tea service.

When I once again tuned in to what was happening in the other room, I was surprised to hear my mother's voice. She was chiming in on "the crazy fluctuations in gas prices." And she said it as if she had honestly begun paying attention and perhaps even pumped her own gas. My mother is a lovely lady, but gasoline might as well have been her kryptonite. Learning she had potentially touched a gas pump made me bobble the spoons I was holding. Two of them fell to the floor with a clatter that brought Fifi to her feet.

"Everything all right in there?" Mom called.

"It's fine." I crouched to retrieve the spoons then tossed them into the sink, making an even louder *clatter-clang-clunk*.

"Do you need a hand?"

"It's fine," I repeated. And it was, wasn't it? I didn't really need help putting together some tea; it wasn't like I was trying to get a Thanksgiving dinner on the table. Tea was certainly something I could do on my own without parental assistance. I was an adult, wasn't I?

They kept on with mundane, polite talk while I buzzed in and out of the kitchen, setting out teaspoons and cloth napkins and placemats on the aged table in the dining room. From the sideboard I grabbed four china dessert plates and my grandmother's pastry dish off their shelf. Some wistful voice in the corner of my awareness whispered about how nice it was to be able to include Grandma in this new family gathering.

Back in the kitchen, I sneaked Fifi a tootsie roll from Grandy's not so secret stash before giving the milk glass pastry dish a swipe with a damp dish towel, just in case. My mind hop-skipped past my current activity and settled on memories of the morning, memories of David Rayburn gasping for breath on the cold autumn ground. I shook my head to bring myself back to the moment and placed the pastry dish carefully on the counter then stood looking from plate to teakettle, trying to remember what I was supposed to do next.

As I opened the cabinet where I keep the loose teas, Fifi let out a little whine. I looked first to her, then in the direction her head was turned.

Friday had ventured out of the downstairs workshop and taken a few tentative steps toward the living room. Her fluffy white tail twitched and her ears seemed to angle forward, as if she was trying to take the measure of the strangers in the living room. She let out a particularly grown-cat *mrrooww* and crept into the living room, out of view.

Quietly, I moved to the doorway and poked my head around to see where she was going.

"Oh, this must be Friday," Mom said. "My goodness, what a pretty cat." Mom had tucked herself into the curved corner of the antique horse-hair couch, one hand resting on Ben's thigh as he sat beside her. She leaned down and brushed her thumb against her fingers in that strange action that routinely lured curious cats. But not my cat.

Friday curled away from my mother then sidled up to Ben and gave his calf a nose-to-tail rub. "Oh. Could you please, Georgia, the . . ." Ben shifted his weight, moving closer to Mom. He lifted his feet a few inches off the floor and checked the gold brocade fabric on the couch cushion as if wondering if it was safe to put his feet up. "Oh boy."

Friday U-turned and went in for another strike, and I rushed from the kitchen.

Ben lifted his feet higher off the floor and leaned over into my mother's lap. Gaze locked on the not-at-all-dangerous cat at his feet, Ben didn't see the displeased grimace on Grandy's face. I had no time to try and determine whether he was unhappy with his new son-in-law or with my cat. Quickly as I could, I scooped up Friday and gathered her in tight to my chest. Her long, silky fur slipped between my fingers. "Sorry," I said over her offended *mrroowww*.

"Troublesome beast," Grandy muttered. But his tone carried no malice, and he held out his hand to me, curled his fingers in a signal I knew well.

"Sorry, Ben," I repeated as I passed Friday to Grandy. The moment Grandy took her in his hands, she started purring. "She's really very sweet."

My mother gave Ben an affectionate pat on his arm. "First the dog, now the cat. Did you spill something on those pants when we stopped for lunch?"

"There now," Grandy murmured, scratching beneath Friday's chin. "You stay with me."

Starting soft but rapidly growing in volume, a sound reminiscent of bagpipes filled the room. Grandy smiled. "That'll be the tea."

Ben's eyes went wide, as though he suddenly feared he'd arrived in a twilight zone, but he stood and headed for the dining room along with Mom while I went into the kitchen to switch off the light beneath the kettle. The sound of bagpipes faded away. I pulled open the deep drawer beside the refrigerator and took out the box of cookies. Tied with red-and-white baker's string, the box was decorated with predictable generic text: BEST IN TOWN, BAKED FRESH, FOR YOUR ENJOYMENT. But the generic text was fine. I didn't need the name of the bakery emblazoned across the cardboard to remind me the cookies came from Rozelle's.

Setting the box on the counter, I let out a breath. Sharp memories rushed at me again, images of the morning arranging cookies on platters scattered throughout the riverside tent. Those were followed shortly and powerfully by more thoughts of David Rayburn. I hoped that he had recovered, that he was resting comfortably at home—or at least had a nice private room at the hospital—and would be none the worse for wear. But a niggling in my gut warned me that wasn't the case.

I huffed and pushed away the mental fog, and once again arranged Rozelle's delicate cookies on a platter. I poured boiling water into the waiting teapot then carried pot and platter into the dining room, announcing, "Tea's ready," as I went.

Ben took a seat at the end of the table nearest the entry to the kitchen, with Mom at his right. Not to be outdone, or lured away from his favorite chair, Grandy sat at the opposite end of the table, straight and proud so there was no doubt which end of the table was the head.

This left me in an unexpected predicament. The rectangular shape of the table meant I was left choosing to sit closer to my mother, or closer to my grandfather. I had the sudden, sinking feeling that the upcoming week might fall short of the ideal family get-together.

I set down the platter of cookies nearer to Ben and Mom then shifted the steel trivet to the center of the table and put down the teapot. I dropped into the chair nearest to Grandy and smiled a little apology at my mom.

"Look at these cookies," Ben said, pulling the platter close for inspection. "They look too good to eat."

Mom took in a breath that ended in a blissful sort of smile. "Are those from Rozelle's?" she asked.

"Of course." I was happy the cookies somehow pleased her and I forced down memories of the morning, not wanting thoughts of poor David Rayburn to further distract me.

"My gosh. How I used to love her cookies. Is she still alive?"

"I beg your pardon," Grandy said, his tone lighthearted despite the stern look on his face. "I'll have you know Rozelle is younger than I am. Why would you presume she's dead?"

Mom paused in her reach for a cookie. "Sorry, Dad. I didn't mean anything by it. Rozelle's been making cookies since I was a kid." She selected a rainbow square and transferred it to her plate. "Does she still make those little cream puffs? You know the ones I mean, Dad, with the chocolate shell?"

"Yes, she does," Grandy said. "And your daughter won't let me have any of them."

Mom smiled, the same smile Grandy had—equal parts happy and mischievous. She took a delicate bite from her cookie and her eyes slipped closed. "Mmmm."

"Someone needs to make sure you don't have too much sugar in your diet," I said as Fifi, strangely late to the party, wandered in from the kitchen and stood on the threshold, looking back and forth between me and Ben. The confusion in her big brown eyes said it all: I was not sitting where I should be. She let out a doggie groan and lowered herself to the ground midway between us.

"You know I was just reading that almost thirty percent of Americans over the age of sixty are suffering with Type 2 diabetes. Thirty percent. That's almost one in every three people," Ben said. "Pass the tea, please?"

I flicked a glance at Grandy, transferred teapot and trivet to Ben.

"Georgia takes good care of me," Grandy said.

I waited for his customary complaints about how I hid his butterscotch candies and threw away any single-serve cakes he brought into the house. No complaint came.

"I am glad to hear that," Ben said.

Mom winked at me—her own unique way of showing her agreement and approval.

"I hope you're paying attention to her lessons," he said, tipping the teapot over his cup. "You'll need to remember all she's taught you once she moves out."

"I'm moving out?" I asked. "What exactly did I miss while I was in the kitchen?" I looked to Grandy. Strangely comforted by the confusion I saw on his face that I reasoned mirrored my own, I turned my surprised expression on Ben. "What are you talking about?"

Ben put the teapot back on the trivet and slid it toward me.

"I'd like some tea," Mom said.

Ben muttered an apology as he pulled back the teapot. "I understand that you needed some place to stay until you got back on your feet. But from what your mother tells me, you've had some success selling your stained glass pieces. I can only imagine you've put aside enough now to be able to reestablish yourself in an urban environment."

I didn't think my eyebrows could lift any closer to my hairline. "An urban . . . Why would I move? I like it here."

"Georgia, as much as I like knowing you're looking after Dad I have to agree with Ben. You're a CPA," Mom said. "You'll have far more opportunity in a city than you do here."

"And what's wrong with here?" Grandy asked, his voice shifting into a growl.

"Absolutely keep making stained glass pieces." Ben reached toward me, as though he was going to put his hand on my arm. But I was seated just far enough away to be out of his reach. "It's an excellent source of income while you work your way back up in the corporate world."

I had to do it. I had to close my eyes in some hopeless wish that when I opened them, this moment would have turned out to be part of a dream. A wish that I was going to wake up warm in my bed with Friday curled behind my knees and a blanket of stars visible from my window.

But of course that didn't happen. Because nothing rotten in my life ever turned out to be a bad dream.

"I don't really want to go back to corporate America." I half stood from my chair and brought the teapot and plate of cookies to my end of the table. "Besides, I didn't exactly leave it under the most auspicious of circumstances."

"I told you, Ben, remember?" Mom asked softly. "The scandal?"

Ben waved his hand, dismissing her comment. "It's been long enough now no one will care."

"They'll care," I snapped. I had spent enough months searching for work after the big blowup at Washington Federal that had cost me my career, my home, and my fiancé—though that third turned out to be no great loss. I knew firsthand how much a financial scandal could wreck the career of an accountant. It was a matter of trust.

"Give it another try," Ben said. "I think you'll be surprised."

I gritted my teeth, forced a little smile onto my face. This was my mother's husband. What would it cost me to humor him and keep the peace? "I'll think about it."

"Forget think about it," he said. "Do it. Get back out

on your own. Be an independent adult again. See how it feels."

The wooden creak of the chair as Grandy shifted his weight was the only sound in the ensuing silence. I certainly didn't know what to say to Ben, and my mom had helpfully stood and poured my tea so even the simple act of asking for the pot to be passed was unnecessary. But Grandy . . . Grandy was never at a loss for the right thing to say.

"Georgia never stopped being an independent adult," he said. "And she doesn't need you to tell her how to continue being one. Now pass the damn cookies."

Little Miss Independent Me, who spent her days watching her grandfather's diet, picked up the plate and passed it over. "Help yourself," I said. "The jelly fingers are especially good."

3

The older generations had stayed up talking long after I crept into bed. As owner and proprietor of the Dine-In Theater, Grandy was accustomed to late nights and sleeping-in mornings. Secretly I thought Ben wouldn't admit to being tired in the face of Grandy's age and apparent ability to stay awake all night long and had thought to outdo him. Whatever the reason, they were still up chatting when I nodded off some time after midnight, gratefully escaping the tumult of low self-esteem battering the corners of my mind.

In the morning I moved as quietly as I could so as not to wake anyone. I put a fresh bowl of food down for Friday, took Fifi for her morning walk, and gathered from the workshop the dozen pairs of earrings I had made, all without disturbing the peace. Everything went smoothly right up until I grabbed my car keys and stepped out of the house.

Grandy had left his Jeep parked at curbside, the branches of the proud old cedar tree on the front lawn reaching out to keep the SUV in shade. I had been left to pull the previously owned sedan I had finally invested in into the driveway, exposing it to sunshine, bird strike, and most problematically, being blocked in by Ben's luxury sports car.

Wincing in anticipation, I turned back to the house and slipped my key in the door. As expected, Fifi sent up a vocal alarm. It made no difference that I had only left the house moments before, that I lived there, and not only fed her the best dog food in Pace County but also pretended never to notice when Grandy sneaked her bits of baked chicken from his own plate. To her, I was an unexpected intruder and the whole household needed to be alerted.

"Hush hush hush," I said softly as I stepped into the house. I slipped my keys into the ceramic bowl by the door and lifted out the spare set of keys to Grandy's Jeep. Fifi rushed toward me, her bark subsiding into what I could only call a welcoming growl. "It's me," I whispered. "I didn't go anywhere yet, you goof."

I patted her on the head in the same moment a door upstairs clicked open.

From where I stood and because one doorknob sounded much like another to me, I had no way of knowing who Fifi had awakened. Much as I wouldn't have minded seeing Grandy or Mom, there was an equal potential the person moving around up there was Ben, and I was in no mood to hear more of his thoughts on what I should be doing with my time and my life.

I ducked out of the door and double-timed it to the Jeep with only the slightest swirl of guilt disturbing my digestion. I simply wasn't ready to repeat last night's delightful conversation.

Key in the ignition, engine engaged, I tore away from the curb with a haste rarely experienced in Wenwood. Though I'd had a good night's sleep, and most of life's tribulations seemed easier and more manageable in the morning, I felt the need to put a physical distance between myself and the emotional stew I had ingested the night before.

I liked Wenwood. I was rapidly nearing the love point. I had begun to believe in staying in the small town long term. And in the span of one conversation, all the doubts I thought I had overcome came crashing back.

Funny how I never considered living with Grandy as being dependent. Maybe because I paid my share of the bills, did the bulk of the housework so that Grandy didn't have to, and shared in meal preparation tasks I saw myself as equal in the arrangement. I wondered, perhaps far later than I should, if the rest of the world saw me as a family member moved back home or as a family member sponging off her grandfather. But then, did how other people saw me really matter?

I could tell myself no, it didn't. But that didn't stop the wicked little voice of self-doubt in my head that suggested I was using my list of chores and cooperations as a means of lying to myself, making up excuses to stay with Grandy instead of facing the truth: Not only was

I a thirty-two-year-old woman with a string of part-time jobs and no home to call her own. I was a failure.

Yes, extreme, I know. I did say that little voice was wicked.

Feeling less than happy with myself and thus wholly unwilling to be sociable with others by the time I reached Wenwood's version of downtown, I avoided the road that bisected the village. Instead of my customary activity of parking behind the market and walking up to the lunch-eonette for a cup of coffee and some gossip before heading to Carrie's shop, I guided the Jeep along the access alley that ran behind the stores. With the road not as well kept as the public street, the Jeep swayed and bounced along the uneven and potholed pavement until at last I came to a stop, nose against the fence dividing the alley from parkland.

I grabbed the canvas tote in which I'd put the earring sets and climbed out of the SUV, eyes already on my destination, the back door of the village's newest retail establishment, Sweets and Stones.

Having been through this particular drill before and knowing full well that I could knock on the steel door until my knuckles bled and still no one inside would hear me, I turned my back to the door and "knocked" with the flat of my foot.

As I turned back, Regina Henry stood in the opening door, one hand on the frame, the other on her hip. "This some kind of incognito visit?"

I smirked. "You could say that. I'm just not in the mood to bump into anyone I know and have to be nice." Too late

I realized how I sounded. "I didn't mean you. I'm sorry. I meant . . ." I sighed. "I'm having a crap day."

Regina smiled, threw the door open wide, and waved me in. "Right this way," she said. "I have just the thing."

I moved into the comparatively dim lighting of the back room and waited while Regina closed and bolted the door.

"Come on out front," she said, and led the way through the storage area and out to the sales floor.

As a result of a vote among the Wenwood Town Council and those residents interested enough to attend town meetings, Sweets and Stones had won the right to rent the space previously occupied by the hardware store—closed due to the untimely and criminal death of its owner. They had faced some competition from a nationwide chain of liquor stores who proposed to open a discount wine shop in the village, and in my present mood, I wasn't entirely convinced the liquor store was a bad idea. Somehow a drink sounded like just the thing.

And yet reaching the sales floor, I became a believer.

"Hot or cold?" Regina asked as she ducked behind a glass-cased counter. The L shape of the counter tucked into the back corner of the shop precisely duplicated the location of the cashier's table from when the shop was a hardware store. But the lighted shelves of gourmet chocolates were a vast improvement over displays of ant spray and nails.

"Hot or cold what?"

"Chocolate, of course," Regina said.

"Oh. Um. Thanks, but I don't need—"

"Do we need to have the chocolate and endorphins talk again?" she asked. "You need this. Now. Cold or hot?"

"Hot, please," I said. I took a deep breath, inhaling the sweet, decadent, and comforting fragrance of fine chocolate. Boxed chocolates in various weights decorated the wall opposite the display case where Regina prepared my hot chocolate, while the displays in the front of the shop combined those same classic bon bon boxes dispersed among costume and trendy jewelry. The little fairy chime earrings I made for the shop were ordinarily scattered atop a curling blue ribbon, but from where I stood, I could spy only one pair.

I wandered across the cream and robin's egg flooring and peered into the case. An additional pair was tucked at the end of the ribbon, a pair done in shades of coral and pink that, looking at them, reminded me of cheesy seventies movies. What had I been thinking?

"What's got you down?" Regina called a split second before she switched on a quiet blender.

"Nothing," I said automatically. We got along well enough, Regina and I, but sharing serious thoughts and giggling together were still a ways off. "Family stuff."

"Oh, girl." She pulled open the drawer of a small dishwasher and lifted out a pale blue porcelain cup. "Every family has its crazy. You're not alone."

"I suppose," I said, wandering back. I unzipped my coat and took a seat at the single small cafe table. "Doesn't make it easier to go through."

"Maybe not, but you get all kinds of sympathy." She grinned. "And free chocolate."

"Well, that *is* worth the aggravation," I said.

"All right. All right. You bring me more earrings to sell?"

"Indeed." I placed the tote bag on the table and reached inside.

"Good, I had some woman in here yesterday bought two pair."

I wondered if it was the same woman I had encountered at the groundbreaking, but couldn't work up the energy to describe her to Regina and ask. "Well, I have twelve for you today," I said. "That's probably all for a while. I need to make some Christmas pieces for Carrie."

"You're not doing jewelry for her, are you?" Regina asked, her face stern but her tone teasing.

"Picture frames," I said. "Don't worry. I'm not creating any competition." Ben's words about my glass work being an excellent source of income stomped through my memory. "I don't want . . ." I let my words trail away, blew out a breath.

I don't know what Regina saw when she came out from behind the counter, mug of hot chocolate in hand, but she placed the mug down on the table in front of me without a word. She smoothed her hands over her thighs before sitting down opposite me. "Drink up," she said. "Did you hear about what happened yesterday at the groundbreaking ceremony for the new shopping complex?"

I nodded, lifted the cup to my lips. "I was there."

She shook her head. "All kinds of gossip over at Grace's about that poor David Rayburn. I can't imagine what might have happened. They say he might have had some kind of condition, but I tell you that man was as healthy as they come."

I met her gaze over the rim of my cup. "You know him?" I asked.

"Not well," she said, and pointed to the cloth-wrapped package I had taken from the tote. "These for me?"

I lifted my chin in the direction of the package. "Go ahead," I said.

She slid the cloth across the table and lifted the top fold.

"Why would you say Rayburn is a healthy man if you don't know him well?"

She looked up at me. "I met him quite a few times but we never talked about anything other than his crusade to stop that strip mall getting built."

"Shopping promenade," I said.

One eyebrow lifted. "Strip mall, promenade, what's the difference?"

I'd been spending a lot of my spare time with a man whose business was construction. I had been educated on the difference, but didn't think the distinction would matter much to Regina. I shrugged. "Okay, so why was he talking to you about the, um . . ."

"His whole 'Save the Shoreline' movement," she said. She peeled back the next layer of cloth, exposing the first half-dozen pair of earrings nestled within. The decorative gold wire crisscrossing the drops of colored glass winked in the illumination of the overhead lights, looking as if the glass contained some secret magic that the wire was keeping in place. "He spent a lot time trying to get me and Stella to swear that if we didn't get this location we're in now, we wouldn't go on and rent a space in the new shopping place. As if we could wait the how-ever many years it's going to take to build that thing."

She took a pair of earrings between thumb and fore-finger and, holding them aloft, turned so they were backlit by the light of the display case. "I don't know how you make these so delicate and beautiful," she said, a note of something akin to reverence in her voice.

I shook my head, shook off the compliment. They were bits of leftover projects, slivers of memories bound to-gether with golden wire to tempt someone else into taking them home. To my thinking, they didn't merit praise.

"I don't know why he kept talking to us, thinking we'd change our mind," Regina said. She put down the first pair of earrings and lifted the next. "And then once we got approved for this location here, he wanted us to sign on and protest so that we didn't have any place coming in that might siphon off our business. We got plenty of time to build up a loyal customer base, I figure. But boy, that man must have believed plenty deep in his cause."

"He wasn't the only one, though. He had a pretty large group of people with him at the groundbreaking," I said. "With the way the town is supporting new business and getting behind the whole rejuvenation movement, I'm surprised there's anyone around who's opposed."

She lifted a shoulder. "People get all kinds of ideas in their heads, but that David Rayburn"—she shook her head—"he was charismatic, you know what I'm saying? And he had the physical strength to go with his convic-tions. I can't believe he had a single thing wrong with him to make him collapse like that."

"Well," I said, "sometimes there's illness on the inside that never shows on the outside."

"I suppose that's so. Still, you gotta admit, there's something fishy about a man like that keeling over eating a Danish."

I took another sip of the smooth, liquid sin that filled my cup. "Yeah, something fishy," I said. "Without a doubt."

"Good, you're back," my mother said.

I was two steps inside the front door and had yet to close it behind me. Fifi, having ceased her vigorous intruder-alert barking, danced gleefully at my feet. As far as the dog was concerned, I had been gone for weeks rather than a couple of short hours. While I patted her head with one hand, my other hand held the keys to Grandy's Jeep inches above the bowl where he kept the spare set. My expression must have conveyed a question, because my mother continued.

"We need to go to the grocery store," Mom said.

I let go the keys, and they hit the bowl with a *clink-thunk*. "I did all the grocery shopping already. There's barely any space left in the fridge. What else would we need?" Kneeling in front of the dog, I unzipped my coat before taking her wide head between my hands and ruffling her jowls.

"I just want to pick up a few things." She slid open the closet door and tugged her seasonally appropriate coat off its hanger. "I thought we could go together."

Her statement set off conflicting desires. Spending some time with her, even doing something as mundane as strolling the supermarket, would be pleasant. I had not gotten in a good visit with my mother in months. And yet I had work to do—patterns to evaluate and an inventory of the glass I had on hand, which I could completely do while obsessing over Tony's interest in meeting the family. Wandering the supermarket for the second time in as many days was not in my plan.

"What's the problem?" she asked.

"There's no problem," I said, maybe too quickly. Are all mothers clairvoyant? If I should ever have children of my own, would I be able to read their minds with such ease? Or will I have used up my allotment of miracles simply by finding a man worth having children with?

"Where's Grandy?" I asked, standing.

She slipped her coat on. "Your stepfather took him to buy some leaf bags and a new rake."

"Don't call him my stepfather," I said. "I'll be a millionaire in Wenwood before I call him Dad."

"Don't be silly, Georgia." She zipped her coat in one swift go. "No one expects you to call him Dad."

"Good."

"That doesn't make him any less your stepfather," she said. "Let me get my purse."

I put a hand to my forehead. My mother and I had wrestled along this path before, and I wasn't eager to trip down it again.

From the dining room, where she was riffling through her purse, she called, "And what's wrong with your cat?"

"What . . . what about the cat?" A beat of fear pulsed through me. My cat? Friday? What could be wrong with her?

Mom bustled through the living room, pulling her handbag over her arm. "She's walking around yowling."

"Yowling?"

"You don't suppose she swallowed some of those pieces of broken glass you keep lying around."

I never kept pieces of glass lying around. I was fastidious about cleaning my workspace, brushing down my table, and putting my tools away where they belonged. Nothing was left to put the cat or the dog at risk, or even a wandering, nosy grandfather. Still, that thread of fear tugged at my confidence.

Sidestepping around Fifi, who was still sitting in front of me hoping for more attention, I passed through the living room and jogged down the few steps to the room I used as my stained glass workshop. Windows wrapped the exterior walls, flooding the room with light, weaker now as the autumn advanced. The worktable at the center of the room was as clear as my recollection of it, with toolboxes stored on shelves beneath. Whatever the cause of the cat—

"*MmmrrrooOOW. MmmrrrooOOOOWWW.*"

Holy cats.

"*MMMRRROOOWWW.*"

"Friday?" I called.

"That's the yelling," my mother said from the top of the stairs.

"Friday?" I called again. The yowling sounded so loud she had to be in the room, didn't she?

"She's up here," Mom said.

As I turned for the stairs, Friday meandered from the direction of the kitchen, heading straight for my mother's denim-clad ankles. Another curdling yowl escaped my previously charming kitten. Friday rubbed the length of her body along my mother's jeans, leaving a trail of white fur behind.

Finding Friday in a beer carton out behind my friend Carrie's antiques shop and deciding to keep the adorable kitten (or more accurately, falling in love and refusing to part with her) launched me on my newfound path of cat ownership. As a kid, my mother and I changed locations a great deal. There was never any chance of a pet that couldn't live its entire life in a ten-gallon fish tank joining our family. When Friday became part of my permanent future plan, I augmented my collection of litter pans, canned fish, and stuffed mice with a few books on cat care. But the noise that came from my sweet kitten's mouth could not be accounted for within the pages.

"Okay, something's not right," I murmured. I knew she hadn't eaten glass—at least none that came from my workshop—but that didn't mean she hadn't eaten something else that was causing her distress.

"Should I take her to the vet?" I asked. For no good reason, I directed this question at my mother. As if she would know. Because moms know everything, right?

Her brow creased in confusion. "We need to go to the market."

I huffed out my frustration. Friday had made similar noises last night, both when Mom and Ben arrived and later when that arrival required us to move from our nice double bed in the corner room to the little single sizer in the tiny spare room. I thought she was offering a feline critique of our temporary quarters. But there she was, out and about and still kitty-yelling. I made up my mind in a snap. "Grab the cat."

"What do you mean, grab the cat? What do you want me to do? You don't want me to pick it up, do you?"

Seriously. What was it about the people in my life and their aversion to cats?

"Never mind," I said. "I'll get her. Just stay still."

Not wanting to spook Friday, I walked calmly up three steps, getting close enough to scoop her up without my mother having to disrupt the cat twining around her ankles.

The cat gave one more curdling *mmrrooww* but allowed me to pick her up and hold her close. She butted her head against my jaw, rubbed her soft fur against my chin.

I gave her a tentative squeeze before setting her down on my worktable. Holding her in place with one hand, I ran my fingers down the length of her little body, feeling for any unusual lumps or protrusions, waiting for any sound of discomfort or protest from her. But I hadn't held her long before she lowered her head to the table, rolled sideways, and began to purr.

I shook my head, bewildered. "I don't see anything wrong with you," I said in a whisper.

Lifting her into my arms again, tucking her against my chest, I opened the door to the garage and reached in to switch on the light.

"Where are you going?" my mother asked.

"I'm getting the cat carrier," I called back as I plunged into the garage, took a right, and continued on to the laundry room.

"What about the market?"

"Vet first," I replied.

I slid the cat carrier off the shelf and dropped it atop the clothes dryer. Catching sight of the carrier, Friday squirmed and did her best to back her way out of my grasp. I held her tighter, flipped open the latches on the carrier. From a bin of clean—and as yet unfolded—laundry I took a bath towel with frayed edges and dropped it into the carrier. I dropped Friday on top of the towel and closed the carrier in a hurry.

"Okay," I said, returning to the workshop, doors closed behind me. "We'll take her to the vet and then stop at the market on the way back."

"Oh, really?" My mother folded her arms and fixed me with a sarcastic glare. "And what are you going to do with the cat while we're in the store? You know you can't leave it in the car, don't you?"

"Of course I know that," I said. She backed away and turned for the front door, struggling for a moment with her hand on the doorknob, trying to tug open the sometimes sticky door. "I'll leave her with my friend Carrie."

Because what are friends for if not to babysit animals they despise so their friends can go shopping?

In the end Mom decided against the potential for waiting around the vet's office and in favor of "wandering around downtown" until I could retrieve her. She made this sound like "downtown" had some sort of urban bustle. I half expected her to be disappointed when we cruised under the town's one traffic signal and onto the stretch of Grand Street that was the whole of downtown. To mitigate that reaction, I pulled to the curb in front of Aggie's Gifts and Antiques. "This is my friend Carrie's shop," I said.

One hand on the door latch, my mother asked, "What happened to Aggie?"

"She moved to Florida."

From the backseat, Friday let out a howl of protest. Though the noise was her customary complaint when confined to her carry kennel, my stomach clenched a little. I frowned, the lowering of my brows and subsequent pulling against the skin of my forehead abstractly reminding me I had forgotten to moisturize. As if dry skin were anywhere near as important as my poor, sick Friday.

"And what's this Sweets and Stones?" Mom put one foot out the door of the SUV.

It would be wrong to push her out, wouldn't it?

I opted for forgo the inevitable charges of cruelty to a matriarch. "It's new. You'll like it. Try the chocolate mint drops."

"Oh, good. I will. Oh, and I want to say hello to Grace while I'm here." She had two feet out and turned back to talk to me through the open door. "Maybe you can pick me up there."

Pick up Mom at Grace's luncheonette. I wondered if Tom would be in his usual place at the counter, perhaps with Terry in tow. That might be too much to hope for, that the men would spend any of their visiting time doing crossword puzzles at the lunch counter. But there had been a to-do at the post-groundbreaking cookies and coffee event. Tom may have overhead some cause for David

Rayburn's collapse, may have news of his condition. "Sounds good," I said. "I'll meet you there."

Mom slammed the door shut, and a whole new breed of dread washed over me.

I wasn't so much worried about David as I was curious what the scuttlebutt was. Oh, holy donkeys. I'd become a small-town resident.

Grasping the steering wheel, foot firmly on the brake, I let my head fall forward until my forehead hit the wheel. My transformation from city dweller to small-town girl was complete.

4

The local veterinarian was only local two days
a week. It said something about the low cost of rent
in Wenwood that keeping the office shuttered for the
remaining days was financially feasible. It also said
something about the pet population.

But I was glad to be able to take Friday to Dr. Bucherati's two-exam-room, one-surgery building at the resi-
dential end of Grand. Had it not been a Wenwood office
day for her, I would have been stuck driving all the way
up to the emergency vet in Newbridge. Fifteen minutes
in the car with a yowling cat was tough enough on my
nerves and my emotions. Forty might have brought me
to tears.

I steered the car into the tiny four-car parking lot span-
ning the front of the building and cut the engine. Without

the hum of the engine and the constant background rumble of the radio, Friday's complaint seemed three times as loud. I wouldn't have been surprised had the hair on the back of my neck stood on end.

Out of the car, with the back door open, I tugged the portable kennel closer and slid my fingers through the top bars hoping to make contact with the soft swipe of gray fur on top of Friday's head. "It's okay," I said, though she pressed herself into the corner and out of my reach. "Doctor's going to take good care of you."

I hauled the carrier out of the backseat and lugged it through the glass door into the waiting room, where a mother and son sat holding the leash of a coal-black puppy. Under normal circumstances I would likely have been rendered motionless by the cuteness. But I had a cat with a problem.

I rushed across the pitted linoleum floor to the reception desk. "Hello," I said, fully expecting the bleached blond woman behind the counter to return the greeting. Or, you know, ask how she could help me.

Without looking up, without uttering a word, the receptionist pushed a clipboard toward me.

"There's something wrong with my cat," I said.

Eyes on the paperwork beneath her fingertips, she asked, "Do you have an appointment?"

"No."

"Is the cat bleeding or showing any signs of broken bones or broken skin, any kind of trauma?"

"No, but—"

"Sign in and have a seat."

I used the office's pen on a chain to chisel my name

on the sign-in sheet affixed to the clipboard then took a
seat on the hard-cushioned bench lining the side wall.
From that point it took nearly half an hour before Dr.
Bucherati called us into the examination room.

Down the wood-paneled hallway I followed the vet
into the second room on the left and put the cat carrier
on the stainless steel table while the doc closed the door.

"And why are we seeing Friday today?" Dr. Bucherati
asked. She stood across the table from me, waiting while
I unlatched the carrier and lifted out the cat.

Holding Friday steady on the table while Dr. Bucherati checked my baby's teeth, eyes, and coat, I explained
Friday's recent vocalizations, confessed my worries,
and even admitted to my mother's broken-glass theory.

Dr. Bucherati—at least one full head shorter than I
was—looked up at me from beneath her brows, her brown
eyes wide with sympathy. "From what you say," she said,
"I have every confidence there is nothing wrong with this
cat. Only that she has come into heat. For many cats . . ."

Dr. Bucherati continued, patiently explaining to me the
birds and the bees as they pertain to felines. I didn't need
a mirror to confirm the heat that was making my cheeks
feel huge was, in fact, a bright red blush. The burning
sensation was one I knew well. She was in heat. Of course.
How had I failed to misread the signs? Some cat mommy
I was.

I became fascinated with everything in the room that
was not Dr. Bucherati's patient expression: the filing cabinet shoved into a corner, the old-fashioned white-painted
aluminum medicine cabinet behind the doc, the glass-
fronted shelves on the wall over her shoulder with their

row on row of containers and phials and little boxes—
sodium something or other, blah blah benzoate, atropine,
omega-3 tablets. Omega-3 tablets? Weren't humans supposed to take those?

"Of course, since you say there is a possibility she
ingested glass," Dr. Bucherati said in a grave tone, "I have
to recommend we do an x-ray, to be certain this is not the
case. After this, we can make an appointment to spay
Friday. You will have her spayed, yes?"

We had discussed the pros (so many) and cons (so few)
of spaying the cat when first I decided to keep Friday.
The choice to spay had been a simple one. But I thought
I'd have a few more months to save up for the fee. And
now, making things even more fun, we would be adding
on the cost of an x-ray, which would no doubt require
sedation to keep the sweet but active furball in one place.

"So x-ray and spay," I said.

"If you choose to spay her, that is correct." She shifted
her head so she was looking at me from the corner of her
eye. "Will you . . ." she began in the manner of a school-
teacher looking for a correct answer.

"I choose to," I said.

Dr. Bucherati's contented nod told me I had chosen
wisely. She scooped Friday up in her arms and deposited
the cat in the carrier with all the effort it took to drop a
piece of bread in a toaster. "We will keep her overnight
for the x-ray," she said. "I will call you with the results as
soon as I am done. Make sure you tell Lee at the front
desk that you need an appointment for spaying next week."

"Wait. Overnight? But—"

"I will have to give her a little sedative so she will

be still for the x-ray. It is best she remain in our care until the effect wears off."

"But you're not here in the morning." Distress squeezed my heart. "How will I be able to bring her home?"

Dr. Bucherati smiled, a surprisingly comforting and sympathetic smile given that she thought I'd allowed my kitten to chew on glass. "It is true I will not be here myself, but there will still be someone here to care for those animals boarding with us. Speak with Lee and she will tell you when it is best for you to come."

My heart ached a little to watch Dr. Bucherati pull Friday's carrier off the exam table and prepare to take her away from me. The little one had slept beside me on my spare pillow (or my neck, depending on her mood) every night since I first brought her home. Hers was the presence that made me feel less alone, that smoothed over the raw patches on my soul and reminded me I could still love another being. Without her close by, how was I going to rest? How could I let Dr. Bucherati take her away from me, even if it was just for one night?

I knew without doubt that she had not ingested any glass. She had never even caught a sliver in her paw. Maybe the x-rays weren't necessary.

I took a steadying breath and mentally shook myself. When it comes to all creatures in your care, better safe than sorry. I could last one night without Friday.

Cat carrier in hand, Dr. Bucherati left the examination room. Shoulders sagging, I departed behind her, steadfastly retracing my steps to the waiting room rather than following the vet across the hall to the door leading to the surgery and boarding area.

In the waiting room I sidestepped a big black German shepherd whose paws, I would swear, were bigger than the steering wheel of my car. The dog whined a little as I sneaked past, and I tamped down the urge to reach out and pet its head; I had no way of knowing if the dog wanted affection or a snack.

I stopped at the counter to make the appointment for the spay while waiting for Dr. Bucherati to appear with Friday's file. The receptionist would need the doctor's notes in order to assemble the charges.

I got a good look at the dark roots beneath the receptionist's bleached blond 'do, easy to notice with the way she kept her head down until it was convenient for her to look up and acknowledge my presence. I studied the clock behind her—old school circular—the calendar below it, and the mini-fridge nestled into the corner. "Hello?" I said.

She sighed but didn't look up. "I don't have the file from the doctor yet."

"I know. I have to make an appointment to have my cat spayed." I rested my purse atop the counter, crossed my arms over it as though keeping my wallet extra safe.

"Tuesday mornings are surgeries here, or you can make an appointment for Monday at the Clarkston office."

"Tuesday would be fine."

Long fingernails clacked away on the keyboard as she brought up the scheduling software. We settled on a time and reviewed the presurgical procedures for the cat, with Dr. Bucherati arriving with Friday's folder and confirming the importance of sticking strictly to the instructions.

With all the information at hand, the receptionist hit me first with the cost of the office visit with x-ray and sedation and then with the estimate for the spay. I clutched my purse tight, willed the sinking dread from showing on my face. My money was going out faster than it was coming in. "Is that all?" I murmured, a squeak of distress lifting my tone.

"I understand," the receptionist said. Her softened voice and a nod of her head made her seem surprisingly sympathetic. "It's not easy living around here, is it?"

"Such a nice area but not enough . . ." I bit back the rest of my complaint. No, I wasn't saving a lot of money. I wasn't going to be rich anytime soon, but I was getting by.

"Not enough work," she finished for me. She set her fists on her hips and fixed her gaze on me. "And do you believe those people who don't want the new shopping center to be built? Unbelievable. I'm a single mother. You know what it's like trying to raise a kid around here? The sooner that thing gets built the better. I'll finally have a chance to work more than two or three days a week and there's people protesting? Please."

I shook my head in vaguely sympathetic agreement. I didn't exactly see the new promenade as providing any kind of employment security, but I didn't want to rain on anyone's parade who did. My own economic pinch was enough for me to worry about. The last thing I needed was a hefty vet bill. But I wanted Friday to have the care she needed, so there was no question of backing out.

I pulled my last-resort Visa from my wallet and handed it to the receptionist. There was only one solution to this money dilemma: I was going to have to cobble together an assortment of stained glass pieces for Carrie to sell . . . and cross my fingers that they did.


Back in the car, I switched the radio station from Grandy's customary all-news programming to what passed for the region's version of a rock station. I was rewarded with the soul-soothing sound of Freddy Mercury's voice singing "Under Pressure." David Bowie didn't hurt the tune any, but it was Freddy's voice that managed to ease both my worry for Friday and my sorrow.

I reassured myself it was only one night that I would be without my fluffy buddy. One night this week, one night next. And as I navigated back roads and side streets on my way to Grand, I marveled at myself, at how quickly and completely I had grown attached to her, how upsetting the thought of being without her. That wicked little voice in the back of my head insinuated my attachment to the cat was the result of my childhood with my mother, the frequent moves and the less frequent stepfathers. I turned the radio volume loud enough to drown out both my thoughts and the sound of my voice. I sang along with Freddy and David, then Steven, then Axl. Song by song, focusing on the lyrics, on what came next in the music and not what came next in my life—or came before, for that matter—I made my way into the village of Wenwood.

The summer was long gone and the seasonal traffic with it. Trees had begun to dress themselves in autumn colors and dropped a few leaves on the brick and cement sidewalks, a preview of the leaf-strewn weeks to come. I slipped the Jeep into an open space right on Grand, a space that never would have remained vacant had August gone on forever.

I held my coat closed rather than spend time on the zipper. A few brisk paces ahead and I ducked through the door of Grace's luncheonette. The welcoming bell jingled overhead, signaling my arrival to those gathered within.

From the entry the lunch counter was ahead and to the left, allowing me to see the faces of those seated there and they could see me—which made things doubly odd that no one so much as looked in my direction. Stunned motionless, I stood at the end of the counter and gaped. There was Tom on his usual stool, his friend Terry beside him. Grace's feet were on the service side of the counter, but her elbows rested on the countertop as she leaned close to Tom and Terry. And there, squeezed between Tom and the wall that divided the luncheonette from its kitchen, was my good friend Diana Davis. Better known as Aspiring Detective Davis.

Diana, at last, glanced my way and nodded briskly, businesslike. Her lips were set in a tight, almost somber line and a quick check of the rest of the group showed her expression mirrored on each of their faces.

The improved mood Freddy Mercury had set in motion faded faster than a cheap dye job doused in salt water. "What's going on?" I asked, moving farther into the luncheonette. "What happened?"

Grace straightened, swiped an imaginary crumb off the counter. "Georgia, honey. Cup of coffee?"

"Sure, thanks." I tugged off my coat and dumped it across the back of the empty booth to my right. "Is everything okay? You all look . . ."

Tom pointed an arthritic finger at me. "You were there. You saw."

"I saw?" I perched on the only vacant stool and leaned forward a tad so I could see the men's faces.

"You saw that man that . . . that . . ."

"David Rayburn," Terry said. He folded his arms across his broad chest, cleared his throat.

I caught Diana's eye. "The guy with the heart attack?"

"Oh, ho ho." Tom smacked the counter with the flat of his palm. "That was no heart attack."

Diana huffed. "Tom, we don't know for sure what it was or what it wasn't."

"Well, now, Diana," Grace said, placing a porcelain mug on the counter. "You did say odds were—"

"I know what I said," Diana snapped. Eyes wide, nostrils slightly flared, she squared her shoulders and stood just that little bit straighter. An observant person could see anger coming on Diana like storm clouds approaching on the horizon. "I said the victim's symptoms were inconsistent with a heart attack. Doesn't make it impossible."

Arms still folded over his chest, Terry turned his swivel stool so he was facing Diana. "That is what you said. But you also said you were down at the bakery. Now, unless things have changed, the bakery still serves coffee and yet here you are, picking up three coffees to go and a couple donuts. Means you're not entirely comfortable with the refreshments on offer down there."

Terry let the statement hang. While Diana's face continued to redden, Grace pushed the porcelain cup toward me without even looking in my direction. Her gaze was locked on Terry. Though the steam was swirling above the cup of coffee, promising warmth and energy all in one tasty package, I didn't want to pull my gaze away from Terry's face long enough to take a sip. I didn't want to miss a thing.

"What are you saying, Ter?" Tom asked, his voice unusually small.

Terry shot Diana a quick glance. "I'm saying that poor man that died—and he did die, didn't he?"

Diana made no response. Terry continued. "That man was poisoned."

I would call the statement a bombshell, but somehow I think bombshells ought to create noise and some measure of havoc. Terry's theory caused a resounding silence. It seemed even the kitchen—whose noises were usually a constant background hum of clattering dishes and running water—had gone still and quiet.

I sneaked a peek at Diana, and her eyes met mine like she was seeking a lifeline. It was a rare expression from her, and one I couldn't ignore perhaps because of that rarity.

I gave Terry a friendly tap with my elbow. "Heck of a theory," I said. "But there were a lot of people in that tent. You and I were among them. If it was poison, how come we're okay?"

"Poison. Bah." Grace produced a counter-wipe towel

from the pocket of her ever-present apron and swiped at the counter with it. "That's ridiculous."

"Right? Not to mention Rozelle," I added in. "Not even possible."

Even Tom shook his head. "I gotta agree, Terry. That's not something Rozelle would do. She wouldn't hurt a mosquito, that one."

Terry raised a hand as though to pause the conversation. "I didn't say anything about Rozelle. But something in that bakery—"

"But we all had that coffee yesterday," I said. "Well, most of us had coffee anyway." There was also tea and cocoa on offer—which is to say an urn of hot water behind tea bags and hot chocolate packets.

"And everyone had cookies and whatnot," Tom added. "Even you."

"Care to make another guess as to why the police are down at the bakery right now?" Terry asked.

If there had been a back on the stool, I'm sure he would have leaned into it. He had that look of subdued pride on his face—the subtlest of smiles and a little glint in his eye.

Diana pulled in a slow, deep breath, eyes slipping closed momentarily. "I really wish I hadn't come in here."

From the open walk-through doorway separating the counter service area from the kitchen, a tall, reedy man ambled out, brown paper shopping bag in hand. He lifted the bag—handles straining against the weight of the sack—and rested it atop the counter. "Here you go, Diana. All set."

"Thank God," she muttered. She took the shopping

bag from the counter, eased out from the corner space she had been tucked into. "Have a nice day, gentlemen."

Tom sat straighter. "You can't go yet. You didn't tell us if Terry's right or not. Was David Rayburn poisoned or wasn't he?"

Her smile was just the slightest bit evil and a big bit smug. "At this time we have no definitive cause of death." She nodded a brief good-bye and took a few steps toward the exit, which put her even with where I sat. "Pour House tonight?" she asked.

"Absolutely," I assured her.

I thought a measure of tension left her shoulders before she continued on her way out of the luncheonette and onto the sidewalk. When she was past the window and headed for the bakery, I turned to Terry. "Do you really think Rayburn was poisoned?"

"What do you think?" he countered. "Tom speaks pretty highly of your skills as a sleuth."

I nearly choked on my coffee. "I don't have any skills," I said. "Not really. Not as a sleuth, I mean. I just have a habit of being in the right place with the wrong people."

He gave me a little sideways smile. "That's not a bad habit to have for a detective."

I held up both hands, palms out. I don't know if I was signaling surrender or hoping to create some invisible barrier that would keep his words away. "Oh no. No thanks. I have a job. I have several jobs. And none of them involve encountering criminals."

Grace laughed, picked up a folded newspaper that I knew from long experience was open to the crossword puzzle. "I wouldn't be too sure about that, Georgia. You never know who's sitting in the dark at your granddad's movie house."

"Oh, thanks," I said as the bell over the door jingled. "That fills me with all kinds of confidence."

"Georgia."

My mother's voice cut through me like a cold shard. There was a certain note her voice hit only when I did something she was going to make me regret, which in the past had ranged anywhere from cutting my own hair to staying out past curfew. A long time past curfew.

I looked over my shoulder to where she had come to stand behind me.

"The police are inside the bakery, and one of them is looking for you. Care to tell me what that's all about?"

5

Life had settled into a comforting routine since last I had to face any member of the Pace County Police Department other than Diana. I wasn't eager to reintroduce the police into my every day anytime soon. Sure, at some point in the future I would no doubt encounter them when the Heaney case went to trial. Until then, I was content to operate like an average citizen who had no need to keep the number for the precinct listed in her cell phone under frequent contacts. There was also the small matter of one Detective Chris "Chip" Nolan, who, when his invitation to dinner had shocked me speechless, wrongly presumed my silence meant I had no interest. Now, whether I did or didn't made no difference. I was as committed to Tony as I could be without, you know, declarations and promises and rings and whatnot. But I hadn't seen Chip since he had taken my statement after the disowned heir to the Heaney estate had threatened Carrie and me at gunpoint. I was uncertain whether things would be at all awkward between us. And yeah, throw in my mother's presence for added amusement.

I gave it my best shot, but there was no convincing her to wait at the luncheonette while I checked in with the police. She walked beside me along the sidewalk, head high, handbag tucked tight under her arm. I might have had a momentary flashback, a long-buried memory of walking with her like this along the halls of yet another unfamiliar school so she could introduce me to yet another principal pretending to be interested. But the scene through the bakery window dispelled those visions from my past.

Rozelle kept only two small tables inside the bakery with a total of six chairs between them. She was seated at one. Detective Nolan was standing beside her.

"Him," my mother said as I suffered a figurative punch in the gut at the sight of the CLOSED sign hung on the door and reached for the handle. "That's the man who was asking for you."

I turned back to face her. "What were you doing down here anyway? You were supposed to meet me at Grace's."

"How was I supposed to know the bakery was closed? I wanted to get some fresh bread for your grandfather," she said. "He likes the rye."

I almost said I know, that I always kept a spare loaf in the freezer in case of emergencies requiring toast or roast beef, but before I could get the words out, Detective Nolan called my name.

"Come on in," he said once he had my attention.

I waved my mother ahead through the door and followed her inside. As predictable as sunrise, the gorgeous aroma of fresh-baked breads and sweet cakes filled my senses, making my mouth water and my belly protest its need of a treat. The misbehaved voice in the back of my mind tried to make me believe since I had to leave my beloved cat at the vet that I deserved something highly fattening to ease the upset. But the display cases filled with Rozelle's amazing baked goods stretched along the right side of the shop, and Detective Nolan stood on the left, hands in his pockets and elbows holding open his suit jacket. I had a feeling the pose was calculated to show off the gleaming detective's shield clipped to his belt.

"I heard you were looking for me," I said, looking away from Nolan and instead searching the shop for Diana. Rozelle remained seated at the little table, hands clasped tightly in her lap, gaze locked on the display counter, and a single uniformed officer stood admiring the cups and saucers that decorated the far wall. Diana was nowhere to be found. "Or someone was anyway. Where's Diana?"

Detective Nolan tipped his head toward the back ovens. "Working," he said. In two long strides he stood before us, extended his hand to my mother. "We didn't meet properly. I'm Detective Nolan, Pace County Police Department."

"Joanne Sutter." My mother laid the tips of her fingers against his palm, as though she was far too old-fashioned to shake hands with a man.

If Detective Nolan was at all surprised to hear my mother refer to herself as Sutter while my last name was Kelly, it did nothing to disturb his impassive cop face. "Why don't you have a seat, Mrs. Sutter? I'd like to talk to Georgia for just a few minutes."

Mom looked from Nolan to me and back again. "What business do you have with my daughter, Detective? Don't tell me she's in some kind of trouble," she said over a laugh.

Nolan treated her to a lightning strike of a smile—a brilliant flash that was gone as fast as it came. "Not that I'm aware of," he said.

I knew he was kidding. I knew I hadn't done anything to warrant suspicion from the police. So why did my stomach knot? What was my conscience guilty of?

"You know when she was a teenager, she had a bad habit of driving without a license," my mother offered.

"Once." I folded my arms. "Once I drove without a license. Once does not create a habit."

Mom gave me an indulgent smile before renewing her efforts at charming Detective Nolan. "She's never been one to follow orders."

His smile then was slyer, almost mischievous, and directed at me. "I never would have guessed."

"Oh, the stories I could tell you," Mom said.

"I'd love to hear them sometime, Mrs. Sutter." He gestured toward the empty chair opposite Rozelle. "But right now, if you wouldn't mind . . ."

Mom finally acquiesced. She joined Rozelle at the little round table, immediately launching into a conversation about Grandy's fondness for fresh-baked rye bread, while Detective Nolan tipped his head toward the front door.

I preceded him out onto the sidewalk, surprised to find that after leaving the sweet, yeasty aroma of the bakery, the early autumn air carried a delicious fragrance all its own, a crisp, clean scent as refreshing as a soft breeze over new snow.

Turning my face to the sky, I took a deep breath, let my eyes slip closed. One deep breath to keep thoughts of my cat and my mother and the question of who had sharper claws from intruding on my thoughts and making it tough to focus on whatever it was Nolan wanted to talk to me about this time. One deep breath to help me face the good detective, just the two of us, for the first time in months.

"So that's your mother, huh?" Nolan asked once the door had shut behind him.

"According to all reliable accounts," I said. "Maybe some unreliable ones, too. It's possible."

I don't know why I expected him to look somehow different since the last time I had seen him. A couple of months would not have changed his appearance, yet I found myself peering close, looking for a few more laugh lines around his eyes, a wider swath of gray at his temples, but neither were there.

"What, um, what did you need to talk to me about?" I asked. Again I folded my arms across my chest, somehow bracing myself.

He met my gaze, eyes locked on mine as seconds ticked away. I nearly shivered with the feeling he was trying to see inside me something I wasn't willing to show. One breath before the situation went from awkward to uncomfortable, he finally spoke. "According to Rozelle, you entered the reception tent early yesterday."

I nodded. "I went to see if she needed any help setting up."

"You want to walk me through that?"

I didn't think there could be anything illuminating in my story of heading for the tent before the speeches were over and offering to put napkins on tables, but for Nolan's sake, I went back through it, step by step, as best I could recall.

"So I helped the girl, Nicole, put cookies out on tables," I finished. "Chocolate chip and oatmeal raisin."

"And what was Rozelle doing while you were doing that? Do you recall?"

The door to the bakery swung open and Diana stepped out onto the sidewalk, a cardboard box with filled bags labeled EVIDENCE tucked under her arm. She kept her head down, avoiding eye contact with both me and the detective.

I watched her for moments only before turning back to Detective Nolan. "You don't honestly believe that man opposed to building the promenade was poisoned, do you?"

He set his hands on his hips, hung his head as he sighed. "That's the preliminary cause of death. It's my job to investigate based on that finding."

"Okay, sure, I understand that part. But . . . Rozelle?

Seriously? Come on. Rozelle runs a little bakery that closes by five. What possible motive would she have for poisoning David Rayburn? You'd do better to look for someone who stands to benefit from the promenade. Like someone in building or construction," I said.

Detective Nolan's brows rose high.

Oh, crap. "Pretend I didn't say that last part."

"Georgia, just tell me what Rozelle was doing while you and Nicole were putting out cookies."

"She was directing," I said. "Or overseeing or whatever else you want to call it. Making sure we separated the cookies and put them on each table."

"That's all she was doing? Giving orders while you did all the work?" Nolan sounded doubtful, as though he couldn't quite believe someone as diminutive as Rozelle would shout out commands.

"Come on, Detective. That's not the way it was at all. She . . ." As I spoke, my mind reviewed the memory of that morning, feeding my consciousness images it deemed relevant. "She was holding a pastry box," I said, my voice betraying me by going soft. "She had cheese Danish. Special made. Sugar free, gluten free. I think they were for David . . ."

Detective Nolan nodded. Had Rozelle told him about them? Had he guessed? No spark of surprise or intrigue lit his face; I was telling him something he already knew.

But it was something I hadn't put together until that moment. The Danish. The one thing not everyone had eaten. The one thing only Rayburn had access to. All at once my head went empty and light. My thighs went weak and my knees threatened to buckle. I reached a hand toward Detective Nolan.

He caught my arm and held me steady. "Georgia, what's wrong? Are you all right? What is it?"

"Grandy," I said, nearly a whisper. "She offered to put some aside that I could bring home for my grandfather."

My gaze had somehow locked on Nolan's detective shield while his hands held me steady and vaguely upright. The shield. The gold-colored symbol of protect and serve. I wanted to find comfort in that symbol, but the glimpse of the grip of the revolver tucked into its holster served only to reinforce the threat of danger.

"It's all right," Nolan said. He slipped an arm across my shoulders—more businesslike than tender—and turned me back to the bakery entrance. "Let's go inside. Have a seat. No one's going to hurt Pete."

I took one step at his urging before digging in my heels in resistance. Straightening, I said, "No, that's just it. She would never hurt my grandfather. She's crazy about him."

His eyes searched mine. I could almost see a question forming in his brown-eyed gaze.

The bakery door banged open and my mother rushed to my side.

"What happened?" she asked. "Are you okay, honey?" She turned and looked daggers at Detective Nolan while trying to pull me free of his hold. "What did you say to her?"

"Are you sure?" he asked me, tone earnest and gaze intent.

"A hundred percent," I assured him before turning to my mother. "I'm fine, Mom. Just a little light-headed."

Nolan nodded sharply. "Could still be the bakery."

"But not Rozelle."

But if not Rozelle, then who?

My mother wanted to drive straight home following my chat with Detective Nolan. She claimed I looked pale. As a redheaded, freckle-faced Irish girl, I always looked pale. It took no small effort on my part to convince my mother I was capable of continuing with the day as planned. At length she determined it was better to go inside the market than to stand on the sidewalk and argue with me, and we spent the brief excursion with her complaining about the lack of selection in between my constant reassurances that I was in no danger of losing consciousness.

I thought once we arrived back at Grandy's house that I could retreat to my room. I needed a few minutes to myself to allow everything that had happened in the past couple of days to sink in. Between the idea of retreating to my single-bed room—the room I was relegated to in the childhood years I'd spent living with Grandy and Grandma—and the fact of my mother driving me around, a flashback to my teen years loomed large and dangerous. Adjusting to my new life as a permanent citizen of Wenwood had been tough enough; losing my sense of adulthood would no doubt cause a setback.

"Maybe we shouldn't tell your grandfather about the police." My mother made the final turn onto Grandy's street, and I smiled, remembering Grandy saying the same thing about telling *her* all those months ago.

"I think he can handle it," I said. "He's pretty used to my run-ins with the police. Besides, the bakery's going to be closed for a while. He'll find out. And you know what a bear he'll be if he even suspects we knew and didn't tell him."

She slowed the car as the house came into view. Cedar shakes in need of a paint job, split-rail porch with a pair of battered Adirondack chairs, and Grandy and my mother's husband, Ben, standing amid the fallen leaves on the front lawn, looking up at the old cedar tree.

"Your grandfather." Mom shook her head, made the final turn into the driveway. "He thinks he's the only one in this family allowed to keep secrets."

She shifted the gear into "Park" and shut off the engine then turned to me with narrow, accusatory eyes. "Not that you're any better," she said. "How could you not tell me about your grandfather being arrested? And on suspicion of murder, of all things."

For the nine-billionth time I said, "We didn't want to spoil your honeymoon. What were you going to do anyway? Cut your trip short? And do what? He already had a lawyer and wouldn't let anyone see him. Besides, it wasn't like he was guilty."

In my haste to escape, I pushed open the door and practically tumbled out of the SUV, bag of groceries in hand. Someday my mother and I would make it through more than forty-eight hours without any reference to Grandy's blissfully brief and completely unjust incarceration. Until then, I fully intended to run away from her every time the subject came up.

"Something wrong with the tree?" I called then slammed shut the car door.

Grandy kept his head tilted back, eyes on the bare branches overhead.

Ben folded his arms and faced me. "I was pointing out to Pete you've got a little fungus up there. It could weaken some of the larger branches. Then all you need is a heavy, wet snow and those branches could fall. They're a hazard."

Grandy rolled his jaw and turned to face me. "We'll have to get a tree specialist out to have a look."

"A specialist?" I repeated. "Because a general practice tree doctor won't be good enough?"

"What's wrong with the tree?" Mom asked, joining us in the middle of the lawn.

"Apparently it's a hazard," Grandy said.

"You don't want to wait too long," Ben said. "You folks get snow pretty early up here, don't you?"

"Not that early," Mom said. "And besides, Dad has a snow blower."

I felt my eyes crease in equal depth with my confusion. I had been in and out of the backyard shed about a billion times over the summer, planting, pruning, fertilizing. And the garage held every implement too delicate or valuable to be left in the shed. "There's no snow blower," I said.

"Of course there is," Mom said. She looked to Grandy. "You bought one two years ago, didn't you?"

Grandy shot quick daggers at me before he pursed his lips and turned his gaze to the branches overhead.

"Dad?" Mom prompted. "Dad! Who's been shoveling the snow?"

"I'm capable of shoveling snow, Joanne," he said. "I'm not an invalid."

"At your age—" Mom began, but Ben cut her off.

"Pete, you know that for every five years over the age of fifty, a man's risk of heart attack increases by twenty percent. You shouldn't take chances."

"Don't worry about it, okay?" I said. "I'm here. I can shovel the snow."

"You don't have to shovel the snow," Grandy said. "I'll hire someone."

"That's what you said year after year, Dad, and it was a lie every time. You finally agreed to buy a snow blower, and then that turns out to be a lie, too." My mother raised her arms, let them fall with a slap against her thighs. "What am I going to do with you?"

"How about we go shopping for a snow blower later in the week, huh, Pete?" Ben suggested. "Give me a chance to see more of the area."

"Please, Ben," Mom said, and for a minute I thought she was going to ask him to stay out of the conversation, but no such luck. "Maybe if you're there, he'll really get a snow blower."

"I can shovel the snow," I repeated. "There's no reason to spend all that money on a machine."

"Don't be silly," Ben said. "What happens when you move out? A snow blower will make things a hundred times easier."

"Why—" I began, but Grandy met my eyes, shook his head ever so slightly. "No harm in looking," he said. He pointed to the reusable grocery bag I held. "More food?"

he asked. "I don't suppose you got me any more of Rozelle's cookies."

I noted that he avoided asking about cookies for us. Us would include Ben, who had eaten his way through all but the one mini Linzer tart Mom had eaten, leaving Grandy with none for his after-dinner indulgence.

"Rozelle didn't open today," I said.

"And the police insisted on talking to Georgia." Mom sounded angry about it, as though her taking offense somehow proved the insanity of the police.

Grandy shrugged. "The police always want to talk to Georgia. Don't worry," he said with a grin. "You get used to it."

Mom looked back and forth between us. "The two of you!" She huffed. "I have groceries to put away."

I had a bag of groceries, too, and would have to follow her into the house. Just how lucky could one girl get?

6

In the days and early weeks after I had arrived in Wenwood, I divided what belongings I hadn't put into storage between my bedroom and my workshop. My summer clothes and personal items I unpacked right away. My stained glass supplies I left in boxes but labeled each carton carefully and kept them unsealed. Glass wasn't the sort of thing you left lying around. But I had worked my way through much of my stash in making pieces for both Carrie's shop and special orders, and when I moved the last carton out of its corner in the spare room—the tiny room to which I had been banished thanks to Mom and Ben's visit—three remaining boxes were exposed. Each bore the same scrawled word: AUTUMN.

Now after leaving the boxes sealed like there was

some final slim chance I would cart them back to the city before the temperature dropped below seventy, I dragged the boxes out of their corner and tore open the tape keeping them closed. I needed sweatshirts and sweaters, a proper coat to keep me warm, and maybe a nice pair of boots. It didn't occur to me to view the opening of the cartons as some sort of defiance over Ben's conviction that I should be leaving. I supposed if I asked him, he would have recommended keeping the boxes closed until I found a new place as a means of adding an urgency to my move.

So when I found a paper-wrapped bundle of glass sheets tucked between a bulky cardigan and a Florida Gators sweatshirt, I got the shivering sense that whatever was in the package, I needed to use it to make something for me, for this new phase of my life.

I set the package of glass on the bed and tore away the masking tape holding the folds of paper together. Carefully pulling away the paper, I sucked in a surprised breath.

Van Gogh glass. How had I forgotten? How was that possible? The glorious swirls of blue and gold were painted on the glass with metallic auto paint, its opposite side sealed with a layer of black paint—a method used when making mirrors that gave the glass the same illusion of depth. Unlike most of the glass I worked with, this was opaque and not intended to have light shine through to bring out its beauty. I had fallen in love with it the moment I saw it. How could something so unique have escaped my memory? But of course, the placement within a box of clothes answered that question. I had bought the glass after all my other supplies had been packed and left in storage, when I was job hunting and sharing a two-bedroom apartment with three other girls and I should have been conserving my funds for rent and food. And yet . . .

Sometimes when life is at its toughest, finding a thing of beauty makes the struggle easier to bear.

The sheets of glass were not bank-breaking expensive. They were, in fact, reasonably, even low priced. The glass contained no precious metals to drive up its value, and held no rarity. And yet the swirl of color had reached right to my heart and I couldn't resist, even though I really didn't have money to spend on glass. That made the Van Gogh sheets an indulgence, or perhaps an investment in the belief that I would land on my feet somewhere and either have space big enough for a studio or enough money I could rent a corner in a glass shop at which to work.

With a mix of reverence and determination, I rewrapped the glass and left it on the bed. It had been forgotten in a box long enough.

Returning my attention to the carton, I selected a half-dozen sweaters and placed them, folded, upon the end of my bed. I dug a little farther until I came up with a pair of sweatpants and a faux-shearling-lined jacket and tossed them to the other end of the bed, reasoning that would be enough to keep me warm for the next month, at least. After tucking the box top folds so that the flaps wedged tightly together, I took the sweaters and the paper-wrapped glass in my arms and crept down the stairs.

Fifi was sound asleep in the low sunbeams streaking

through the living room window. Her legs were stiff straight, her tongue lolling against the side of her muzzle. When she'd first come to live with us, Grandy and I had each, separately, taken this position to mean she'd either dropped dead of a heart attack or the cat had scared her stiff. Fortunately, all it took was a few seconds of careful focus, and the rise and fall of her chest became easily visible. At which point, both Grandy and I decided she was trying to give us, or the cat, a heart attack.

But looking at Fifi renewed my awareness of how long it had been since I'd left Friday at the vet's. Those were low sun beams coming through the window, and my dog was sleeping when she might otherwise be chasing the cat.

Of course, I was carrying large sheets of glass, so rushing was out of the question as was dropping everything to call the office to check on Friday. I continued on my way, making the turn and taking the stairs down to my workshop. There, I gently set down the paper-wrapped glass on my worktable before carrying my sweaters down the few steps to the laundry room. I tossed them in the dryer and threw in a scented fabric softener sheet. With the dryer set to "Fluff" and the stored-in-cardboard scent of my sweaters on its way to being evicted, I was finally free to make the call.

I raced back up to my room to grab my cell but waited until I was once again in the workshop before I scrolled for the vet's number and hit the "Dial" icon.

Listening to the phone ring on the other end, I reached for the scrapbook storage box in which I stowed glass patterns and design ideas and kept beneath the worktable.

"Wenwood Veterinary. Can you hold?"

"Sure," I said.

I tugged the lid off the box, reached inside, and lifted out a stack of papers. Folded glass patterns mingled with pages torn from magazines and printouts of images found during one computer search or another. Back issues of stained glass "newspapers" peppered the collection, each featuring a free pattern-of-the-month. I evaluated the page on top of the pile—an image of a peacock paper-clipped to a copy of its crinkled and folded pattern. The peacock was one of those pieces I intended to make "someday." I collected patterns the way some people collected books, with plans of taking the time at some point in the future to lose oneself. I turned the peacock aside to reveal another "someday" pattern, this one of water lilies and reeds. I would have to consider making them for Carrie's shop, but first, I wanted something suitable for the Van Gogh glass.

I turned aside the water lilies and a wistful sigh escaped me. There sat not a traditional pattern, or cartoon as they were known in the stained glass world, but a list of measurements. At the left edge of the page I had clipped a picture of the finished project: an elaborate, albeit miniature, greenhouse, its style reminiscent of Great Britain's Crystal Palace. The pattern called for nothing but clear glass and a steady hand with lead. It was the need for perfectly straight lines and delicately angled corners that made the piece challenging. That, and the fact that once complete, it wasn't the sort of piece to be packed up and moved from place to place. It was a piece for a permanent home.

"How can I help you?" The voice on the other end of the phone broke clear through my wandering thoughts.

"I'm just calling to check on my cat, Friday. Last name Kelly," I said. "I left her for x-rays. I wanted to be sure she was all right."

My shoulders sagged as I held the greenhouse plans, ready to turn them aside. I had a flash of a vision where the completed greenhouse sat upon the sideboard in the dining room . . . in Grandy's dining room. But Grandy's house wasn't part of "someday," was it?

The voice said, "Okay. Friday. Feline. Yeah, you can come pick her up anytime."

I blinked. "Are you sure she can come home?" I asked eagerly. "Dr. Bucherati said she'd be there overnight."

"Says here she can be released. She's been ready for at least an hour."

I gritted my teeth momentarily, squinted one eye shut. My cat could come home and no one called me? "I'll be right there," I said, and switched off the call. I dropped the greenhouse plans back in their box without another thought. Stained glass could wait. I wanted to know if my cat was okay.

In the car, with no distractions other than the occasional falling leaf or passing vehicle, I couldn't stop myself from replaying the conversation on the lawn, with highlights of talk from the night before. It was strange for me to realize that once I'd stopped planning on returning to the city, I had also stopped thinking of moving, well, anywhere. What Ben and Mom were saying about me leaving Grandy felt like all new thoughts. Move out? I had long since decided I was staying in Wenwood for as long as I could keep my head above water financially. I had succumbed to its charm, its quirks, and its nearly tangible sense of community. And while the idea of moving out didn't necessarily mean leaving Wenwood, it did mean leaving Grandy, and that was a whole different issue.

Sure, when I'd first arrived at his doorstep with a U-Move-It trailer filled with a selection of my personal possessions and a key in my pocket to a storage facility that held the rest, I viewed my upcoming stay with Grandy as temporary. At that time I had envisioned "back on my feet" as back to the city—any city—back to the accounting department of some faceless, soulless corporation whose ultimate goal was unimaginable wealth and perhaps world domination. Wenwood, and Grandy in particular, in a short while had taught me that life really could be better without an expense account and an apartment in a building with a doorman. And me and Grandy, we made a good team, a good family. I had no desire to leave.

But then . . . maybe Grandy wanted me to go. Maybe he'd had enough of me and my glass and my propensity to bring home strays. Maybe he was eager to be on his own again and didn't have the words to tell me. Not that Grandy was one to keep his thoughts or his emotions to himself. He was a pretty straightforward guy, not known for pulling his punches. So what would stop him from being honest? Unless he worried he might hurt my feelings. Really hurt my feelings. Not like he did when he told me even Fifi would refuse to eat my lentil salad in favor of a classic bologna sandwich. A deeper hurt. The kind that risked driving an immovable wedge between us.

I couldn't quite believe that was the case. But once the idea took hold in my mind, it would be a challenge to dislodge.

Sighing, I slowed the car and turned into one of the three vacant spots in front of the veterinarian's office. I needed to stop letting Ben's commentary get under my skin. I had bigger things to worry about. Probably.

The glass rattled in the door as I pulled it open. I hustled inside the waiting room of the vet's office and straight to the reception desk. "I'm here to pick up Friday," I said.

The receptionist looked up and for a moment I was convinced she was going to tell me to sign in and wait. Instead she nodded toward the benches wrapping the waiting room. "Have a seat. I'll tell the doctor you're here."

Having studied earlier in the day the chart of dog breeds and the reasons you needed to care for your pet's dental health, I did what I'd become increasingly inclined to do while waiting. I pulled out my phone and texted Carrie. We still on for tonight? I wrote.

As I hit "Send," I realized just how much I was looking forward to seeing my friends for our regular girls' night out. Ordinarily, spending an evening with Carrie and Diana was relaxing good fun. I had a feeling tonight's get-together for me would be more like therapy.

"Friday?"

I looked up to find Dr. Bucherati standing at the end

of the reception counter, folder in hand. She smiled and waved me toward her. "Come on back."

She led me into a different exam room than the one we had been in that morning. This one was slightly larger, with a window in the wall opposite the door and a wall of cabinets above and below a countertop facing the aluminum exam table. Atop the table was my pet carrier, and Friday crouched within it growling softly.

"Her x-rays are clear," Dr. Bucherati said, opening the folder. Checking what was written there, she continued, "There's no evidence she ingested any foreign substances and her bones show normal growth."

As confident as I had been that Friday hadn't swallowed glass or worse, still I went a little limp with relief. I popped open the carrier door and peered in at her.

She growled louder, clearly not as happy to see me as I was to see her.

"She is due, though, for her second dose of FeLV. Do you want to do that now or wait until you bring her for her spay?" Dr. Bucherati had already stepped back to the cabinets and pulled open a drawer. From where I stood, it was easy to spy the collection of prepackaged injections arrayed in containers.

"Um . . ." I stalled, guilt awakening in my belly.

Dr. Bucherati smiled gently. "You already paid for this one when we did the first."

I shook my head, lowered my eyes. "I'm sorry. I hate to reduce things to money. Yes, if you can do the injection now, that would be fine."

"Don't worry," she said, turning her back to me as she

sorted through the selection of paper-wrapped syringes. "I understand the cost of pet care can be prohibitive. We can always work out a payment plan if it becomes necessary."

"Really?" I said. "But . . ." I looked to the door, which was about all I could do to convey the idea that the receptionist had a different perspective.

"Don't worry about Lee," she said. "If I tell her it's okay, she'll set up the plan. I don't want anyone to risk their pet's health because they fear the cost of care. Now. If you could take her out of the carrier and hold her, this will only take a moment."

Gratitude rose an unexpected lump in my throat. Swallowing against the threat of tears, I carefully extracted Friday from the carrier, thanking Dr. Bucherati as I did so. It hit me then that my day had been a roller coaster of emotions from family to pets to police.

I was definitely in need of a night among friends.


Back when I told Terry I had no leanings toward being a sleuth, I might have been bending the truth. No, I had no great desire to hang out a shingle as a private detective or join the police force and patrol the county with Diana. However . . .

Yeah, the first time I went knee deep into a crime investigation, it was more of an accident. Grandy had been arrested on suspicion of murder. Sure, the victim and Grandy were definitely on the outs at the time the man was killed, but I knew Grandy was innocent. So I did what I could to figure out who really wielded the murder weapon. My grandfather . . . Well, I didn't have a lot of family. I wasn't going to lose him.

The second time, okay, I stuck my nose into that one on purpose, too. But the nut job not only trashed my best friend Carrie's antiques shop, but also broke into her apartment, burned down her ex-husband's office, and murdered the ex-husband's law partner. If there was anything I could have done to help identify the miscreant before Carrie got hurt, I was more than willing to give it a try.

Still. I didn't know David Rayburn beyond recognizing his face from the local paper. Even if he had been the victim of foul play, I was content to let the police handle the investigation.

"But what about Rozelle?" Carrie asked when I announced my resolution to keep my freckled nose out of it. "How can you not help her? What happened to being a useful resident or a valuable citizen or whatever it was you wanted to be?"

We sat in one of the few booths at the Pour House, Wenwood village's one and only watering hole. Its décor was all exposed wood and dark leather, and its clientele was as well aged as the top-shelf Scotch. Carrie, Diana, and I met there every Thursday for our girls' night out. With each of us only just north of thirty, we were routinely the youngest demographic in the bar. "Carrie, really. Rozelle? There's nothing to help her with. You know as well as I do she had nothing to do with David Rayburn's death. Everyone knows that."

"Yes," she said. "But can we prove that? As I recall, the police are pretty big on proof."

I shook my head and sighed. "The police took a boat-load of samples out of the bakery and I can pretty well guarantee you they won't find anything in the flour other than, you know, flour. I'd take that as proof."

"I suppose I would, too. You're right. This is Rozelle after all." She took a ladylike sip of wine. "What does Pete have to say about all this?"

"I don't think he knows yet. If he does, someone else told him."

"News travels fast around here."

"You don't say." I grinned. Briefly. Wenwood was a small town. News traveled faster through its streets than it did on social media. "Well, if he knows, he hasn't said anything to me. Not that he's had a chance with—"

"Oh my gosh! That's right. Your mom is in town."

"You mean my mom is in my bedroom." I grimaced. I know, I know. There are way bigger issues in the world than my frustration at having to surrender my room, with my nice, big bed, for the week or so Mom and Ben planned on staying. But it's hard to keep perspective when you haven't slept well.

Carrie chuckled. "It's not that bad."

I was saved from arguing—and displaying how truly shallow I can be—by Diana's arrival. She dropped her purse on the seat next to me then pointed to me then Carrie and back again. "Sorry I'm late. You guys ready for another?"

Our standard was one drink. One drink was enough to relax and be social and feel like being out was some-what special. If conversation was really rolling, we'd move on to club sodas for me and Carrie and diet cola for Diana.

"More wine, please," I said.

Carrie's eyes widened in surprise.

"Carrie?" Diana asked.

She shook her head—"No thank you"—and waited for Diana to move to the bar before furrowing her brow at me. "A second glass? That's not like you."

"There's nothing wrong with a second glass of wine."

"I didn't say there was. I just said it's not like you. What aren't you telling me?"

Worried about what my eyes might give away if I continued to allow Carrie to study me, I angled my head so I could see Diana at the bar tapping her foot while she waited for the bartender to bring her wine.

"Georgia . . ." Carrie tried to sound stern—she always sounded like she was holding back a burp when she attempted this—but failed to pull it off.

"Nothing," I said. I tried to catch the score on the hockey game playing on the flat screen at the end of the bar. Instead I caught the eye of one of the Pour House regulars. Not wanting to give the impression I was interested in him, I glanced away quickly.

Carrie took in a noisy breath and sat back. "You know, I have a mom who comes to visit, too. It's not easy."

I flapped a hand at her, dismissing her comment. "I'm fine with my mom visiting. I'm just being a baby about the bedroom thing."

She narrowed one eye at me.

"There's nothing," I insisted.

In the same moment, Diana lifted the two glasses of wine from the bar and headed back to our booth. "What's nothing?" she asked.

"My mother being here," I said before Carrie could. "Apart from the fact that I'm stuck in the tiny guest room for the duration, I'm fine with it. Now tell us what's going on with Rozelle."

Both of Diana's brows rose high on her forehead. She slid into the booth beside me, gently placed the wine glasses down on the table. "I . . . I don't know what you mean."

It was my turn to huff. "I was telling Carrie about how you guys took a bunch of samples from the bakery this morning."

"Don't listen to her," Carrie said. "She's trying to change the subject."

"That so?" Diana asked.

"No," I said.

"Yes," Carrie countered.

"Look, I'm fine with my mother visiting. It's strange, I know, but I do actually get along with her."

Diana shifted in her seat so she could face both Carrie and me somewhat equally. "Is it your stepfather then?"

I held up a hand. "Okay, whoa. There is no way we're going to refer to my mother's husband as my stepfather."

Wrapping a finger around a low-hanging brown curl, Carrie said, "You know, technically, the man your mother marries—"

"I don't care about technically or legally or historically. We will be referring to Ben only as he relates to my mother, not to me, got it?" Wrapping one hand around the glass of wine Diana had brought me and keeping hold of the remains of my other glass, I lifted my elbows onto the table and pulled both glasses in close. "I've had enough stepfathers," I said, my voice sounding small even to me. "I prefer not to get attached."

The wood grain of the tabletop wasn't particularly fascinating, but I spent a little while tracing the swirl with my eye, keeping my head down. Too many frequently buried feelings were threatening to rise to the surface. Old-habit emotions that had no place in the present day.

Neither Diana nor Carrie spoke. The typical Pour House soundtrack of sports television, old man laughter, and out-dated jukebox surrounded us and amplified their silence.

"Okay." Diana tapped her fingers against the tabletop. "Now that we're all clear on what we can and can't talk to Georgia about."

I opened my mouth to protest but she grinned and shook her head. "I'm only teasing."

"Yeah," Carrie said. "It's okay if you don't want to talk about your mom and your step— Ben."

There was no stopping the sigh that escaped me. "It's not that I don't want to, it's that there's nothing to talk about."

"Sure," Diana said.

"Okay," Carrie added.

Maybe, just maybe, there was a little voice inside that warned me I was wrong, a little voice that knew there was something troubling about my mother and Ben. But it wasn't offering up any specific wisdom, and I had other things to fill my time than trying to chase down answers that were probably best sought in therapy.

"So can we get back to Rozelle? Please?"

For a handful of breaths the noise of the bar was once again the only thing dispelling the silence. I was afraid Carrie wouldn't agree because she was a deeply caring person who could never pass up an opportunity to be the shoulder her friends cried on. And I was afraid Diana would resist on some sort of police department principle. I wasn't sure which surprised me more. Carrie echoing my request with a "Yeah, what about Rozelle?" or Diana asking, "What is it you want to know?"

I settled back in my seat. "All those bags you took from the bakery this morning, you're testing for poison, right?"

Diana shrugged lightly. "You knew that. Nolan told you this morning."

"So what happens now?" I asked.

"Yes, what's next?" Carrie echoed.

"Well, the Department of Health is going to do their thing," Diana said. "You know, go in with their inspectors and poke and test and all, but it's really a formality at this point."

"Because no one else even got sick?" Carrie asked.

Diana nodded. "No one else got so much as the hiccups."

"Then, how long until Rozelle can reopen?" I took a tiny sip of wine—mostly because that was all that was left in one of my glasses—then slid the empty to the far side of the table.

"She doesn't technically need to be closed," Diana said. "Or she only needs to be closed as long as it takes to clear out any opened flour and sugar and all that, give the place a good cleaning, and bake up some new tempting treats."

Carrie tapped her fingers against the tabletop, lips pursed as she shook her head in slow tempo. "But she'll wait," she said. "Rozelle isn't the type to take any chances, you know? I mean, we know and everyone else knows she wouldn't intentionally . . ." She made small circles with her hand and waited for us to fill in the blank.

"Poison?" I suggested.

She tipped her head to the side. "Or make anyone fall under the weather."

Diana rolled her eyes. "Way to tap dance, Carrie."

Carrie moved her wineglass a finger-length closer. "What I'm saying is, even if some sort of, like, crazy germ got into the dough, Rozelle wouldn't take a chance on anyone else getting sick. And she wouldn't want any of her regular customers to worry. She'll wait until there's some kind of lab result."

"*If* there's some kind of result," I said. "And what if there's not? What if there is?"

"We're investigating this death," Diana said. "We're looking at more than the samples from the bakery. That's just a logical place to start. But if the samples don't tell us anything, that doesn't mean we give up. I mean, c'mon. Give us a little credit."

"Wow." I leaned back, away from the table, out of Diana's reach. "Things getting a little tense down at the precinct house?"

Diana took a long drink of wine, banged the glass back down on the table. "Nolan might be all smooth and friendly with you, but let me tell you, that man can be a complete jerk."

"He's kind of like your boss now, right?" Carrie asked.

"He's supposed to be my mentor. He's supposed to train me, and help me get ready for the detective's test. I doubt how he takes his coffee is on the detective test."

"Okay, so not your boss," Carrie said. "How much longer until the test?"

"It'll be four weeks from this coming Monday."

"And by that time you'll have solved the case of who killed David Rayburn and it won't be Rozelle," I said.

"Absolutely," she said. "Or *you'll* have solved it while I was back on restricted duty for assaulting a police detective with a cup of coffee-black-no-sugar."

I lifted my glass. "Here's to solved cases."

# 7

Huddled in my bathrobe and some newly unearthed sweatpants, I carried a fresh cup of coffee down the stairs to my workshop. *Fleece-lined slippers*, I thought. *What I need is fleece-lined slippers*. Only October and already the overnight lows made walking through the house without a hat and scarf a questionable activity.

Shuffling to the table, I set the mug of coffee down then stood and watched the steam rise for longer than I should have. Some mornings weren't meant to be started in a hurry. Some were meant to be eased into like a leisurely stretch.

Beside the door leading to the yard, I kept a small bookcase. Its shelves were filled with old books on art and gardening that belonged to my grandmother, a couple of volumes I'd picked up at museums, and a very few soft-bound books filled with stained glass designs. I ran a finger along the stapled "spines" of the design books until I came to the one with the pine green cover. That one I pulled from the shelf.

It wasn't titled *The Big Book of Christmas Designs* but it may as well have been. Poinsettias and holly, angels and candles, candy canes, snowflakes, cardinals, and Santa Claus. If the symbol represented Christmas even remotely, it was incorporated into a pattern within that book. Even snowmen. Why was it snowmen were associated with Christmas when those round and frosty giants hung around all winter?

Shaking my head, I carried the book over to the table and set it down at the center. I was going to have to do an Internet search to find patterns suitable for Chanukah.

Carrie had suggested I create small holiday pieces for the shop. Handmade ornaments and sun catchers that celebrated the season and she could sell as the perfect gift for someone who has everything. Or in my opinion, the perfect gift for someone you don't know well enough to buy for. In fairness, that opinion had come up toward the end of my third glass of wine.

Lifting my coffee cup with one hand, I flipped open the cover of the pattern book with the other. While I sipped at my coffee, I studied the images on the inside of the cover. Santa, holly, candy cane. Red, green, silvery white.

The beams overhead creaked, and I let out a sigh. Someone was up. And not someone as in Grandy, who first of all rarely got up early in the morning. And on the rare occasions he did get up early, he tended to leave me in peace. With Mom and Ben visiting, all manner of disturbance was possible.

I held my breath and listened, hoping the footsteps I heard would follow the path to the bathroom, but no such luck. The squeak of floorboards moved down the hallway and down the stairs.

Mentally preparing myself for an eventual interruption, I flipped to the inside back cover of the book. Here there were angels and snowflakes and a Christmas tree. More green, some blue, clear.

Images of the clear glass greenhouse came to mind, but I shook them away.

The greenhouse required perfectly clear glass. Snowflakes, on the other hand, were none so plain. They required a textured glass—maybe glass with smooth lifts and curves like the surface of water, or that ripple-looking glass usually found in bathrooms. I took another sip of coffee, a big one, but still the proper name for the ripple glass escaped me. No matter. I would have to make a trip to the glass store to stock up on the holiday colors I would need. I could look at the clear glass options then.

As I flipped to the book's centerfold, where a pattern for a Santa in a half-moon spanned both pages, someone sneezed.

That someone was not me.

I turned in time to see my mother stepping slowly down the stairs, her own cup of coffee in hand.

"Bless you," I said.

She smiled her thanks as she reached the bottom step. "Am I interrupting anything?"

I looked from her to the book opened up on my table, gave the question a moment's thought. Apart from my morning peace and quiet time, I wasn't exactly involved in anything that required concentration. And once she and Ben were on their way north in the next week, I would have that quiet back again. It was not a sacrifice to give one morning to my mom.

"I was hoping we could talk," she said, shuffling into the room and coming to stand beside me at the table. "Just us. What are you working on here?"

I lifted a shoulder. "Nothing yet. Getting ready to start in on some Christmas pieces for Carrie's shop."

She let out a breath that other people might have turned into a low whistle. "Christmas already? Boy, it gets earlier every year, doesn't it?"

"Early for carols and egg nog, yes. But by some crafters' standards I'm already behind. Handmade takes time."

"I'm sure it does." She gave me a brief one-armed hug before passing behind me and circling around the far end of the table to where a work desk and chair sat tucked beneath the corner windows. With an audible sigh, she lowered herself into the chair. "You enjoy this stained glass thing then?"

I grinned. "Yes, I enjoy this *thing*." I glanced down at the open pattern, admiring the curved shapes used to form Santa's beard.

"And you're making money at it, your grandfather says."

"Some." I nodded without assurance.

"What are you working now, Georgia, three jobs?"

Trepidation set in. I turned the page in the pattern book slooowly. "What's on your mind, Mom?"

Leaning forward, she said, "Don't you think it's time to get back to, you know, the life you had? Get back to living?"

"I am living," I said. I took a sip of coffee.

"This isn't living," she said with a sweep of her hand.

"What are you talking about?" I felt my forehead crease above the bridge of my nose. If I wasn't careful, my face was going to freeze like that.

"This is not living. A handful of part-time jobs and no place of your own isn't living, Georgia. It's hiding. This is you hiding out in your grandfather's basement waiting for the thunderstorm to pass." Her eyes blazed into mine. "It's passed. It's over. It's time to get out and enjoy life again."

I took a breath, scratched at my head. "I am enjoying life," I said. "I like it here. I have good friends, I—"

"You have friends in the city, too, or do you not keep up with them?" She did not pause for an answer. "You had a good job and a successful fiancé. You were on the verge of having a wonderful life."

"Yeah," I said over a laugh. "And then I lost my job and my fiancé kicked me out and I was on a whole different verge. Thanks, but I'll pass on that wonderful life."

She started to lift her coffee cup to her lips but stopped along the way. "All right. So things took a bad turn. That doesn't mean it will happen again. But you'll never know what heights you can reach unless you get out there and try."

I sighed. "Look, Mom, I don't think . . . That life I

had, it's not what I want anymore. I'm not sure it's what I wanted then."

"That's just the bitterness talking."

"Is it? What if it's more truth than bitterness?"

Her eyelids lowered ever so slightly, enough to give her the appearance of a wise old woman. "It's easier to let yourself believe you didn't want something than to face the pain of losing it."

"I faced the pain," I said, not a little bit dramatically. "I'm over it."

"Then get back out there. You have an excellent degree, go do something with it. Get back to civilization. Go to museums. Meet people. Ben says the urban environment in Los Angeles is really on the rise and it's ideal for young professionals like yourself. It could be perfect for you."

"Los Angeles? California?"

She pulled in a breath and her eyes lit. "You could go for a visit. See for yourself. I bet you'll love it there. A couple of weeks in the sunshine and you won't ever want to come back here."

"What is it with you and Ben?" I snapped. Finally. "Why are you so dead set on getting me out of Grandy's house? What is so all-out awful about me being here? Isn't it a good thing I'm here? Doesn't it ease your mind at all to know I'm watching out for Grandy? And he's watching out for me? We're family. Why are you so bent on me leaving?"

The telltale sound of doggie nails on wood warned of Fifi's approach, and more, it warned that Grandy was awake. But Mom didn't know that.

"Because I don't want you to get stuck here," she said at last, coming to her feet. She closed the distance from the chair to the table with the speed of a mother rescuing her child from danger. Coffee sloshed as she banged her cup down on the table. Palms on the tabletop, she leaned across the surface and said through gritted teeth, "This town will pour cement around your feet if you let it. It will drag you in and drag you under and you'll be stuck here in this decrepit little hamlet while the world gets smaller and smaller around you. I want more for you."

Fifi raced down the steps and commenced her morning let's-go-outside dance at my feet, rising up on her back legs and bouncing back to the floor.

"You deserve more than run-down old luncheonettes and pharmacists that still dispense Coke syrup and a house that can't hold in heat," Mom continued. "This town will suffocate you, and I won't stand here and watch that happen."

"Standing and watching was never your way," Grandy said. At the top of the half staircase he stood with his hands in the pockets of his deep blue bathrobe, looking more imposing than a five-star general in full dress uniform. "You were more the don't-look-back type."

He took each step with an intimidating sense of purpose, bringing with him a cloud of anger that shuddered through the room and woke a seed of fear deep within me. Even Fifi stopped her happy morning dancing and pressed herself against my legs in hopes I would protect her.

"Dad," Mom said. "What are you doing up so early?"

"The dog," he said. "Knew someone was awake and

wanted out." He had yet to look at me, instead keeping his gaze locked on my mother. "I know how you feel about this town, I know you never liked it, thought it was a second-rate, hick place to live, and you couldn't wait to leave. You took every opportunity that came along."

Shaking her head, she lifted her coffee cup. "It's too early to do this, Dad."

"Is it? It's too early for you and I to talk but not too early for you to denigrate my town? My house?"

"You don't mean talk, you mean argue," Mom said. "And we'll only say the same things we always do and end up angry at one another like always."

"I wouldn't be angry if only you'd stop talking about my home like it's something to be avoided at all cost."

"And now you're exaggerating," she said on a sigh. "So can we do this another time? If you don't mind, I'm trying to have a conversation with Georgia."

Grandy turned to me then, his jaw tight, but said nothing.

I pulled in a breath, reached one hand down to the smooth fur on Fifi's head. "I have to walk the dog," I said.

"Georgia," Mom said.

I held up a hand, long-buried memories of the two of them shouting at each other floating to my awareness. "If I remember right, this is where I make myself scarce," I said. "Let's stick with the script, huh?"

I snatched up the pattern book from the table, avoiding eye contact with both Grandy and my mother. "Come on, Fifi. Let's go outside. Outside? Yes? Yes, let's go."

I kept up my monologue of pet-owner speak as I jogged up the stairs, ignoring my mother repeating my name and my grandfather telling her to let me go. The living room seemed to tilt and freeze as I stutter-stepped through. It might have been déjà vu. It might have been the memories coming awake, making me see that I'd been in this place—this emotion—before.

There was a difference this time, though. I knew it as I pulled Fifi's leash down from its hook then snapped it onto her collar. This time I was an adult, and making myself scarce didn't limit me to my little yellow bedroom. I had all of Wenwood to get lost in.

By a miracle of full house, needy bulldog, and cat in heat, there was enough confusion for the early morning that there simply was no opportunity for my mother and me to revisit our conversation. No surprise, that was fine by me.

I managed without interruption to pack a fisherman's tackle box that I had repurposed to carry some stained glass supplies. The deep main compartment easily held two types of cutters, a ruler, marking pens, a spool of lead, a soldering iron, and assorted other tools I liked to have on hand. I used a basic cotton tote bag to carry sheets of glass and a roll of poster paper and carbon paper and I tucked in *The Big Book of Christmas Designs* as well.

All of this I loaded into the car with the intention of heading into the village and using the back room at Carrie's antiques shop to get some Christmas pieces started.

Through the summer, when weekends could get crowded with antiques hunters, I had spent long hours working out of Carrie's back room. Doing so allowed me to be on hand to help out should a rush of customers arrive while at the same time allowing me to keep busy with my own work during lulls. And though I was pretty sure there wouldn't be any big rush at the store and Carrie truly wouldn't need me, I was certain she wouldn't be averse to me hiding out in her back room.

I briefly considered bringing Fifi with me—the shop had become a second home to her—but decided against it. After thinking I had all of Wenwood to wander through, I didn't want to limit myself to places where dogs were allowed should I decide against staying at Carrie's.

The mail was in the box as I left the house and I grabbed it and carted it along with me into the car. There were no pieces of personal mail in the bunch, only a post-card from a real estate agent, the weekly coupon circulars, and the latest issue of the *Town Crier*. I tossed the lot of it onto the passenger seat and headed on my way.

Feeling the urge to put a little distance between me and my mother, I opted to take the drive out to the fancy coffee shop up on the highway and there pulled into the line at the drive-thru.

As I waited my turn to place an order, I picked up the *Town Crier* and forced myself to flip through the pages one by one rather than turning directly to the classifieds at the back, which I knew was what I really wanted to do. Denial is a powerful thing.

No, I had really had no plans to leave Grandy's, though I can't say why I didn't. Until my mother's arrival I had assumed I was simply happy where I was. And for all that I insisted as much to her, still, she was my mom.

That meant whatever she said to me, right or wrong, carried extra power. So of course I faced the little itch of doubt that insisted Mom was right and I was staying with Grandy more to hide from life than to learn to live it happily again. Maybe it really was time to get back out on my own.

Wenwood was a small town with a low population. Its neighboring towns were not much larger. You had to go up to Newbridge to get any sort of real numbers. Because of this, the *Town Crier* covered not just Wenwood but most of the eastern side of Pace County. This wider coverage brought the listings of available apartments and rental houses up to almost two full columns.

Finally reaching the window, I ordered an iced latte and paid the tab before letting my foot off the brake long enough for the car to roll forward a whopping four feet.

I returned my attention to the classifieds and the properties listed for rent. Studio and one-bedroom apartments seemed the most predominant and the most affordable. With my limited earnings, renting a whole house was out of the question. But then again, wasn't renting almost anything out of the question? I had Friday and Fifi to think of. I didn't see a single "pets welcome" notation on any of the listings.

All right. Maybe that wasn't something that got listed but was something that was negotiated after. In which case, there were a smattering of studio apartments in Edgewater that I might be able to afford. And Edgewater was a . . . well, a bit more run down than Wenwood but not too run down as to be scary.

Edgewater. Studio. Just me and Friday and Fifi.

In Edgewater.

Alone.

I let the car inch forward into the space that had opened up before me. Almost there. A frothy, caffeinated beverage was almost in my possession.

I looked back at the paper.

Edgewater.

Suddenly it seemed so far away. It couldn't have been more than forty minutes from Grandy's house and yet somehow that seemed a vast and challenging distance. It would be a long drive from Edgewater to Drew's law office. Even longer out to the Dine-In. I'd be spending a lot of time in the car.

Alone.

And that was the bottom line. That was the reason I bunched up the *Crier* and tossed it to the floor in front of the passenger seat. That was the reason my stomach was coiling itself into a knot.

I wasn't staying in Grandy's house because I was hiding, or because I didn't have the drive to go searching for a better job somewhere more urban than Wenwood. That wasn't it at all. I was simply and genuinely happy where I was. One of the largest components of that happiness, one of the hardest for me to admit even to myself, was that I didn't want to be alone. Living with Grandy had given me the sense of permanence I missed having as a child, the sense of family I longed for in those months when it was Mom and me leaving Grandy and Grandma behind and heading off for the next great destination that my mother believed would be perfect.

A gap opened ahead of my car and I rolled forward

little by little until my window was aligned with the serving window on the side of the building. I accepted the latte the barista handed to me and slipped it into the vehicle's cup holder before settling into the renewed business of driving.

As I made the turn out of the coffee spot's drive-thru and back onto the road, I flicked one last glance at the *Town Crier* bunched up on the floor. Until Grandy asked me to leave, I was determined to stay put.

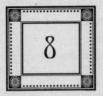

8

As I was growing up, my mom and I relocated pe-
riodically as she went from job to job and, to a lesser
extent, husband to husband. At the time I thought that
was normal. Later, I blamed it on my mother's inability
to put down roots. Now that I knew one of her primary
motives was staying out of Wenwood for as long as possible, things made a little more sense. None of this is to
say that Mom could in any way be described as flaky or
irresponsible. She was a good mother, even with our constantly changing addresses. After my dad—my real
dad—died when I was two, Mom took every chance she
could to improve her and my situation. Those chances
didn't always turn out for the best. Those were the times
we'd land back in Wenwood, bunking in with Grandy—
and with Grandma when she was alive. We stayed as long

as it took for Mom to get back on her feet or until the school year ended or, I guessed, until she couldn't tolerate small-town living for another moment, and we were off again, Nomad style. There was no money to buy or space to store comic books, and for some reason libraries weren't big on them.

A very long way of explaining why I had no idea who Iron Man was. Or Captain America. Or that Thor had an entire incarnation outside of a mythology book. Now, all grown up and helping out Grandy—and my bank balance—by waiting tables two nights a week at the Dine-In Theater he owned and operated, I was finally being exposed to the world of superheroes, twice on Fridays and three times a day on Saturdays.

"All right. What about Tony Stark?" Liz asked. We stood at the back of the theater, tucked into a corner where we could see the movie screen and—mostly—keep an eye on the tables of patrons. All the food orders had already gone out, giving Liz and me a short reprieve as the evening's waitress tag team.

"What about him?" I asked, keeping my voice soft without going all the way to whisper. Those Marvel movies can get loud.

"Would you date Tony Stark?" Liz was a petite brunette in her late twenties filled with inexhaustible energy that revealed itself in quick speech and unending motion. Even as she asked about Stark, one eye on me and one on the screen, she rocked back and forth with a little bounce thrown in.

"You mean if he were real?" I asked.

She giggled. "Yeah, or if you were a comic book character."

"Do I get to pick which character I am?"

"Would you know which one to pick?"

She had me there. I was still working on learning the mundane names for all the supers and didn't quite agree that the Hulk looked like a Bruce. "Is there a reason I wouldn't want to date Tony Stark?" I asked. "He's a bazillionaire, right?"

Liz tipped her head side to side as she considered. "Yeah, but he is kind of a womanizer."

"But not since he started a non-work relationship with Pepper Potts," I pointed out. "Indicating he does have the capacity to commit himself to one woman. That kind of devotion can be appealing."

She narrowed her eyes at me. "Wow. I never pegged you for a romantic."

Her gaze flicked to an unknown point behind me a split second before a tap on my shoulder made me gasp in surprise. When I turned, the high school student who ordinarily manned the candy counter—and had clearly left her post in order to try and scare me to death—was standing behind me, pointing toward the lobby. "Some guy is asking for you," she said. "He'd be kinda hot if he weren't so old."

Liz and I locked gazes. I imagined the perplexed expression on her face mirrored my own. Hot but old?

"Go ahead," Liz said. "I'll keep an eye on your tables."

"Thanks." I followed the candy girl out of the theater, saying a silent prayer that the guy who was waiting for me wasn't my mother's husband thinking he might smooth over the tension the morning's family gathering caused.

She held the door open for me as she passed back into the lobby, and I followed her into the gray and navy area where patrons ordinarily milled about before the auditorium doors opened for their show. Now, with the crowd in their seats, the lobby was empty save for one man. Standing in the center, hands clasped behind his back as he studied an old one sheet for *Casablanca*, was Tony Himmel.

Old? My boyfriend was old? Not to me at least. Certainly Grandy would declare him a man in his prime. Still, I supposed to a high school girl he might appear old. She couldn't be more than—

It hit me with a sickening turn of my stomach that the girl's father technically could be the same age as Tony. Could that make me the same age as her mother?

I pushed down the shock, the nausea, and the frightening sensation of life passing me by and made myself grin big. "Tony. What are you doing here?" I practically gushed . . . and realized that the gush stemmed from being genuinely pleased to see him.

He turned to me with a smile. Hair damp, cheeks smooth from a fresh shave, blue eyes bright, he sort of glowed and I felt a little warm tingle right down to my toes. "I thought I'd surprise you." He leaned down and kissed me, a brief PG-rated hello that wouldn't give anyone gossip fodder. "Maybe talk you into going out after work."

He could have knocked me over with a thought.

"After work?" I repeated. "Don't you have to be at the site in the morning?"

"I do."

"And by 'morning,' we're talking before sunrise, right?"

He nodded. "Typically."

"Tony, I'm not done here until after ten, if I'm lucky. Correct me if I'm wrong, but don't you like to be asleep by then, so you can be sure you're at the site on time?"

"Where's the fun in being the boss if you can't show up late once in a while?"

I might have blinked half a dozen times while I waited for his comment to sink in. Since we had been together, while he always made time for me—for us—that time had always been evening. I took soft hold of his arm—or more accurately, the fabric of his jacket. "What's going on? Is everything all right?"

His smile was gentle, warm. "Everything's fine."

"Are you lying to me?"

He pulled my hand free of his jacket and gave my fingers a squeeze. "You know I'm always honest with you."

The door to the auditorium opened, letting into the lobby the explosive noises of a superhero destroying a city in the name of justice. "Yeah," I said, lowering my head a bit so I could look up at him from below my brows. "You're honest about the big things. But how do I know for sure you don't fib on the little things?"

"You'll just have to trust me." He lifted his gaze from mine, looked over my shoulder as his warm smile transformed into one that was more polite, somewhat reserved. "Pete," he said.

I turned to find Grandy crossing the lobby toward us. He held his small, old-school ledger book in one hand, reached out the other to Tony. "Well, hello there, young man."

See? Not old.

They shook hands in a way that seemed to define their relationship to each other: Grandy, the elder, the wiser; Tony, the younger, the student who had yet to earn the approval of his teacher.

"You've missed the start of the show, I'm afraid," Grandy said.

Tony grinned. "I'll have to come back and see it another time. Tonight I'm here for Georgia."

"Really? What trouble has she caused this time?"

"You know as well as I do she's never any trouble."

"She's standing right here," I said.

Grandy made a face that could only be described as a smirk. "Yes, and as long as you're standing there, you're not getting into any trouble. The minute I turn my back, you'll be off trying to figure out who killed that—what's his name—Rayburn something."

"David Rayburn," Tony said.

Grandy pointed a finger at Tony. "That's the one."

"I only saw the guy once," I said. "I have no intention of trying to figure out who poisoned him." I turned narrowed eyes on Grandy. "But can you honestly say you wouldn't want me poking around if the police weren't already convinced Rozelle had nothing to do with it?"

He folded his arms across his chest. "Let's be grateful

for the wisdom of the police in this case. I take it your friend Detective Nolan is involved? He seems to always be in the middle of these things as well."

I cut a glance at Tony, whose eyebrows rose at the mention of Detective Nolan as my friend. I waved a hand as though to brush away any potential thought of jealousy, though I supposed calling Nolan a friend was a fair, if not entirely accurate, assessment. There was a chance the good detective may have been even more than a friend had it not been for Tony.

All at once it hit me that Nolan knew Grandy well, and had even met my mother, neither of which occurred over the most congenial of circumstances, while Tony, who had asked to be introduced, who wanted to get to know my family, had yet to be given the chance. A goose-flesh feeling of guilt crept over me.

"Diana is assigned to the case," I said, sidestepping any question of Nolan's involvement.

"That explains this newfound common sense the police department possesses," Grandy said.

"Listen, Pete," Tony said. "I know you usually ride home with Georgia. Will you be all right if I drive her back tonight? That is, unless you came up here in Georgia's car?"

Grandy squared his shoulders, stood straighter and taller than most any eighty-year-old could achieve. "I have no problem driving at night, or driving Georgia's car, and I'll thank you not to insinuate any differently."

Ducking his head, Tony held up his hands. "I apologize wholeheartedly. It was thoughtless of me to imply . . . anything."

Grandy lifted his chin, rolled his head like an Old West gunslinger—as portrayed in film, that is. "Apology accepted." He looked to me. "Go ahead, then. I'll see you at home."

"Wait, no—" I began.

But Grandy had already returned his attention to Tony. "I'll expect you for Sunday dinner. Five o'clock. Don't you dare be late."

"No, no," I said.

Given his earlier campaign to meet my family, Tony kept his expression surprisingly neutral.

"You don't get to argue who I invite for dinner," Grandy said.

I shook my head. "That's not . . . I have no problem . . . I think dinner is a great idea," I said, and mostly meant it.

Tony peered at me from the corner of his eye. He may have doubted my sincerity, but he was too much of a good guy to call me on it in front of my grandfather.

"Then what are you protesting?" Grandy asked.

Visions of the morning's set-to between Grandy and Mom gave me the shivers. "I don't know if now is the best time. We're all still getting used to one another," I said. "I mean, with Mom's new husband and . . ."

"All the more reason for your man here to join us now," Grandy said. "Better to get to know us as we really are, don't you think?"

No, I didn't think that at all. I thought Mom and Grandy snarling at each other had the potential to scare Tony away. And that was something I did not want to happen.

But Tony was smiling patiently . . . and a little worriedly. I might have been scaring him away all by myself. "You're right," I said to Grandy, forcing my voice light. "He should meet us as we are. Does this mean I don't have to dust?"

He grinned. "We'll get your mother to dust. Now, get going, you two."

"Um, Grandy?" I pointed to the auditorium doors. "I have a shift to finish."

Grandy nodded, smiled as though this was a new and appealing revelation. "So you do. Well. This is a conundrum." Then he reached out and gave Tony an amiable slap on the shoulder. "Why don't we wait in my office until Georgia's done? We'll have a nice chat."

There are vulgar terms for the type of triumphant grin Tony shot me, and he went happily off to Grandy's office. I waited in the lobby for a minute or more, trying to figure out if I was worried about the two of them being alone together.

I had no fear of them trading stories about the brilliant things I'd done—whether brilliant was meant in honesty or sarcasm. The sense of unease I felt . . . I couldn't tell where it was coming from, couldn't pinpoint its source with any precision. There was something behind the idea of Tony meeting my family, something so . . . serious, so formal, so . . .

. . . so once burned twice shy.

I took a deep breath, ran my hands down my thighs, smoothing the black fabric of my slacks. From the corner of my eye, I spied the candy girl leaning across the counter.

"That's your boyfriend, huh?" she asked.

I didn't think an answer was strictly necessary.

"I guess he's the right age for you," she said.

I was pretty sure she had just called me old.


Past the Dine-In Theater, in the opposite direction of Wenwood, there was a retail center that featured a chain restaurant.

"Wow," I said when Tony pulled into a vacant parking spot at the rear of the establishment. "You really know how to show a girl a good time, huh? They have two-for-one appetizers here and everything."

He switched off the engine and smiled. "Play your cards right and next time I might just take you to a restaurant with cloth napkins."

"Oh, be still, my heart."

I hadn't forgotten, not for one minute of our drive, that Tony had something on his mind, something big enough or important enough to warrant staying out past his bedtime. Sure, he had said everything was fine. But the funny thing about "fine" is that it's almost always a lie—in varying degrees perhaps, but a lie all the same.

He took my hand as we circled the exterior of the restaurant. The night had grown cooler, and his warmth was reassuring.

We were shown to a table outside the bar area, where the hostess warned the kitchen would close within the hour so we should order any food straightaway.

Tony ordered coffee and a slice of cheesecake; I ordered tea and a brownie. Ordinarily I would avoid anything so sweet, so sugary. Somehow being around Tony made my resolve weaken.

"So what did you and my grandfather talk about?" I asked.

"Is that really what you want to ask me?"

I ducked my head, took a deep breath, and kept my eyes on the grooves worn into the wooden table. My cheeks warmed. "You're right," I said, not wanting to look up. "I want to ask why you said you were always honest with me when you were obviously lying."

"Georgia," he said on a sigh.

"Or maybe it's like that old brain teaser about the man who says I always speak the truth but how do you know he's not lying when he says he always speaks the truth?"

"Georgia, look at me."

I did as he asked, risked meeting his eyes, so blue, so earnest.

"Everything is fine." He took a sip of his ice water, all the while holding my gaze. "You know, the interesting thing is, there is a connection between what I discussed with Pete and why I wanted to see you tonight."

My stomach did a funny flip while every muscle in my body went tense.

Tony chuckled. "Relax. This is not a marriage proposal."

I let out my breath in a noisy rush.

"You don't have to look so relieved." He glanced around the restaurant, eyes moving from pop culture décor to tiled floor to the televisions suspended over the bar showing a broadcast of a West Coast baseball championship playoff game. From where we sat, the score was little more than a blur. "And you could give me a little more credit than to think I'd propose someplace where beer is routinely spilled on the floor."

I smiled and shook my head. "It's just . . . you know . . ."

"I know," he said. "Any mention of the future makes you nervous. You can play private detective and face down murderers, yet the idea of commitment sends you into a panic."

"Not a panic," I said quickly. "And not commitment, just . . . okay, maybe commitment." Because really, who knew? Maybe I would indeed turn out to be commitment averse. The potential for discovering my inclination had yet to arise.

"So what is it then?" I asked. "What's so important it couldn't wait until tomorrow? And required a face-to-face instead of a phone call?"

Our waiter arrived at the table, set down one tea, one coffee, and an assortment of sweeteners, and assured us he'd be right back with our desserts.

"And milk," I said.

The waiter snapped his fingers and pointed at me like his hands were six-shooters. "You got it."

Tony, the big tough construction guy, took a sip of his coffee, black and unsweetened. I, the delicate stained glass artist, suppressed a shudder.

"So?" I prompted. "What's the urgency?"

He shook his head. "Not urgent, no. But . . . The face-to-face, that's what's important." He sighed and leaned in, resting his elbows on the table. "Here's the thing. The marina project is wrapping up. There's no reason for me to be there every day anymore but—"

"I know," I said, nodding. "It's your dream project. I can't imagine how amazing it must be to see it completed, and how hard it must be to walk away."

"You might have something there. I'm not going to go get psychoanalyzed to see if you're right, though."

I grinned. "Fair enough. Go on."

"The project is wrapping and I need to look ahead to what's next."

The waiter buzzed by, sliding a minuscule pitcher of milk onto the table as he passed. I grabbed up the pitcher a little too forcefully; the cold metal of the handle bit into my fingers and I splashed too much milk into the tea. My mind raced in a multitude of directions. Part of me wanted to know what Tony planned for his future, part of me didn't care, part of me cared too much.

"What are your options?" I managed.

"That's just it," he said. "It's not about the options. Well, it is, but more importantly . . ." He reached across the table and took my hand in his. I froze. He grinned, bent his head toward mine. "Still not a proposal."

I laughed, relaxed a fraction.

"But I realized I have these options. I have these choices. And . . ." He furrowed his brow. "I wanted to talk to you about them."

He appeared perplexed, and that emotion may have been contagious. My own brow wrinkled as I tried to determine the cause of the confusion.

"That's . . ." I began. "I don't . . . understand why that made you shower and shave and show up at the Dine-In."

"Georgia, I make these decisions all the time. I move from project to project on strictly business choices, all numbers and spreadsheets. But this time all I keep asking myself is what would Georgia think. For the first time in I don't know how long, someone else's opinion is important to me, important enough that I don't want to make these choices on my own."

I was almost disappointed. All that lead-up and the only thing he needed was a second opinion on his next business move?

"I don't really think I'm qualified to advise you on your next . . . whatever," I said, hedging.

"It's not about qualifications, babe. It's about . . ." He lowered his head, huffed out a breath before continuing. "About the whole idea that I wanted your input." He looked up then, eyes clear and fathomless. "That's a first for me."

"But you, you have business partners and whatnot and probably an adviser tucked away somewhere in your files. They're the ones you should be talking to."

He sighed. "You're missing my point."

No, I wasn't missing it. Try as I might to dodge it, still it grazed its mark and I pretended I wasn't hit. There was something serious, something next level about being asked to add input to your boyfriend's business decisions— something I didn't know if I would handle well.

"Or maybe I'm not explaining this right. Bottom line, I need to start setting up the next project. I can do that here, or fairly close to here, or I can do that in Virginia or North Carolina."

Our desserts arrived, pausing the conversation while

Tony assured the waiter we had everything we needed for the moment and while I tried to work out how I was supposed to respond, if I was supposed to respond.

"So, which project appeals to you the most?" I asked, keeping my voice even, almost light. I thought I could offer input without dwelling on what it meant to be asked. "You like to lead projects that you've got something more than time invested in, so which one fits that bill?"

"Still missing the point."

"Boy, I'm not getting anything right tonight, am I? I guess it really is a good thing I'm not poking around the Rayburn murder." I used my fork to break off a piece of brownie. "Speaking of, what do you know—"

"No. No speaking of. Don't change the subject."

"Okay. All right. So what's the point?" I asked. "What am I missing?"

He grimaced, as if he couldn't believe he had to spell things out for me. Or more accurately, that I was making him spell things out because my own personal issues prevented me from admitting I knew what he was getting at. "It's more than the project, Georgia," he said, his voice soft despite what had to be frustration igniting the blue in his eyes. "It's what you would think, how you would feel, if I choose to stay."

Yes, I knew that's where the conversation was headed. No, I was in no way ready to talk about it. Maybe this wasn't a proposal, but it was most certainly a great big What If step. I lifted my fork, poked at my brownie, while avoiding his gaze. "It's not about me," I said. "It's your business, it's your choice."

"But it is about you, Georgia. It's about you and it's

about us. It's about the question of if there will still be an us."

I looked up at him then, but the melting in my heart only served to increase the clenching in my gut.

"I don't want to scare you away. Look, I know . . . you told me about what happened with your fiancé. As thankful as I am that you didn't marry him and came here instead, I know that whole experience has left you gunshy. And I don't want my talking about staying to force you into running in the opposite direction."

"I wouldn't," I said. But if I heard the uncertainty in my voice, Tony did, too.

"You might," he said, nodding to affirm the truth. He sat back and chopped at his cheesecake with the side of his fork.

I slipped a sliver of brownie into my mouth, where the chocolate tasted weak and dry. I washed it down with a sip of tea and only then did I risk meeting Tony's eyes again. "It's not about you," I said.

"For now," he said. "For now it's about you. But sooner or later it's going to start being about me, about whether you can overcome those fears because I've made you forget them. But it's not that time yet. Right now, I just want you to know that it's time for me to make a choice, and you're a big factor in my decision."

"Oh, is that all?" I said over a light laugh.

He smiled. "I was hoping to slowly get you used to the idea. So this is, you know, planting the seed." At last he forked a piece of cheesecake into his mouth.

"Planting the seed, huh?"

He nodded, spoke around a mouth full of dessert. "Maybe more like pouring the foundation."

In that moment, I ached to grab him and hold on for as long as I could. At the same time, I wanted to drop my fork and run. Damn, but he had me figured out—maybe better than I had myself figured out.

"All right," I said. "I'll start getting used to the idea."

He grinned, bright, happy. He pushed the plate of cheesecake toward me. "Try this," he said. "I think you'll like it better than that brownie."

Yup, he had me figured out. Now if I could just figure out how I was going to become accustomed to the idea of him staying. Which is not to say I'd given a great deal of thought to the reality that one day his project would be completed and he would pick up and move on to the next one. Basically I'd been going along one day at a time. But now . . . now . . . what if . . .

9

Late-night dessert and coffee had made me worried about Tony being late to work Saturday morning, but of course, he made my worries unfounded. He got up on the first alarm, stopped at the drive-thru coffee shop on his way to drop me off at home, and still arrived at the marina site on time. Me? I made the mistake of lying back down "for just a minute" after my shower and ended up dashing out of the house in a panic with Fifi at my heels. With my hair scraped back into a French braid to keep it from exposing its pillow-dried wildness, I headed into Wenwood village without so much as an apple in my belly to keep it from rumbling—despite my mother's insistence that I shouldn't dash out on an empty stomach and with a wet head to boot.

The plus side of my rush was not having time to try

explaining to my mother that I was a grown-up and knew where to find food, and not having to think about Tony's talk of staying in the Wenwood area or giving up his rented house and hitting the road.

Okay. Not having to think *deeply* about Tony. Obviously considerations of him and his decision continued to float on the surface of my thoughts. Even as I unpacked what amounted to a portable stained glass studio from the trunk of my car and pounded on the back door of Carrie's shop, fresh memories of Tony talking about whether to break camp and move on or renew his rental house agreement occupied my awareness.

The door creaked open and Carrie held it for me, smiling down at Fifi as we passed through into the back room of Aggie's Gifts and Antiques. "Let me guess," she said. "You overslept."

"Sort of." I set my modified tackle box down with a thump then released Fifi from her leash. Body rolling side to side, Fifi trotted back to Carrie, plunked her back end on the floor, and gave a quiet woof. I started unzipping my jacket before I thought better of it. "Did you eat?"

Grinning, Carrie pulled shut the door then bent to scratch behind Fifi's ears. "Ah. You spent the night at Tony's again, huh?"

I held up a hand, palm out. "I don't want to talk about it yet."

"Oh. That's mysterious and intriguing." After giving Fifi a final pat, she turned and reset the alarm on the back door. "I can't wait until you're ready."

"Meanwhile," I said, "food?"

"I ate." Carrie ranged up beside me and we walked together onto the sales floor with Fifi leading the way. She trotted ahead to her favorite resting place behind the cash wrap and looked over her shoulder at us as though she didn't understand what was taking us so long. "But if you're going to pick up some food, would you bring me back a cup of tea?"

I raised my eyebrows. "As if you had to ask me?"

Pushing through the front door of the shop, I let my gaze wander across the street not to Grace's luncheonette but to Rozelle's bakery. The large plate glass window in front was dark, and for the first time in memory there was no Saturday morning line snaking out the front door. I couldn't say with certainty that the sign in the door remained turned to CLOSED but I reasoned it was a safe bet.

Not for the first time I felt a little pang of sorrow for Rozelle. It seemed there was no doubt in anyone's mind that Rozelle had nothing to do with the poisoning of David Rayburn. And yet her shop, her livelihood, was closed, waiting for the Department of Health to come along and inspect it and prove what every resident of Wenwood already knew. Whatever had killed David Rayburn it didn't originate with Rozelle.

But if the poison wasn't delivered with one of Rozelle's Danishes, how did the poison get into Rayburn's system? And who put it there?

I shook my head, shook the thought away, and, checking both directions first, proceeded across the street to the luncheonette. Whether or even if there was poison involved and where it originated were none of my concern.

The police were working on the Rayburn case. Diana was working on the case. This time I could peacefully mind my own business and let the authorities do their job.

As ever, when I pushed open the door of the luncheonette, the little bell overhead jingled. Heads swiveled, the regulars lined up at the counter turning to see who had entered. I hadn't taken two steps inside before my mouth watered and my stomach ached in anticipation. Morning at the luncheonette meant the savory aroma of coffee and bacon and fried potatoes filled the air, and I was instantly aware of how long it had been since my last meal.

"Well, good morning, Georgia," Tom called from his usual counter stool. He lifted a hand in added greeting and waved me over—as if there were somewhere else in the little six-booth shop I would be going. Every booth was occupied and several people were wandering around the stationery-goods side of the establishment as though killing time waiting for their turn at a table rather than shopping.

I took up position at the end of the counter, between the register and the first stool, where at least there was room to stand. "What's going on in here?" I asked.

Seated on that first stool, Tom's friend Terry looked up at me and opened his mouth to answer. In that same instant, Rozelle bustled out from the pass-through behind the counter that led to the kitchen. "Oatmeal raisin, one dozen, McAnn," she called.

One of the men wandering amid the shelves of boxed envelopes and index cards rushed forward, hand in the air. He wore a black-and-red-checkered jacket and smelled vaguely of horse. "Right here," the man said.

Terry inclined his head toward the exchange taking place between Rozelle and the man in the plaid jacket. "Cookie sales," Terry said.

Rozelle nodded in my direction, a wide grin on her face. "Good morning, Georgia." She turned back to her customer, accepted the ten-dollar bill he held out. Sliding her hand into the pocketed apron at her waist, she pulled out a folded wad of cash and peeled off two singles before slipping the ten into its place. She handed the man his change and spun back toward the kitchen. "I've got to get the next batch."

I looked back to Terry, my brows raised in a manner that typically conveyed a question without using words.

Yet it was Tom who addressed my silent query. He leaned in front of Terry to say, "Grace is letting Rozelle use one of the ovens to bake cookies in the mornings."

"Only until she gets that bakery open again." Grace herself strode through the kitchen bypass, two plates of eggs balanced on her forearm. She set down one each in front of two women occupying the stools beyond where Tom sat before joining us at the opposite end of the counter. "She sings in the kitchen, did you know that?"

I pressed my lips tight to hold back a giggle.

"And it's not a melodious sound. Not by a lot." Grace pulled a cloth from the white apron she wore with her robin's egg blue cotton uniform dress and brushed stray crumbs from the countertop.

"It's a nice thing you're doing," Terry said, lifting his coffee cup in salute.

Though Grace grimaced, her eyes remained warm. "It's madness. We have enough cooks in that kitchen as it is," she said, then looked to me. "One coffee, one egg sandwich?" she asked.

"And a tea?"

She nodded and buzzed back to the kitchen to put in the order.

"So, Georgia," Tom said. "What'd you find out about that David Rayburn fella?"

"Uhh . . . nothing?" I said. "It doesn't concern me. I have other things going on."

"Oh, I know that. I know that," he said. "You're busy. You got your mom in for a visit and all."

I didn't even want to try and work out which Wenwood rumor mill had served that information to him.

"It's only that I figured you'd have the inside scoop from Diana," he finished.

Terry took a gulp of his coffee then set down the cup. "I keep telling ya, Tom, it doesn't work like that. The police aren't going to speculate and they're not going to give out any information if they're in the middle of an investigation."

I nodded along as Terry spoke. "It's true. Diana hasn't shared anything, except to say it's going to take a few weeks before any of the lab reports come back on Rayburn."

"Exactly." Terry jabbed a finger at the air. "Until they know exactly what killed him, everything is on hold."

"But wait," I said. "I thought it was pretty well accepted that he was poisoned."

"But with what?" Tom said.

"And by who?" Terry said. "That's the million-dollar—"

He cut himself off and I almost prodded him to continue. But Rozelle had reappeared behind the counter—

he must have seen her approach the pass-through—and he gave her a great big smile as she bustled by, bakery box in hand.

She smiled back—a little nervous, a little shy—before looking out across the luncheonette and calling the next name on her cookie order list.

Terry kept his focus on her as she went through her transaction and I admit I had to take a fresh stock of Rozelle.

Since I met her, I had thought of Rozelle only as the nice woman who owns the bakery and is sweet on Grandy. I'd never really looked beyond her gray curls and baker's apron. But standing at the luncheonette, watching Terry watch Rozelle with a fond look in his eye, I saw at last a woman whose gray hair was a pretty, soft-looking silver, whose face was sweetly shaped and relatively unlined, and whose happiness and inner joy were evident in her bright eyes and impish smile.

And then it hit me. What was wrong with Grandy that he couldn't see how lovely Rozelle was? He had to know she had a soft spot for him. He always had nice things to say about her. What was he waiting for?

"Coffee, tea, and an egg sandwich." Grace snapped open a paper bag, and I flinched at my abrupt return to the moment.

"Sorry," I said. "What do I owe you?"

Grace gave me the total. I dug money from the depths of my coat pocket to pay my bill, by which time Rozelle had returned to the kitchen presumably to box more cookies.

"The million-dollar question," Terry said. "Why would

anyone want to poison David Rayburn? You always have to find the motive. Once you find the motive, you can start rounding up suspects."

One hand on the edge of the counter, he spun on his stool to look at me head-on. "What kind of man was David Rayburn? Was he single, married, divorced? Kids? Debt? What did he do for a living? What did he do in his spare time?"

His questions seemed to pin me to the spot. I reached blindly for the change Grace owed me. "I have no idea," I replied.

Terry gave a slow nod. "Learn everything you can about the man, and you'll have a pretty good idea who killed him."

I took one more bite of egg sandwich, happy to have a full belly once again. The rest I tossed to Fifi, whose jowls fairly bounced with joy as she chomped down on her treat.

Eyes on me, Carrie shook her head, a movement of disbelief. "And you see Tony telling you he's considering you in his choices as a problem?"

We were clustered behind the cash wrap counter, Fifi gazing longingly up at us and hoping more food would fall, Carrie and me facing the empty sales floor. It was yet a little too early for the fall foliage vacationers to pass through Wenwood and towns like it in search of true antiques rather than vintage reproductions. Even the local populace, who shopped Carrie's store for unique birthday and holiday gifts, tended not to arrive before noon.

Wadding up the white paper Grace had wrapped my sandwich in, I met Carrie's gaze. "I don't like being put in this position." I tossed the wad of paper into the trash bin, and Fifi grumbled her disappointment. Abandoning her good-dog begging position, she rolled to her feet and meandered out onto the sales floor.

"It doesn't sound like he's put you in any sort of position." Carrie lifted her tea, took a moment to blow a cooling breath across its steamy surface. "Sounds like he wants to know where you stand. In fact, it almost sounds like he wants to know whether you think you guys have a future together."

My stomach muscles seized. I reached for the paper cup of coffee, immediately needing something— anything—to hold, to assist in keeping me conscious and upright.

"Why does that make you anxious?" Carrie asked.

I shot her a glance. "Why do you have to be so observant?"

"Well, I hate to tell you this," she said, tipping her head in a motion that indicated sympathy. "But I'm not that observant. It's completely obvious. And if I can see how that makes you nervous, so can Tony."

"Carrie, you know—"

She held up a hand. "Yes, I know. Evil no-good loser fiancé, broken heart, messy life, I know. I understand all that. But this is Tony we're talking about, not the other guy. Tony, who lets your drool-y bulldog slobber on his car seats and picks you wildflowers from the riverside. You have to know by now Tony is nothing like your ex. You must have learned at least that much."

The echo of her words and their reminder of what could be learned brought Terry's comments about David Rayburn back to the forefront of my mind. I held up a finger while I took a deep sip of coffee, letting thoughts of Tony and his dilemma wander back into the mental strongbox I had set up for them.

Setting down the coffee cup, I asked, "Did you know David Rayburn?"

Carrie closed her eyes, shook her head, exasperation evident. When she opened her eyes, she gaped at me like I'd lost my mind. "I can't believe you're trying to change the subject."

"I don't know why you're surprised. You know the idea of Tony staying in Wenwood to see how things work out between us stresses me." I forced a smile. "Please? Let me change the subject this time?"

She blew out a dramatic sigh. "Fine. But we're coming back to this topic before the day is over."

"Thank you," I said.

"You're welcome. Now tell me about your mother's husband instead."

"Tell me about David Rayburn," I countered.

"Oh, come on. You don't really want to know about him, do you?" She took a half step back from me. "Or are you going all Jessica Fletcher on me again? I need to know if you are because I might have to leave town. I'm sorry, I'm your friend, but I just don't think I can go through that again."

The bell over the door jingled. Two women entered the store, one middle-aged, the other clearly her daughter. They had the same dirty blond hair, high foreheads, and narrow shoulders.

"Hey, you were caught up in the Heaney affair all on your own. I didn't do anything to drag you into it. If anything, it was the other way around." I pitched my voice lower so as not to be overheard by the mother-daughter shoppers. "Now tell me about Rayburn. Did you know him?"

Carrie followed my example, keeping her voice soft. "Not really."

"Town gossip?"

She shrugged, eyes on the ladies moving slowly through the shop. "You'd know as much as I do. He was the loudest mouth behind the anti-promenade movement, predicting doom and disaster for local businesses once all the retail opens on the riverfront."

A long-forgotten memory surfaced: Liz and me outside the kitchen at the Dine-In, with Liz announcing she wanted to open an antiques store on the promenade. I'd worried then about what impact such a business would have on Carrie, but had been too shortsighted to wonder how it may affect other business owners.

I looked to Carrie. "What do you think? Do you think Rayburn is—was—right?"

She edged behind me, sidestepping her way out from behind the counter. "I think as long we keep the big chain stores out, then a little competition can actually be good for business. I hope." With a quick grin she slithered around an inlaid entryway table and past a cherrywood washstand and greeted the shoppers.

Coffee in hand, I wandered my way toward the back room. I snapped my fingers and whistled badly as I walked, and by the time I set my coffee cup on my worktable, Fifi was standing at the threshold between the sales floor and the back room. She looked at me then looked behind her, evidently trying to choose between me and Carrie.

"You don't want to come back here with me?" I asked.

Fifi licked her chops, looked over her shoulder.

"Carrie doesn't have any food," I said. I slid my repurposed tackle box to the right edge of the table and flipped open the latches. "You may as well stay with me."

She made a noise between a whine and a growl then turned and waddled back onto the sales floor.

"Traitor," I called.

Bit by bit, piece by piece, I unpacked the assortment of glass pieces I had brought with me. Dozens of red poinsettia petals and an equal number of green leaves were followed by a roll of copper foil, a small pair of scissors, and a purple fid—a hard plastic tool that oddly resembled a thick emery board. Reaching out to my left, I grabbed hold of a classic vinyl bar stool and dragged it close. I pulled my cell phone from my purse, prepared to open the application for streaming music, but the message light was blinking in the corner.

Unlocking the device, I saw the message was from Tony and I was smiling before I read a word. The message was a simple one: a reminder to have a nice day and assurance that he'd see me later. It didn't need to be elaborate to ignite an inner warmth.

I kept my focus on that sweet feeling. Streaming audio open, I lifted the first poinsettia leaf and freed the end from the spool of the copper foil. Carefully I pressed the adhesive side of the foil against the edge of the leaf then rotated the glass in one hand while wrapping the foil with the other. When the leaf edge was wrapped entirely in copper foil, I snipped the roll free.

"I think you know what you want to tell Tony," Carrie said. She stood in the doorway, arms folded and leaning against the jamb, watching me.

"What makes you say that?" I pinched my fingers against the sides of the foil, flattening the edges of the foil onto to the front and back of the leaf.

Carrie gave me her best know-it-all tone. "You're singing."

"So?"

She sighed and rolled her eyes to the heavens. "You're singing a love song."

I opened my mouth to protest—not the fact that I had been singing along but her implication over the meaning behind my action—but a tiny little thought that she might be right grabbed my words away.

"Fine," she said. With a tip of her head toward the sales floor, she said, "Terry's here to see you."

My face rumpled, a reflexive reaction. Why would Terry be at the shop? Especially when I had just seen him at the luncheonette.

I set down the red glass leaf, switched off the audio, and followed Carrie back through displays of antique plates and pitchers to the center of the store, where Terry stood bent over Fifi. She had her belly up and her tongue lolling out of her mouth while one foot thumped against the floor at rabbit speed.

"You found the tickle spot, I see," I said.

Fifi didn't bother to look up at the sound of my voice. Too much doggie euphoria, I guessed.

"Fine dog," Terry said cheerfully. "Old friend of mine, Mike Heaney, used to keep a bulldog."

Carrie and I exchanged glances. We had no way of knowing how he might react if either of us told him that Fifi had belonged to Mike Heaney's widow, Margaret, and had only come to me after Margaret passed. He might think it a nice thing that someone had taken in the dog, but the news of Margaret's demise might be an unwanted reminder of his own advancing age.

"Carrie said you wanted to see me?" I said, opting not to risk spoiling Terry's mood.

Terry left off scratching the dog's belly. He stood straight and met my eye. "Wanted to talk to you about who killed David Rayburn."

I may have then tried to avoid his eye. "I don't . . . I don't know anything about—"

"Never said you did." His eyes had a glint in them I wasn't accustomed to seeing in men over fifty. "But I'm hoping you'd be interested in learning along with me."

I sneaked another glance at Carrie. Big help she was. All she did was open her eyes wide and ever so slightly shrug.

I ducked my head to the side, focused my gaze on Fifi— who remained belly-up on the floor and was moments away from snoring. "Look, Terry, I appreciate you thinking of me and, you know, asking me, um . . ." I blew out a breath.

"I made you a copy of my notes." Terry pushed his hands into the pockets of his twill barn coat. "Ever since he's started those new vitamins, Tom's been pretty good at remembering things. He filled me in on what ol' David has been up to."

He pulled a rumpled and folded piece of paper from his pocket and fought to catch the edge in order to unfold it. The slight tremor in his hands made it difficult.

I moved a step closer to him, reached out to stop him trying to open the page, but he misread my intent and handed me the paper. "Some things on there I'd like to see for myself. You know, once a private investigator always a private investigator," he said. "Problem is, I can't drive. That's where you come in."

The bell over the door jingled, and Carrie edged away from us, off to keep an eye on her new customer in case help should be needed.

Before I caught myself, I had the paper open, trying to decipher Terry's handwriting.

I shut my eyes tight, held out the page to him.

"No, now, that's for you to keep."

"I can't do this. Terry, I'd love to help you . . ." I blinked as though I'd lost my focus somehow. "What is it you're planning to do? Solve the case? What about Tom? You're supposed to be visiting with him, aren't you? How would he feel if he knew you were out investigating a crime without him?"

"Not to worry," he said, holding up a hand. "Trick to a good long visit is not spending every second in one another's company. But I do have to go now because he's my ride home and he's waiting on me. You keep hold of those notes." He winked. "We'll talk." Then he turned and stepped over a sleeping Fifi on his way out of the store.

I was stuck holding a piece of paper that I didn't want to look at . . . or did I?

No. No. Absolutely not. It was going to take a lot more than a bored old gentleman to get me caught up in sleuthing again.

I folded the paper in half one more time and gave it a sharp crease with my nail. Telling myself I'd dispose of the paper as soon as I came upon a recycle bin, I shoved the piece of paper deep into the pocket of my jeans and returned to the back room with the realization that Fifi snoring sounded a lot like Fate laughing.

10

By 2 p.m. Sunday I had finished helping my mom clean up after a brunch she hosted at Grandy's house so she could catch up with all her old friends at once. I'd done my bit to smile and be polite, and refrain from shouting at women that it was none of their business why I wasn't married yet and who the new man in my life was or if I thought we had a future. By 3 p.m. I was pouring a glass of red wine for me and a glass of red wine into the beef sauce I was preparing with Ben's help while Mom took a ride with Grandy up to Newbridge to buy some pastries. By 4 p.m. the beef was in the oven, Mom and Ben were in the living room working on the Sunday crossword puzzle, and Grandy was watching baseball in his bedroom, cursing the umpires. I took advantage of the lull to tiptoe down to my studio with a gallon of tap water.

With the water set on the table for the moment, I went to the corner of the room and switched on the radio. Technology may have changed the way we acquire and listen to music, but that old tabletop radio with its manual dial and physical antenna worked just as well today as it had when I was a kid.

I tuned to a station that played not-quite-golden oldies then turned back to my worktable. No doubt about it, the butterflies were waking in my belly the lower the sun sank. Its rays slanted through the corner windows of the workroom, bathing the floor and the lower half of the opposite walls in golden afternoon light and increasing the anxiety poised to race through my blood.

Pulling in a slow, deep breath that I told myself would be soothing, I ducked into the garage. Beneath the worktable where I kept my glass grinder was a carton containing the last piece of stained glass equipment I had bought myself before my job, my engagement, and so much more went down the drain. And then there I was, pulling out that box on the very same day the new man in my life was meeting my family.

I tried to remember the true meaning of irony, tried to figure out if my situation fit. Mulling over definitions made it easier to keep thoughts of Tony in company with my mother at bay.

While my brain was occupied with pointless thoughts, I carried the box to the workshop and got busy unpacking and setting up my ring saw. I filled the basin with the water I'd brought down, mounted the saw, checked the blade . . . All the minuscule little tasks it took to get the saw working took focus. It was an ideal distraction.

But once the saw was ready and I'd given up on irony, there was nothing left to stop my mind from returning to Tony and his imminent arrival.

I raised the sheet I used to cover the table and lifted the marked square of glass I had left there. Poinsettias were characterized by the contrast in their leaves. The flower, in fact, was the cluster of tight yellow buds at its center. I'd selected a yellow shot through with gold and traced on the glass a series of small circles.

The wheel of the traditional, hand-held glass cutter was set in a fixed mount. From model to model the type of grip changed from standard to pistol grip to pencil hold. The one feature they all shared was the inability to curve, making cutting circles a tough task. Not impossible, but tough. And the smaller the circle, the harder it got. There were tools made specifically to cut circles, but I had chosen to go with a ring saw and its ability to cut complicated or deeply curved patterns, patterns that really would be impossible to achieve with a simple cutter.

With safety goggles in place, I reached for the first piece of glass and switched on the saw.

Friday scared a curse out of me as she bolted from some secret space I hadn't spotted her in and streaked up the stairs like a Great Dane was after her. I pressed a hand to my heart and blew out a breath.

Returning my attention to the saw, I watched as the water flowed through tubing that led from the reservoir below to the edge of the diamond grit saw. Keeping both glass and saw blade cooled with water was mandatory.

Assured everything was working as it should, I lay the sheet of glass on the platform above the water reservoir and guided the glass gently toward the spinning saw blade.

The trick to cutting on a ring saw was maintaining even pressure and moving in straight lines—forward and back, side to side. Cutting a circle meant always pushing in a forward direction, and following the curve by turning the sheet of glass rather than turning the blade.

"Georgia!"

The trick was also not to have your mother shouting your name.

I switched off the saw and lifted my goggles to rest against my forehead, turned to my mother.

She stood at the top of the half-dozen stairs, hands on her thighs as she bent to look at me. "What are you doing? What is all that noise?"

I imagine my face must have shown my disbelief. "Cutting glass," I said. It was perfectly obvious to me; I wasn't sure where the question came from.

"Do you have to do that now?" she asked.

I opened and closed my mouth without any words escaping. I blinked. Twice. "I thought I'd get some of this done, yes."

Huffing, she clomped down the stairs, her feet heavy with the latest thick-soled athletic shoes. "Can't you do this another day? During the week maybe?"

"It's sort of one of my jobs," I said. "Among the two others you think are taking me nowhere. I need to get this done while I have the time."

She gave a shallow sigh and folded her arms. "Why

must it be now? Can't you come up and visit with Ben and I? We're only here for a few more days. I feel like I've barely seen you."

She had a point there. Of course, she hadn't seen me because I'd mainly been avoiding her. A person can take only so much of her mother telling her she isn't living up to her potential. "That's the whole purpose of tonight," I said. "Visiting, relaxing, talking."

Tipping her head a fraction to the side, she said, "I want a few moments when it's just us. Just the family."

Just the family. Me, Mom, and Grandy. And Ben. I tugged the goggles off and tossed them onto the table. "Okay. We'll visit."

"Georgia," she began in a very don't-get-smart-with-me tone.

I forced a smile, backtracked to the corner of the room to switch off the radio. "You're right," I said. "We should visit. Just us."

The smile seemed to appease her, seemed to mask my insincerity sufficiently that she smiled, too, and preceded me up the stairs. "I'll open some wine," she said. "You get your grandfather."

"Um, Grandy's watching the ball game." I stopped my progress up the steps.

Mom continued to the top, turned around to speak to me. "I'm sure he can make an exception."

"It's the play-offs," I said.

"Family," she said, "is more important than baseball."

I looked to the heavens. Honestly, it was like she didn't know her own father. More important than baseball indeed.

* * *

Grandy was sunk in his favorite chair, a classic leather club chair with nail-head accents. The chair was ancient. On more than one occasion Carrie had eyed the chair with the appreciation and borderline greed of an antiques dealer. On this occasion, Grandy was staring at the television that sat in the corner, his teeth clenched, the muscles of his jaw bunching and rolling. The television screen was black.

"But it would make better sense," Ben said, "to get a full-time job, one with benefits. That way you can build a career at the same time you're securing your future."

On those same occasions Carrie eyed the furniture, she also turned a knowledgeable eye on the crystal, with its sharp cut glass and heavy stems. Those sharp edges she admired threatened to leave permanent indents in my hand as I gripped the bowl of the glass tighter with each word Ben uttered.

I took a steadying breath, tried to inhale calm. "I'm not averse to a full-time job," I said. "I am actively looking for one. In the meantime, I pick up what work I can get."

Ben's eyes slipped closed as he shook his head. "No. You'll never find a job while you have one. Finding a job is full-time work. You need to do away with these little diversions and focus on the job hunt."

"I need to pay bills," I snapped. "I need to put gas in my car. And I have an inconvenient fondness for food."

"Now, Georgia," my mother said. "Ben's only trying to help. You should be grateful for his advice."

My jaw fell. I looked to Grandy, hoping for help from his corner. The muscle at the back of his jaw twitched. At the same time I wanted him to leap to my defense, I appreciated his allowing me to defend myself. In that moment when I was close to feeling like a child again, it was nice to know someone believed I was an adult.

"Maybe," Ben said, his voice at an almost gentle pitch, "you ought to consider looking out of state. There's bound to be more opportunities for an accountant in a larger town, or even a city."

"But I like it here." I didn't like the soft sound of my voice. I cleared my throat and repeated, "I like it here." I felt, all it once, like I had said the same words a hundred times, but no one seemed to hear them.

Fifi picked up the sound of the car door first, earning her keep by behaving like a proper watchdog. From her napping position beneath the kitchen table, she scrambled to her feet and bounded to the door, barking her warning along the way.

"Ah. That must be your gentleman friend," Ben said.

Grandy's eye twitched briefly, and I bit back a "thank heavens" while I set my glass of wine down on the coffee table and stood.

Mom pushed to her feet, faced me across the table. "I'll get it, Georgia, you sit."

"It's fine, Mom. I've got it."

An even-measured thump sounded from the porch— Tony jogging up the steps—and Fifi mixed a little whining in among her barking.

"It won't do to look too eager." Ben raised his glass as

though his words were a toast. I raised my eyes to the heavens and ducked out from behind the coffee table.

"I've got it," I repeated.

The first chime of the doorbell hadn't completed before I yanked open the door and slipped outside.

Startled, Tony looked at me with concern in his eye. "What's wrong?" he asked.

I shook my head, tugged the door closed. "You don't want to go in there." My hand against his chest kept him from advancing. "Really. Trust me on this one."

He grinned, and rested his hand over mine. A cool evening breeze wafted the scent of his cologne toward me. "What are you going to do to stop me?"

"Give me a minute. I'm sure I can come up with something."

"Can I make suggestions?" he asked. There was a tease in his voice and a hint of mischief in his eyes—if only for the split instant before the door whooshed open behind me.

"Well, hello there," Ben said.

I might have flinched.

"You must be Tony," he said. Then he was out the door and standing beside me on the porch, as Fifi wriggled through the gap left in the door. "Ben Sutter." He stretched out a hand toward Tony, and Tony the traitor, dog snuffling at his slacks, obliged.

"Anton Himmel," he said. He released Ben's hand then bent to pat Fifi on the head.

"Happy to meet you. Georgia's told us nothing about you."

My mother appeared in the doorway. "We were beginning to think you didn't exist," she said.

I was obliged to shuffle to the side to let my mother join the growing huddle on the porch. My movement disturbed Fifi from her inspection of Tony's ankles. She waddled off down the porch steps and onto the front lawn.

"In or out," Grandy called. "But shut the door. I'm not paying to heat the whole neighborhood."

Mom reached behind her and pulled the door closed. She took a breath and looked out across the yard. "Georgia, call the dog back before she wanders into the street."

"She won't wander into the street," I said. Fifi, her canine priorities intact, located a patch of fading sunlight and flopped onto the ground.

"Oh, now, you can't be too careful," Ben said.

Tony shifted his stance, legs wide, arms crossed. "I installed an electric fence. Poor dog's owner had passed away. Georgia may have told you. We didn't want to risk the dog trying to get back to its original home and getting hurt. She won't leave the lawn unless she's on a leash."

A silence of unusual magnitude overtook the porch. Seconds ticked away at the pace of hours. At last, Mom put on one of her broadest smiles. "That's right. Georgia told us you're in construction. I imagine putting in an invisible fence would be a piece of cake for someone like you."

"Well." Tony gave a lopsided grin. "Every task has its challenges."

This was a highly delicate way of referring to Grandy's

supervisory skills, which Tony had borne with an endless supply of good nature.

"But isn't there some concern with those fences not really keeping a dog in if it spots something it wants to chase, like a squirrel or a cat or another dog?"

Ben directed the question at me, whether because it was my dog or because he'd decided not to tangle with Tony.

I made an effort to duplicate my mother's smile. "Why don't we all go inside?"

With a call to the dog, I followed Mom and Ben into the house, Tony's hand gently at my back.

Fifi pushed past me and bumped up against Ben, making him take a stumbled step to the side. I determined to share my portion of beef with her.

Stepping back into the house from the clean air of the outdoors, I was enveloped by the savory scent of beef tenderloin, which filled me with a feeling that was more than appreciation, more than hunger. In some unnameable way, the aroma comforted me.

"Dad." Mom stood at the edge of the living room, hands planted on her hips.

Grandy remained in his favorite chair but his expression no longer looked like he'd been chewing sour lemons. He had the television remote clenched in his fist and the ball game showing quietly on the TV.

"We have company," Mom said.

"It's just for a minute. I only want to see the score." Despite his words, he shifted so that his upper body bulk blocked the remote from anyone foolish enough to try and grab it from his hand.

Mom glanced at the screen, where the score showed clearly in the upper left corner. "It's right there. It's three to two. Will you turn it off now?"

"Three to two?" Tony said. No doubt I was the only one who realized he spoke somewhat louder than usual. "Who's ahead?"

"Red Sox," Grandy grumbled.

Tony gave a say-it-isn't-so huff. "Yankees left two men on base?"

Grandy made an agreeing grunt. "They haven't had a decent cleanup batter since Jeter retired."

"No kidding." Tony moved past me, threw a wink over his shoulder, and sat himself down on the sofa end closest to Grandy. He kept to the edge of his seat, eyes on the game. "I thought they had a shot with Freeman, but . . ."

Grandy scoffed. "Lot of good he turned out to be."

And they were off, two avid sports fans solving the league's problems from a living room in Wenwood. At length, Ben took a seat and focused on the television. His brow furrowed as though he was deep in thought, or trying very hard to behave as if he were interested.

Mom lifted her hands in surrender. "They're all the same. I give up."

Together we retreated to the kitchen. Mom poured another glass of wine and I got to work chopping and dicing and grating for the salad. By the time dinner was ready for the table, the Red Sox had a four-run lead on the Yankees, and the men were happy to switch off the disappointment of the game and join us in the dining room.

Fifi took up her traditional place at the corner between Grandy and me while Friday perched on the back of the club chair, keeping a wary eye on the humans and an eager eye on the broccoli in cheese sauce.

"Everything looks delicious." Tony flicked open his napkin and laid it in his lap. His gaze bounced from dish to dish until it landed on the same broccoli dish that held Friday's attention. He glanced over at me and smiled. "Nice touch."

I grinned back and raised my glass. "Something told me you might like that."

The room filled with the clatter of silver, the pleases and thank-yous of passing platters, and finally the appreciative noises and compliments on tasty food.

It wasn't long before the silence that accompanied people digging in to their meals edged over into the silence of people who didn't know what to say to one another. Or what to say that was safe. No politics, no religion. Something polite that was neither cold nor prying.

"So you're a Yankees fan?" Grandy said. "Were you raised in New York or were you a bandwagon fan?"

Tony flashed a smile. "When you're a kid, it's hard not to be a bandwagon fan. It takes a good amount of self-confidence to be a fan of a losing team and I think kids are generally lacking that. Or I was at least."

"But not a New Yorker?" Grandy slid a healthy cut of meat into his mouth and instantly washed it back with a sip of cold tea.

"Not by birth. Only a temporary resident."

"Oh, you're not a local?" Mom asked.

"No, I'm not. Just the son of a man who was fond of scenic road trips. That's how I found Wenwood and the brickworks."

Ben sipped his wine, set the cup down on the table with a thump. "So you're, what, a contract worker? Where's home if it's not here?"

"If you mean where did I grow up, the answer is New Jersey. Warren County to be exact." He lifted his knife and cut with gusto into the meat. "If you mean where's home now, the answer is Asheville, North Carolina."

I may have imagined the silence I thought I heard—or didn't hear, as it were. I may have imagined the paused breath, the reluctance to make a single movement. That's what it feels like when time is suspended.

"So," my mother began, drawing out the word. "You'll be heading back there when the marina's done?"

I wanted to keep my eyes on my plate, wanted to continue my avoidance of the topic.

But I couldn't let Tony answer the question without giving any indication that his answer mattered to me.

I lifted my chin, met his fixed blue gaze waiting for mine.

"I might. Nothing's definite yet," he said.

Grandy's fork clattered onto his plate. I looked quickly to him. His smile was swift in coming and going. "My apologies," he said. "Slipped right out of my hand."

He left the fork where it was, reaching instead for the glass of wine he had, up until that point, left untouched.

"So you're thinking of staying in Wenwood?" Mom had one eye narrowed, brows slightly furrowed.

Poor Tony. He'd finally gotten to take a bite of food before her question.

"Can we do twenty questions later?" I asked. "Let the man eat."

"Georgia, your mother's just making conversation," Ben said.

"There are other people at the table she can make conversation with," I snapped. And just as quickly, I sighed. My regression to teenager was unending. As an added bonus, my boyfriend was a witness.

I let my eyes slip closed. "Sorry," I said. "It's just that I would appreciate it if you—"

Beneath Grandy's chair, Fifi scrambled to her feet, sounding the canine alarm. Friday came to her feet on the back of the couch, eyes wide, fur puffed. She took a panicked leap off the couch and disappeared in the general direction of the stairs. Fifi's nails scratched against the hardwood floor, digging grooves into the wax until she got her purchase and scurried to the door.

No humans moved. We were all still trapped in the freeze frame my outburst had caused.

A loud rap sounded against the door, and Fifi's defensive bark grew more purposeful. And still we sat, looking at one another like gunslingers at high noon, waiting to see who would make the first move.

At last, determining the silence and the impromptu game of statues were mainly my fault, I tossed my napkin beside my plate and stood.

My chair scraped as the backs of my knees pressed against it. The awful noise was enough to snap the rest of the family into action. Glasses were lowered, knives and forks dropped, and chairs were pushed back in a cacophony of noise while I headed for the door.

Fifi pressed her nose to the sliver of air sneaking between the bottom of the door and the top of the saddle.

Her barking subsided to be replaced by a faint whine and the side-to-side wobble of her back end that meant someone she wanted to see was on the other side of the door.

It was based on that behavior, the wisdom of a dog, that I didn't think twice before I pulled the door open.

# 11

The inward whoosh of the door brought with it the crisp scent of a deepening autumn and the woody aroma of Detective Nolan's cologne. He stood with one hand in his pocket, the other resting on his thigh, in a suit that looked somehow limp and unkempt, as though he had been in it for days. Beside him, Diana bent to try and stop Fifi from jumping against her with glee. Fifi was probably Diana's biggest fan.

Happy though the dog was, and indulgent though Diana was, I took hold of Fifi's collar and tugged her back into the house. I barely got a hello out of my mouth before Grandy was at my elbow. "What are you doing here?"

I hauled Fifi back behind the gathering of family at the door and ordered her to stay.

"Who is it, Dad?" Mom asked.

I turned back to find my mother on tiptoe, trying to peer over Grandy's shoulder. "Oh, hello there, Detective," she said.

"Detective?" Ben repeated, alarm in his voice.

To have Diana drop by on a Sunday evening was not that unusual. She often stopped for a visit, sometimes talking through her week or venting about her frustrations working toward detective status with Nolan as her assigned mentor. She was especially fond of being around while I was working with glass—she was always eager to help break things when needed. But to have her here unplanned? With Nolan? That couldn't mean anything good.

"What's going on?" I asked, then became instantly annoyed with myself for having echoed Ben in any way.

Nolan opened his mouth to speak. In the brief pause before words emerged, I felt Tony's hand at the back of my waist. With the five of us huddled in the doorway, we must have made quite a familial sight.

"Sorry to interrupt your evening, folks," the detective said. His gaze bounced off mine and settled on Grandy. "We won't keep you long."

I shifted my attention to Diana, looking for some clue in her posture or her eyes. Her shoulders were relaxed, her lips halfway to a smirk, and her eyes wide in what was likely an effort to keep them from rolling. I couldn't guess at whether she thought Detective Nolan was lying about the prospective duration of their stay or whether some conversation had transpired between them earlier that caused her attitude.

Tony edged marginally closer to me, his warmth

making me all the more conscious of the cool air breezing across the porch.

"What can we do for you?" Ben asked, all puffed and official.

The muscle at the back of Grandy's jaw bulged.

Nolan kept his eyes on Grandy. "We were wondering if by chance you had seen or heard from Rozelle Schurz." It was somewhere between a statement and a question, and I glanced from him back to Diana.

The smirk and sarcasm had faded.

"Rozelle?" Grandy repeated. His spine stiffened and he shook his head. "I've not spoken to her since . . ." He raised his eyes to the lintel, as though that was where he stored his memories.

Despite the comfort of being surrounded by family and friends, a shiver of cold discomfort worked its way through me caused either by Nolan's careful control or Diana's uncharacteristic quiet. She was as accustomed to making herself at home here as Fifi was. Something was keeping her on the visitor's side of the door.

"Who's Rozelle?" Ben stage-whispered.

"She owns the bakery," I said. "I saw her yesterday at Grace's. Grandy, I don't think you've mentioned going into the village since—"

At eighty, Grandy was too old to blush. But the careful way he avoided my gaze, the subtle shrinking in his bearing, told me he was keeping something from me, keeping something from everyone.

"Friday lunchtime," Grandy said.

Friday? Lunchtime?

"Did she give any indication she would be away for

the weekend?" Detective Nolan reached into the inside breast pocket of his suit jacket and produced his worn leather notepad. From the same pocket he pulled out a pen. "Mention anything about visiting friends or family?"

Blowing out a noisy breath, Grandy folded his arms. "What business is it of yours?"

Mom leaned forward a fraction, trying to make eye contact with Grandy from over my shoulder. "Dad," she said, using the same tone she favored when accusing me of pushing my luck.

"Pete, you might consider speaking nicely to the police," Ben said.

Grandy turned his scowl on Ben. "And you might consider not telling me what to do in my own home."

"Pete," Diana said softly. The very gentleness of her voice, so unlike her, turned the shiver of cold I had felt earlier to heated fear. "No one has seen Rozelle since she left the luncheonette yesterday morning. A bunch of us are getting kind of worried."

"So you see why it's important," Detective Nolan said. He took a moment to shoot a quelling look in Ben's direction before looking back to Grandy. "Did Mrs. Shurz tell you anything about her plans for the weekend? Have you heard from her at all?"

To the unfamiliar eye, Grandy would have appeared unmoved, unconcerned. I had been living with him long enough to qualify as being quite a familiar eye. For me, there was no hiding the worry bubbling beneath his stoic exterior.

"Not a word. Why would you expect her to tell me?" Grandy asked.

Diana smiled. "Rozelle's got a thing for you, Pete. We figured if she was going to share her plans with anyone, it would be Grace or you."

"And she said nothing to Grace?" Tony asked.

Detective Nolan's gaze snapped to Tony, bounced over me, and returned to Grandy. "If Grace had any information, we wouldn't be here."

Grandy unfolded his arms, slipped his hands into his trouser pockets. He shook his head. "She never said a word."

Silence hung in the air as though we each waited for someone else to offer some tidbit of information about Rozelle.

Detective Nolan produced a business card from the back of his notebook. He held it out toward Grandy. "If you remember anything, if anything comes back to you, give me a call."

I opened my mouth, intending to remind Detective Nolan that I had his cell number so the business card was unnecessary. Luckily I kept that thought to myself.

"Of course I will," Grandy said. He kept the card in his hand as good nights and promises to call with any news of Rozelle were exchanged. Diana and Detective Nolan turned to head down the porch steps while Mom, Ben, Tony, and I backed away from the door so Grandy could close it.

Head down, I reached out for Tony. He caught my shoulder as I ran my arm around his waist, concern for Rozelle unnerving me, making me seek that extra support.

But Tony stopped short, and I lifted my head to learn the cause. I didn't even have to ask. All I had to do was follow the direction of his gaze.

Atop the dining room table, Friday stood beside my dinner plate batting a piece of broccoli across the table-cloth and toward the edge to where Fifi sat below, eyes begging, tongue lolling, waiting for the food to drop.

Grandy huffed out a sigh. "Turn your back for a moment and your whole world spins into chaos."

I waited until the following morning to return the serving platters and good dishes to the sideboard. I wanted the work done before anyone in the house awoke and so I moved from the kitchen to the dining room as quietly as possible, clutching the plates tightly to keep them from rattling. All that effort and I nearly dropped them to the ground when Grandy said, "Georgia."

I had the presence of mind to slide the plates onto their shelf before turning my death glare on Grandy. "You scared the bejeezus out of me, Grandy," I said.

He shushed me, pressed his palms downward on the air. "Keep your voice down," he whispered. "You want to wake the whole house?"

"If I wanted to wake everyone, would I be tiptoeing?" I straightened, grabbed Friday off the table, and put her on the floor before edging closer to Grandy so I could speak softly but still be heard. "What are you doing up?"

"I wanted to talk to you alone, without the possibility of your mother or . . ." He ran a hand over the stubble on his cheeks, and it was only at that moment the thread of unease began to unspool.

Without looking, without conscious thought, I

reached for a chair back and grabbed hold, tried to look casual. "All right. What's up?"

I could almost picture the words coming out of his mouth, drifting into a speech bubble above his head. *It's about Tony Himmel*, the words would say. But what he said in reality was, "I know I've told you time and again not to stick your nose into police investigations."

Relief flooded through me. I let out more breath than I'd taken in, my spine softened, and my shoulders sagged. "Grandy, don't worry I—"

"This time I . . . I have to ask you to, well, stick your nose in."

Good thing I hadn't loosened my grip on the chair. I could have been knocked down by a heavy sigh. "You want me to . . ." I shook my head. "Grandy, you . . . Why?"

And there was that heavy sigh. "I haven't been precisely forthright with you about my relationship with Rozelle."

My brows rose high. "Can you be forthright now?"

He scratched again at the stubble gathered on his jaw. "I didn't see any reason to tell you I'd been seeing Rozelle socially. It was only lunch now and again."

"Lunch," I repeated dumbly. How could he have been leaving the house to meet Rozelle and I had never noticed? But of course, he had already given me the answer. "Let me guess," I said. "You and Rozelle met for lunch on days I was working at Drew's law office."

His nostrils flared as he exhaled, and that was all the confirmation I needed.

I wanted to be angry with him, wanted to feel some

sort of offense at his unwillingness to share this development with me. Instead, I felt the stirrings of what could only be hurt. "Why didn't you tell me?" I asked, my voice almost impossibly quiet.

Friday leaped onto the table again, her paws landing with a thud that seemed thunder-loud in the stillness of the room.

Grandy glanced in her direction but made no move to shoo her away. "It's my business," he said, voice gruff. "My personal business."

I supposed I could understand the sentiment. "But—"

"I don't have to tell you everything," he said. "I'm allowed my privacy."

The sense of being on the wrong side of the conversation threatened to make me dizzy. Those were my lines, weren't they? Words the younger of the household had been uttering for eons.

I closed my eyes for a moment, taking the time to allow all the news to sink in. "Okay, so you've been . . . lunching . . . with Rozelle." I nodded—another move to encourage sinking in—and finally smiled. "That's so sweet. I'm so happy for you. It's nice to know—"

"Which is exactly what I didn't want." His voice practically boomed in the hush of the room, startling Fifi out of her resting place under the kitchen table. The sounds of her nails on the linoleum as she lumbered to her feet gave away her movement. "I don't want you giggling with your friends about how cute it is or pushing for information or, heaven forbid, telling your mother."

I pulled in a deep breath, preparing to defend myself—and my friends—from his impressions when the deeper implication struck me. Nolan and Diana had showed up at the house looking for news of Rozelle, which meant . . . "Who did Rozelle tell?" I asked.

"Georgia, can you focus, please, before the whole house is awake?"

"I bet she told Grace," I said. "And Grace told Diana—"

"Georgia . . ."

"Which is how Chris Nolan knew to come here."

Grandy's wispy gray eyebrows popped high. "Chris?" he asked. "I didn't realize you were on a first-name basis with the officer."

"Detective," I corrected automatically.

"Well, good." He folded his arms and glared down at me. "That will help you get the information you need to find Rozelle. Won't it?"

"Grandy, I doubt Rozelle is truly missing," I said as gently as I could. "She's probably taking advantage of the bakery being closed and she's gone off to a friend's house."

"And told no one?"

"Maybe she's got the same approach to life you do," I said, "and she wants privacy."

"She would have said something," he insisted. "Maybe not to me, but certainly to Grace or a member of her staff. She wouldn't just up and disappear. There's something not right about her going missing."

I thought to argue his point, telling him maybe a little time alone was just what she needed most after all the upset with the death of David and the suspicion cast on the bakery. But it was that very thought that stole the argument from me. For someone like Rozelle to vanish might be unbelievable. For her to vanish at the same time her business was at the center of a police investigation was chilling.

No doubt Grandy saw the understanding in my eyes. "You'll help, won't you?"

I reached out and grasped his arm. Squeezing lightly, I said, "I'll do what I can."

In the past when I got myself into the middle of a police investigation, I had a ton of insider knowledge to work with—with Grandy falsely accused of murder, I had a lifetime of background information. With Carrie and her ex-husband as targets of a murderous arsonist, I had Carrie helping me out by sharing all the knowledge I may have needed. But with Rozelle . . .

Rozelle was something of an unknown to me. She was the kind old lady that ran the bakery and had been sweet on Grandy since before I returned to Wenwood. Because of Carrie I knew Rozelle and her husband had divorced after only a few short years of marriage when Rozelle was in her forties. She had no children, a sister who had retired to Boca Raton ages ago, and a brother who had passed away in the late nineties. In short, Rozelle was alone.

Except, of course, for those clandestine lunches with Grandy.

By the time I got in the car to head to work, I was giggling over their secret rendezvous. Despite his marshmallow center, Grandy was a big, gruff, manly kind of man. It made me smile to picture him knocking on the back door of the bakery so he and Rozelle could lunch without witnesses.

I made the drive into downtown Wenwood with those images in my mind and worry for Rozelle in my heart. It wasn't until I pulled into a vacant space along Grand Street that I acknowledged the addition of the crazy hope that I'd walk into Grace's luncheonette and Rozelle would be in her temporary spot behind the counter handing out fresh-baked cookies and muffins. Crazy though it was, the hope was there as I crossed the sidewalk and pulled open the door to the luncheonette.

The aroma of frying bacon and fresh coffee assailed me the moment I stepped inside. It was both comforting and aggravating. Aggravating because my stomach went a little tight and spiky with hunger; comforting because I'd spent so many mornings at the luncheonette that the particular mix of smells had the soothing effects of the familiar, almost like home.

If the fragrance of breakfast food was familiar and normal, the quiet of the luncheonette seemed unnatural and somewhat alarming. It was the quiet of an old-style Hollywood Western, when the troublemaking gunslinger swung into the saloon and everyone stopped talking and the piano went silent.

A half-dozen sets of eyes turned to me, took me in, and showed a glimmer of disappointment before turning away. That was enough to tell me Rozelle wasn't lurking in the kitchen fighting the grill cook for counter space. Everyone was still waiting, hoping for Rozelle to come bustling through the door.

I followed my usual path, turning left at the spinning rack of faded postcards and edging up to the lunch counter. Clutching the handle on a mug of black coffee, Tom met my gaze, nodded, and turned away with a sigh.

Grace's usual space beside the cash register was vacant, and I perched on the empty stool next to Tom and waited for her to appear.

At the tables behind me, conversation had started up again. Subdued voices accompanied the tap of cutlery on plates, the thunk of coffee mugs being lowered onto tables. It was this quiet conversation that made me tap Tom's arm. "Where's Terry?" I asked. "He didn't go back down south, did he?"

Tom shook his head. "Under the weather, he said. He's back at the house, still in his pajamas."

"Oh." I thought to continue the conversation, make small talk about how long Terry planned to stay in Wenwood and when he planned to head back to his daughter's house in North Carolina, but with Rozelle as my number one concern, I couldn't muster the energy to pretend interest in Terry's travel schedule.

And yet . . . Terry had been a private investigator during his years in Wenwood. No doubt he would have some solid ideas on how to go about locating Rozelle. Such as where to begin.

Grace ambled through the pass-through, plates of food stacked along both arms. "Be right with you, Georgia," she said and continued to the opposite, open end of the counter and out to the table of waiting patrons.

I rested my elbows on the counter and leaned in, canting a bit in Tom's direction. "Do you think . . . I mean . . .

would you mind if I gave Terry a call at your house? Would you give me the number?"

He looked at me first from the corners of his eyes, then slowly turned his head until his nose was in line with his pupils and he was looking at me full on. "Why would you want to do a thing like that?" he asked, suspicion in every syllable.

"I'd like to talk to him."

"Are you sure that's all?"

I didn't know whether to be surprised or confused. That is, I thought I knew what Tom was inferring, but I couldn't be right, could I? "You don't think I have some sort of romantic interest in Terry, do you?"

Tom sniffed, turned his attention back to the window on the opposite side of the counter. Only a few cars rolled by; no one was out on foot. "Terry's a good-lookin' fella," he said. "Might make a fine catch."

Terry was, of course, old enough to have gone to kindergarten with Grandy. That alone was enough for me to overlook him as a potential paramour. I opted not to share that with Tom, though, and went instead with a simpler truth. "I'm sure he would," I said. "But I've already caught myself a man." I tried a grin, to add a bit of levity.

Tom shrugged, almost like he thought I was lying but he wasn't going to call me on it.

"Now then." Grace rounded the end of the counter and stopped in front of me. "Coffee and an egg sandwich to go?"

"Please," I said.

She went on through to the kitchen to put the sandwich order in and I tried again with Tom. "If I promise

I'm no threat to Terry's status as a bachelor, can I have the number?"

He shook his head. "Don't understand why you want to talk to him."

"I want to pick his brain about some old cases he worked on," I said. I wanted to ask him if he had any experience with people who'd gone missing, how one went about finding them.

Before I could get further, Grace returned from the kitchen. She set a paper cup on the counter and filled it from the ever-present carafe of coffee. "I hear Diana went by your house last night," she said.

I sneaked a peek at Tom.

"He knows," Grace said. "Everyone knows."

"Everyone knows the police were at my house?" So much for Grandy's secret.

Grace gave a sad shake of her head. "Everyone knows about poor Rozelle."

Poor Rozelle.

I didn't know whether shivering or shuddering was the right physical response.

"Did Diana mention anything to you about theories? Any ideas of where Rozelle might be?"

Tom lifted his coffee cup to his lips. "Her car's gone and so is she. She maybe wanted to get out of town for a while, until all the Rayburn nonsense blows over." He sipped noisily from the cup.

Forgoing her typical good-hearted yet cutting remark, Grace grimaced briefly at Tom then looked to me. The glistening of her eyes made my stomach sink beneath a heavy heart. "Diana hasn't said anything other than what the department allows," she said softly.

She capped my coffee cup as the cook popped his head out from the kitchen, my paper-wrapped sandwich in his hand. I fished in my purse for a five-dollar bill. By the time I came up with one, Grace had my sandwich and coffee secure inside a brown paper bag.

"If I hear anything," she said, trading a single for my five, "should I let you know?"

A demurral was ready on my lips, but there was no sense in lying, was there? "Yes," I said. "As soon as you can."

12

Working for Drew Able, Esquire, meant dressing in a semiprofessional manner. Sure, I was a kind of back-office girl, the accountant who did occasional copying and filing because her boss was a bit too scatterbrained to pull that off in a timely fashion. But in the small, in-house office it wasn't uncommon for me to cross paths with his clients and it wouldn't do for me to greet them in yoga pants and an I LOVE NY sweatshirt.

I parked my car across the street and down a ways from Drew's, leaving the space in front of his house vacant for clients. At the peak of summer when I started working for Drew, parking at a distance hadn't been a problem. Now, with summer gone and mornings biting cooler, the air against my legs made me lament that my professional wardrobe consisted primarily of unlined trousers and pencil skirts, and made me think fondly of those yoga pants back at home.

Hurrying up the walkway, I clutched the hot cup of coffee in one hand and the bag holding my egg sandwich in another. I jogged up the few steps and faced the door to his private home ahead of me and the door to the office on my right. With the hand holding the bag, I tried to turn the knob on the door that led to the office but found the door locked. Having been in this predicament before, I knew Drew hadn't squirreled away a key inside a hollowed-out rock or beneath a decorative Wenwood brick. I also knew that the window in the back room where I worked was never locked and in a pinch I could climb in through there—as long as I wasn't wearing a pencil skirt. But in order to pull that off, I would have to put down my coffee, and that just wasn't going to happen.

I rapped on the door and waited in the cold for Drew to let me in. I tried not to think about the winter that lay ahead, but if I pushed those thoughts to the side, I would revert to worrying about Rozelle, so for the moment, thoughts of winter dominated, followed closely by and intertwining with thoughts of Tony.

Alone on the steps, I shook my head. After the visit from Diana and Detective Nolan, it was a little tough to return to the dinner table with the same somewhat relaxed attitude as before. Talk, as expected, turned to speculation on where Rozelle might be and whether the police involvement was necessary or extraneous. Small wonder Grandy didn't volunteer any information about his burgeoning relationship with Rozelle. Ben would

have had that out and dissected along with his speculation over whether looking for missing persons was a
waste of taxpayer money. All in all and given the circumstances, the evening hadn't provided any hints at
how well Tony did or didn't fit in with the family.

I caught the inside of my lip, asked myself why Tony
fitting in was even a consideration. Certainly it was too
early in the relationship to—

The door swung open, dragging a rush of morning air
past me as Drew stood on the other side of the threshold,
sandy hair mussed and green eyes almost frantic.

"What's wrong?" I asked, practically pushing him
back into his office waiting room as I advanced. "What
happened?" What with everything that had gone on in
Wenwood since I moved in with Grandy, my imagin-
ation could go to some troubling places. My heart was
prepared to lodge in my throat and adrenaline dumped
into my bloodstream. "Are you all right?"

He pushed a hand through his hair and swung the door
shut. "It's the . . . stupid . . . toilet again. I can't . . ." He
sighed and looked at the ceiling. "I'm going to have to call
the plumber."

I squinched one eye shut to keep it from twitching.
"You're having a plumbing emergency?"

"The toilet's clogged," he said. He rolled down his
shirtsleeves as he passed through the doorway from the
waiting area to his office. "To me, that's an emergency."

I followed him inside, set the paper bag with my egg
sandwich inside on the edge of his desk. Drew fell into
his chair and I took a bracing sip of my coffee then said,
"I take it you haven't heard the news?"

He paused in rubbing his hands over his face, peering at me between his fingers. "What news?"

"About Rozelle? About her being missing?"

"Rozelle?" he asked, wrinkles of memory strain forming on his forehead. "From the bakery Rozelle?"

"That would be she."

"What do you mean, she's missing?"

One-handed, I dragged one of the visitor chairs closer and settled in to tell him the story. I kept to the few details I knew—that Rozelle hadn't been seen since Saturday morning, the police thought Grandy might know where she was, and oh yeah, someone ate a pastry Rozelle had made and didn't survive the night.

"So it's all very . . . strange and unsettling," I said, summing up. "And it makes your clogged toilet seem a bit trivial in comparison."

Drew folded his hands and sat back, the tall backing of his leather desk chair giving him the look of a framed portrait. "In comparison." He pulled in a noisy breath. "And you're sure the police weren't suspicious of Pete in any way?"

I opted to answer with a glare.

"Okay, okay." For a brief moment he appeared lost in thought. I stood from the chair, reasoning that perhaps he was going to spend some time absorbing all I'd told him. But instead of leaving his office and starting in on my own work, I said, "Just out of curiosity . . ."

I waited until his gaze met mine, then continued. "If I were to say, go have a look around Rozelle's house, just to be sure she wasn't there, what would the legality be there? Out of curiosity."

Drew lowered his hands. "Strictly outside the house?"

"Well." It was my turn to study the ceiling. "I'd have to stay outside if the door was locked, wouldn't I? I wouldn't want to be accused of breaking and entering or anything. But if the door happened to be open . . ."

He grimaced and shook his head. "First of all, you could only be charged with trespassing. New York doesn't list breaking and entering as a crime. But more importantly, I'm sure Pete wouldn't be too happy to hear you were nosing around in matters that aren't your business."

The temptation to tell him my nosing around was Pete's idea in the first place rushed through me. To keep from blurting out that tidbit, I kept to the law. "So what's the difference between breaking and entering and trespassing?"

"In those states that recognize it as a crime, the police can charge you with breaking and entering. For trespassing, the owner of the property has to press charges."

I nodded to show I was following along. Drew interpreted the action as me plotting something.

"Georgia, I wouldn't recommend trying to let yourself into Rozelle's house," he said, voice stern and expression serious. "The law may be on your side, but you don't want to be sitting in jail waiting for me to remind the authorities of that."

"Awww." I grinned. "You'd really come try and get me out of jail? That's so sweet."

"Of course," he said. "I'd be there right away. And I'll bring your grandfather so he can offer his opinion on your situation."

In other circumstances the threat may have worked. In this one, however . . .

"Don't forget to call the plumber." I picked up the paper bag, long since resigned to the impending need to warm the sandwich in the microwave, and scooted through the door that led from his office to the back room. I had work to do . . . and plans to make.

Comfortable in the quiet of Drew's back office, I'd calmly progressed to the point of sealing the envelope on the last ready bill when my cell phone broke the silence. Idina Menzel's soaring voice, usually so exhilarating, so brilliant, startled the breath out of me.

"Carrie," I said, no doubt sounding like I'd just finished a marathon. "Hi. What's up?"

"You know Tom's friend Terry who was in here the other day?" she said.

"What about him?" I sat up a little straighter.

"He's here. He's looking for you." Her voice had a flattened sound to it, as though she were cupping her hand over the speaker so no one would hear. I had an instant visual of her hiding in the back room, whispering on the cordless. "He says you wanted to talk to him. That's what Tom told him, he says."

"He's there now?" I stood, gripping the phone with one hand and gathering the outgoing mail into a stack with the other.

"He's out on the sales floor," she said. I gave myself a mental high five for being right about Carrie hunkering in the back room. "So is it true? You're looking for him? Why?"

Grabbing my purse from the back of the chair, I used a combination of foot and hip to slide the chair into place beneath the table. "I wanted to talk to him about—"

I hadn't prepared myself for telling anyone but Terry what I intended. Certainly I hadn't meant to keep anything from Carrie, but I kinda didn't want to fess up to going off snooping.

"Georgia Kelly, are you planning on going off snooping without me?" Carrie demanded to know.

I froze. "Absolutely not?"

"Georgia!"

"Carrie, honestly, last time wasn't enough for you?" I asked on a sigh. Back in motion, I shoved a hand into my purse to blindly feel around for my car keys.

Her responding huff came across the line sounding like mild static. "I want to at least know what's going on. Are you and Terry going to go poking around the David Rayburn thing?"

Mascara, lip balm, old receipts—I was coming up with everything except keys. "That's truly not what I had in mind."

There was barely enough time to draw breath before Carrie said, "Oh, you're going to try and find out where Rozelle is. Good. Count me in. Should I tell Terry you're on your way?"

"As soon as I find my keys," I mumbled. "But, Carrie, you—"

"Great. We'll be ready."

"Wait, Car—" But of course, she hung up before I could get the sentence out. Talking Carrie out of helping would have to wait. Besides, once we were face-to-face, it would be easier to get her to see reason.

C arrie drove.
     The sky had grown overcast while I toiled away at Drew's, updating his accounts and pulling files for his afternoon clients. With the weakening sunshine, the chill seemed to grow, and my toes had gone icy in my thin dress shoes.

"You sure you know where you're going?" Terry asked from the backseat.

"We're almost there, I promise." Carrie's grip on the steering wheel tightened. With Terry along for the ride, I couldn't ask her whether the strain was due to his presence or due to memories of getting caught up in the dispute over the Heaney estate. Regardless the cause, her tension was evident.

She made a right turn and proceeded slowly along a narrow road so chewed up I wouldn't be surprised if the last time it was paved, Jimmy Carter was president. The front left tire caught the edge of a pothole and her otherwise comfortable sedan bounced us around like a dingy on a stormy sea.

"Jeez, what's wrong with this town? Why don't they fix the roads? Criminettely, I'll be glad to get back to North Carolina after this."

Carrie hunkered closer to the steering wheel and I

was saved from commenting by the ping of an incoming text message.

I yanked my cell phone free of the side pocket of my purse and checked my display. Message from Tony. What are you doing today?

I didn't want to lie to him. But telling the truth didn't feel like a good plan either. As I pondered the best compromise, I checked the changing color of the tree leaves as we drove beneath the boughs.

Carrie and I are taking a ride over to Rozelle's. Why? What's up? I typed, then hit "Send."

"There it is," Terry said. "Lakeland Avenue. That's the left."

Carrie blew out a breath and switched on the turn signal.

As she guided the car around the corner, I took a keener look at our surroundings. A part of Wenwood I had never been through before, the area had the classic, aged look the old riverside houses had. But where the riverside houses had been built to accommodate the large families whose patriarchs the brickworks employed, here the houses were small, built perhaps for single men, or newlyweds' summer getaway. Tiny homes in which standard-sized doorways looked oversized and out of perspective.

"All right, everyone look for 624," Terry said.

A peek at the first house number—12—informed us we had a ways to go. It took until we were in the low 400s for Tony's reply to come back.

Done at the site for the day. Dinner?

Dinner.

On the other side of a cross street on which the last house was 418, the first house was 588. "Five eighty-eight? What kind of crazy town is this?" I murmured.

"Now, when we get there, you ladies wait in the car. I'll go look around."

I cut a glance at Carrie to make sure we were in agreement. The pursing of her lips told me I needn't have worried.

Turning in my seat, I gave Terry my best dealing-with-problem-customers squint. "We're doing this to-gether or Carrie's going to drive right on by. I did not come all the way out here to sit in the car. Got it?"

Terry gave a sort of smirk and lifted his shoulders, and I was left wondering if he had been teasing when he said he would go it alone. I didn't have the luxury of wondering for long. As I looked away from Terry and prepared to turn and face forward in my seat, I caught sight of a car rolling along behind us by about half a block. Big and gray, the sedan appeared to be traveling at precisely our speed. Were we being followed?

I shook the thought out of my head and turned around to face front. Thinking we were being followed was para-noia plain and simple. It's not like I had seen the car behind us until now. And clearly other people used the roads.

"This looks like it." Carrie slowed the car and pulled smoothly into the vacant spot at curbside.

The house, like its neighbors, was a mere teabag of a structure—single step to the front door, one large window, and just a suggestion of front yard. But a pot filled to overflowing with two colors of mums sat beside the step, and a shepherd's hook held a bird feeder, half-filled. A statue of an angel at prayer knelt among the ground cover lining the front of the house. Such simple touches were enough to elevate the building to charming.

Eyes on the angel, I climbed out of the car. Terry followed suit, and we stood together on the ragged edge of the lawn, examining the house.

"Welp," Terry said. "It doesn't look like Rozelle has suddenly returned home."

"Why do you say that?" I asked, then answered my own question. "There's mail in the box." An old-fashioned metal mailbox hung vertically between the door and the window, its cover propped open by an array of envelopes.

"Indeed there is," he said. He shuffled forward a couple of steps. "Your friend not coming?"

I looked behind me, turning in the same moment the gray sedan rolled by, its side windows smoked dark. Keeping an eye on the vehicle's progress, I knocked on the window of Carrie's car and she obligingly powered it down. "Aren't you coming?" I asked.

She held up a cell phone. "I'll be lookout. If anything happens, I'm here to call 911."

I thought to question her on her change of heart. After she insisted on inclusion, I figured she would have been right there with me, peering in windows and expecting any minute for Rozelle to come bursting through the door and shoo us away from her property. But maybe she'd come as close as she could to a potential problem. It hadn't been that long ago that her own apartment had been ransacked, her belongings scattered like the leaves littering the roads. If Rozelle's home had been ransacked, the sight may have been more than Carrie was prepared for.

I nodded my agreement on Carrie's lookout plan and turned to get back to snooping.

Terry was already steps from the front window, his head swiveling back and forth as though he expected some hidden assailant to burst out of the neighbor's bushes. But apart from the two of us and our prowling, the area was still, its residents either off at work or locked in the comfort of their homes. The afternoon sunshine was losing its warmth, and I tugged my jacket close around me as I hurried to catch up with Terry.

He stood on tiptoe at the front door, running his fingers over the top of the door frame. I chuckled. "If you're looking for a key, Rozelle is way too short to stash one up high," I said.

Terry sighed. "It never hurts to be thorough."

I knelt beside the front step. Carefully tipping the statue of the angel, I peered at its underside, searching for any sort of seam in the plaster that might indicate a hidden compartment.

Nothing.

For good measure I brushed my hands through some of the ground cover. I had no idea how big those fake rocks were that were advertised late at night, but I was relatively confident they'd be bigger than the average garden stone.

Terry passed behind me, and I got a good look at his scuffed and worn boat shoes as he came to a stop. I considered asking him what he thought of the marina, but thoughts of the marina led to thoughts of Tony, and I wanted to stay focused.

I brushed bits of dirt from my hands as I stood.

Terry held his hands cupped around his face, his forehead practically touching the glass of the large front window.

"See anything?" I asked, duplicating his pose. Irish lace curtains hung inside, the gaps between motifs wide enough to allow a fairly good view.

"She's got a nice big television," he said. "Look at that."

The television was tough to miss. It sat on an angle in the corner, its screen practically dwarfing the more Rozelle-sized furniture—low-back loveseat, mismatched accent chairs, a side table that looked more like a nightstand, all gathered around a circular rug that had to be less than ten feet in diameter.

"Be good for watching the game," Terry muttered.

I made some noise to indicate agreement then stepped forward until my nose touched the glass. Not the tip of my nose, but the flat of it below the bridge. Maybe if I moved closer, I could see better, I could see more, I could see Rozelle.

But there was no movement inside the house. Nothing appeared disturbed. And really, having been in Carrie's apartment after it had been torn apart, I felt I was making an educated observation. No one had been in Rozelle's looking for anything—not her best jewelry, her best recipes, or the poison that had found its way into David Rayburn's Danish.

At the back of the living room, a half wall divided

Rozelle's home theater from her kitchen. From our vantage point at the window, all I could make out were cabinets, with a braid of garlic hung between two pairs of hinges.

"I'm going around back," I said.

I didn't wait to see if Terry was going to join me, but I didn't rush either. Calmly and slowly I walked along the little front garden, past the kneeling angel and the hanging bird feeder. I was looking for footprints, any footprints. Little feet that might belong to Rozelle or big feet that might belong to some miscreant. Either one could provide a clue we needed.

Of course, I didn't actually know how to spot footprints. They always looked so obvious on television. In reality, though, autumn-dried grass tamped down or standing straight in no specific pattern didn't readily offer up any shoe-shaped images. Add in a few fallen leaves, and even if there were prints, the leaves would obscure them.

Rolling my eyes at my own foolishness, I picked up the pace and circled to the side of the house. Dead leaves had blown into the narrow gap between house and foundation and wedged themselves there, and I wondered abstractly who it was who took care of Rozelle's yard. I hoped she wasn't doing her own raking and shoveling, and that somewhere along her street was a neighbor who did these things for her and that they would come along soon and take care of that most recent mess.

Terry ambled up alongside me so that we were side by side when we came upon the next window. From there we had a view into the kitchen, with only a top valance acting as a curtain on this window. The braid of garlic hung above the counter beside a sink in which several large baking tins rested half out of the basin. A cooling rack three levels high sat on the counter, each level filled with—

"Cookies," Terry said. Rather than surprise or even a little wistfulness, his voice was heavy with something that sounded remarkably like dread.

My stomach sank. I understood his sentiment. Cookies sitting out on the rack and cooling . . . Wherever Rozelle was, she hadn't planned on being away from home, at least not for long.

I opened my mouth, thinking maybe Terry was expecting a comment, but words failed me.

At the back of the house another door sat beside the kitchen and gave us a view of the living room from the other side. A small window set with privacy glass could only have been the bathroom, and farther along, at the rear corner of the house, heavy shades were down in what I presumed to be the bedroom.

"Wish we'd found a key," Terry mumbled. "I'd like to get inside, have a look around."

I kicked at a small cluster of leaves. "You think there's any information to be learned there?"

"Always something to learn," he said.

We rounded the rear corner, heading back to the street, and narrowly missed crashing into Carrie.

"You left your cell phone in the car," she said. "How can I be a lookout and call you if there's trouble if you left your cell phone in the car?" She brandished my phone for emphasis.

I could have pointed out that the lookout thing was her idea and she mentioned calling 911 and not me. Instead, I tapped my fingers against my forehead and gave a little smile. "Sorry. I wasn't thinking. But, um, why did you take it out of my purse?"

"It wouldn't stop ringing," she said. "I was only going to put it on vibrate, but when I saw who was calling, I thought you'd like to know."

I reached for the phone as cautiously as if I were reaching for a snake. "Why? Who's been calling?"

Wordless, she held the phone out to me. I grabbed it, thumb poised to bring up the call log, when again the phone rang. There, bold as a billboard across the display screen, were the words PACE COUNTY POLICE DEPT.

My life was such that those words no longer filled me with instant fear or guilt. Dread, though . . . that was hard to put an end to.

Taking a breath, I accepted the call then lifted the phone to my ear. "This is Georgia," I said.

The words had barely left my mouth when Diana's voice blasted through the receiver. "Tell me you're not snooping around Rozelle's house," she commanded.

I let out that breath, shoulders dropping as I relaxed. As I resumed my slow walk around the house, eyes on the ground as I tried to pick up traces of Carrie's recent footprints, I said, "I'm not *in* the house."

"*Why* are you there?" Diana asked. "We've already searched and secured her house and I told you—"

"I know," I said, catching Carrie's eye. "You told us there was nothing to be learned here."

"And to leave this to the police, right?" Diana prompted.

"Uuuhmmm, no, that I don't remember you saying," I said.

"Really? Detective Nolan didn't happen to mention the importance of leaving things to the police?"

My steps slowed. We had reached the front yard and I had yet to spot a footprint, but that was no surprise. The realization that Nolan had told me no such thing rocketed through me. More than that, though . . .

I glanced from the dead and dying grass at my feet to the curb, where Carrie's tan sedan sat smack in front of the house.

"Hey, Diana," I said. "Tell me something. Any luck finding Rozelle's car?"

Her sigh carried a hint of resignation. "Not yet. We're looking. Why do you ask?"

Though she clearly couldn't see me, I shook my head nonetheless. "No reason," I said. "Just trying to put things together."

"Because that goes right along with leaving things to the police," she said, sarcasm dragging her tone of voice lower.

"She left home in a hurry but took her own car," I murmured. "So probably no one stopped by and surprised her. Does that mean she was in a rush? Running late for some prearranged get-together?"

"Georgia, are you talking to me or talking to yourself? Because I'm going to hang up on you if you're talking to yourself."

I considered claiming I had been talking to her, asking her to keep me company along my mind wandering and give a little input. But my thoughts were half formed at best. A sense of certitude told me I was on to something, but I didn't know what. Not yet. "Talking to myself," I said. "I'll let you get back to work."

We said our good-byes and I clicked off the phone, looked at Terry. "Okay. What next?"

13

When Carrie heard Terry's next-stop plan for continuing our informal investigation into Rozelle's disappearance, she instantly recalled an important shipment she had to pull together. A very big part of me wanted to claim she needed my help. But this was my crusade. All I had to do was think of Grandy and my resolve returned. Besides, Terry had some kind of weird faith in me. Or maybe he was just using me for my access to cars and the opportunity to spend a little time reliving the good old days.

Whatever the case, Terry and I went alone to the last place I ever thought I'd visit—the last place most folks visit, come to that: the county morgue.

For half an hour on the road, "turn right here" and "turn left there" acted as brief interruptions to Terry's tales of life in his daughter's house. One particular story involving his grandson, the family parrot, and Terry's denture paste resulted in a complete U-turn. Distracting though it was, his chatter kept me from dwelling on our destination, and I pulled into the parking lot at the county coroner's office far less nervous than I may have been otherwise.

"Are you sure we're allowed to be here?" I asked as we slow-rolled through a mostly empty lot. There were a few cars scattered throughout the lot, and a couple parked directly beside the building. Though signs indicated who was permitted to use the slots, the area gave an impression of abandonment, or a forbidden zone.

"You pay your taxes, doncha?" Terry asked.

I nosed the car into an empty spot in an empty row beneath one of three signs marked VISITOR PARKING. "Of course I pay taxes," I said.

"Then you're allowed to be here. You can park here, walk through those doors there, and have a seat in the lobby." With a wave of his hand, he indicated a pair of brown-aluminum-rimmed glass doors. "Whether you get any farther than that is a crap shoot."

Marvelous.

Silence enveloped us as we stepped out of the car, and the air itself seemed oddly without odor, as if all life had been sucked into a void. I suppressed a shudder and used the key fob to lock the car.

Terry had a bit of a slower step than Grandy, and I had to pay attention and be careful not to overtake him. We walked mostly side by side across the parking lot, a few stray leaves billowing into our path and getting caught beneath our feet. They flattened with a crunch and I had a moment's wistfulness in memories of jumping into a pile of leaves in Grandy's backyard when I was a little bit of a thing with constantly tangled hair. Now all I needed was a pile of leaves and I could re-create my childhood.

Acting the gentleman, Terry opened the door and made a little bow as he waved me inside ahead of him. One step over the threshold and all thoughts of jumping in leaves and other innocent and innocuous pursuits fled my mind. The sensation that I had just entered a hospital washed over me, along with the odorous combination of commercial cleaners and dust. Two steps and I realized I had a leaf impaled on the heel of my shoe.

I proceeded to the counter stretched along the far wall and propped my elbow on its pitted and gouged wood surface for added balance while I removed the dead vegetation. The dark-haired woman behind the counter looked up from her contemplation of the glossy pages of a textbook and laid a pen on the notebook beside it. "Help you?" she asked.

Her tired, returning-student eyes skittered over to Terry when he laid his hands on the counter with a slight slap. "Yes, please, darlin'." Terry gave her a big smile. "Will you tell me if ol' Lucky Hendricks is still around?"

The way he phrased it, it was hard to tell if he was asking if Lucky was still in the building or if he was still among the living.

She flipped a lock of hair over her shoulder then lifted a phone receiver. "I'll check. Who should I say is looking for him?"

"Hank," Terry said. "Hank Fields." He touched his fingertips to my shoulder. "And this here's my grand-niece Bernadette."

With her free hand, she pointed to her left. "Have a seat."

Terry turned in the indicated direction and I gaped at the back of his head. Hank? Bernadette?

He made himself comfortable on a squared-off armchair covered in teal vinyl and pen marks. "Place hasn't changed a bit," he said.

I perched on the edge of a 1970s version of a futuristic couch upholstered in the same scary teal. "What's with the name change?" I whispered.

"What's that?" He set a hand behind his ear and tilted his head toward me.

I huffed, leaned closer so I didn't need to speak louder. "What's up with the new name, *Hank*?"

His brows lowered and seemed to blend into one straight line stretching from one side of his face to the other. "You want anyone who asks to know we were here asking questions?"

I had already taken a breath in preparation of arguing with him, but let it out slowly. He was right. Last thing I wanted was for Detective Nolan to know I'd visited the morgue. At least, I *thought* the news would displease him. My mind spun back to the question of why he hadn't issued his usual "let the police handle it" warning. If he hadn't given me the warning, would he be opposed to my visit with the county coroner?

Before I could formulate an answer—or a theory—the metallic thunk of a push bar on a door echoed through the quiet. Into the waiting area strode a man I estimated to be in his early fifties. He wore neat gray slacks and a charcoal shirt with a black-and-white art deco patterned tie. His dark hair was trimmed short and his smile was almost unnaturally white as he approached Terry, hand extended.

"Hank," he said, grabbing Terry's hand before the poor man had risen from his chair. "Good to see you. How have you been?"

They exchanged the predictable long-time-no-see banter with only a slight pause to acknowledge my presence.

"What brings you by?" Lucky Hendricks folded his arms across his chest and peered at Terry with open interest.

"Need a favor." Terry put his hand on Lucky's shoulder, looked left then right then back again. "Someplace we can talk that's not so . . . public?"

I expected some hesitation, some resistance on Lucky's part, but he kept a smile in place and invited us to his office. "Such as it is," he said.

"Such as it is?" I repeated as we trailed him across the lobby and to the very door he had come through.

As he tugged on the door, it unlocked with a click then he darted through ahead of us. "More like a desk in a corner of a room," he said over his shoulder. "But I can assure you no one else will be listening."

Some stupid, late reality check landed like a fist in my gut. Morgue. We were headed into the morgue. Those no-one-elses who wouldn't be listening were most likely corpses.

Did that cold, tingly feeling across my cheeks mean the blood was draining from my face? I was so used to the heat of embarrassment, I couldn't be sure what its opposite meant.

Without any conscious decision on my part, I slowed my steps until I was trailing slightly behind Terry and Lucky. My plan was to keep my gaze on the backs of their heads, maybe as far as their necks. Under no circumstances did I plan to let my gaze wander elsewhere.

But I kind of couldn't help it. I thought the space we'd be walking into would look like locations I'd seen on television—wide hallways with rooms on either side that were almost like operating rooms only somewhat darker and with metal tables instead of gurneys.

Instead, the rooms on either side of us reminded me of high school, with chicken-wire reinforced glass windows set into wooden doors, posters in the hallway reminding passersby of lab rules and protocols, and an encompassing hush of the sort enforced by hall monitors.

Near the end of the hall Lucky tipped his head to the right and turned toward a door. Terry lagged behind a little until I caught up and we stood elbow to elbow while Lucky produced a heavy set of keys and fed one into the dead bolt in the door. With a turn of the key and a turn of the knob, the door swung inward, opening into darkness.

I wanted to close my eyes, but that would no doubt end in some sort of self-injury. Instead, I squeezed them as almost closed as I could and peered out between the screen of my lashes.

Lights flared on in the room as Lucky strode inside. I crept in behind Terry, doing my utmost to keep my gaze on the ground, but I couldn't do anything to keep my nose closed without drawing attention to myself. The scent of the room impacted me instantly. I flinched backward at the aroma of . . . burnt coffee?

Still shielding myself behind Terry, I cautiously opened one eye.

Lucky had led us into what my one eye assessed as a room straight out of a high school science department. With the other eye open, I was able to confirm that assessment. Though clearly we were not in a high school, the large room contained the same sort of furnishing you would find there. Classic, black-topped lab tables on wooden legs, file cabinets tucked beneath. The tabletops themselves were scattered with stacks of papers, the occasional indoor plant, and an impressive array of coffee mugs.

I was, indeed, standing inside a lab. Not a corpse in sight. Thank heavens for small miracles; I don't think I could have handled the sight of a dead body.

My shoulders sagged as I let go the worry I'd been carrying. I moved level with Terry in time to decline from Lucky an offer of coffee.

"So what can I do for you?" Lucky perched on the edge of what I presumed to be the desk he had referred to earlier, being in the corner of the room and all. His hip pushed aside a half-finished cup of coffee and I reached to stop it from tipping over entirely. He smiled his thanks as Terry said, "Bernadette here had some questions and I told her you'd be the man to ask."

I resisted the urge to punch him in the arm but doubted I kept the surprise from my face.

Lucky looked at me with raised brows and an expectant gaze.

"Umm, yes," I said. "Some questions I hoped you could help with."

He nodded, a motion that meant "go ahead."

Finding no way to stall until the right words came to me, I took a breath and said, "I'm trying to understand how you determine cause of death."

More nodding, but no offer of information.

"That is, I suppose if someone dies of a known medical condition or, say, gets hit by a car, the cause of death is pretty obvious and you . . . wouldn't do an autopsy?"

Lucky Henricks folded his arms. "That's right. We typically reserve autopsy for situations where the cause of death is suspected but not definite or is unknown altogether."

"Suspected or suspicious?" I asked.

Lucky tipped his head, acquiescing. "Both, I guess you could say." His gaze narrowed. "What is this about?"

"Listen, Lucky," Terry began.

But since he was the one who'd thrown me to the wolves, I wasn't about to let him do any rescuing. "I was there," I said quickly, "for the groundbreaking ceremony where David Rayburn got sick. The newspaper says cause of death is undetermined but the suspicion is that it's poisoning."

Lucky leaned back, almost imperceptibly. "That's right."

"So what I don't understand is how it's only a suspected poisoning? I mean, if someone was poisoned, there would be signs, right? Like foaming at the mouth or speaking in tongues or something?"

Beside me, Terry chuckled. I steeled myself against the suspicion that he thought my question to be somewhat simpleminded. After all, what did I know about poison really? It's not that I was likely to come across that information during my education in accounting.

Fortunately, Lucky seemed more interested in educating than mocking. "Most poisons leave very little indication as to their presence. They're not as obvious as, say, signs of drowning or a heart attack or even a drug overdose."

"Then how do you test for them?" I asked. "And what would even make you think to test for them instead of, say, a valium overdose or something?"

Lucky sucked air between his teeth and gave a slight shrug. "Truth is, we would do a panel of blood tests to look for known drugs, known chemical substances. If it's artificial, we'll find it. If it's a naturally occurring substance, then it's a matter of looking at premortem behavior and the clues the body gives us."

"Such as?" Terry put in.

"Things like vomiting, confusion, dilated pupils, swollen tongue, rash, paralysis, a lot of things."

I tried to stop my mind from drawing images of people with dilated pupils and swollen tongues and focus instead on what that list of symptoms would show. "And David, did he have any of those signs?"

Lucky launched into an explanation of the way in which medical treatment for an unknown cause of seizures or paralysis—such as those that David suffered—can sometimes interact with poison in such a way that new and misleading symptoms arise. His mini-lecture included no small number of medical terms and sciency words and he realized soon enough that the technical talk was going over my head.

He shrugged. "Fact is, if it's a natural poison, we won't be able to identify it with any certainty. It's pure guess work."

I held back a huff of frustration. "But the rash and the pupils and the tongue," I said. "Doesn't that tell you anything?"

Lucky sighed for both of us. "That combination, with no heart failure? Could be morphine, could be atropine—"

"Atropine?" I said, my tone conveying my lack of familiarity with that term.

"Belladonna," Terry said.

Lucky nodded. "Correct. Belladonna. Grows as common and easy as hemlock."

"Hemlock," I muttered. Vague memories of my one and only college philosophy class wandered across my awareness.

"Yes, but from a medical standpoint, forget about finding proof of that one." Lucky unfolded his arms, rested his hands on the edge of the desk, and slouched his weight into his arms. "Hemlock doesn't leave a trace."

"But." I put a hand to my head as if that would help hold in all the information Lucky was providing. "How will you know what poison was used against David Rayburn?"

He shook his head. "*If* he was poisoned and *if* the poison was naturally occurring," Lucky said, "I won't."

* * *

The idea that a poison could come straight out of the garden wasn't news. I'd come across any number of warnings about common vegetation as soon as I'd adopted Friday, and the list had only grown after Fifi joined the household. What I couldn't get out of my head was the little angel statue in Rozelle's garden and the proliferation of plantings surrounding it. I had dismissed what growth I saw as nothing more than decorative ground cover, but had I been right?

Snug in the passenger seat of Tony's car, I squinted at the tiny images of poisonous plants I had used my smart phone to find. At that size, the only difference the pictures showed were in the flowers and leaves. But I was snug in the car in part because of the warmth being spread by the heater. Flowering season had long since ended and even the leaves on plants had died back or shriveled in the cold. Any one of those deadly plants could have been in Rozelle's garden. For that matter, they could very well be in mine.

I huffed and dropped my head back until it bonked against the head rest.

"Did I miss a turn?" Tony asked, hand already reaching toward the console-mounted GPS.

"You're fine," I assured him. "This is just one of those moments I wish I had a great big computer monitor in my life."

He made a little snort and grinned. "A nice-sized laptop won't be enough?"

"No, it's got to be huge or it's useless." I dropped the smart phone into the open purse at my feet.

"Are you thinking waiting-room huge or family-room huge?"

"I'm thinking home-theater enormous," I said, then laughed and put a hand to my forehead as I leaned my arm against the window ledge.

"Okay." He did a slow nod. "I'll keep that in mind."

The voice of the GPS broke into the conversation to advise us our destination would be on our left in one thousand feet.

I couldn't guess at whether he was kidding along with me or was actually filing away the preference for some-time in the future. Worse, I didn't know how to ask, or if I even should.

I tipped a chin toward the direction we were headed. "The parking lot is on the side, just before the shop."

"Got it," he said.

After a moment I said, "Thanks. I appreciate you driving me all the way out here."

His smile then was brief. "It's no trouble," he said. And though he didn't continue, the word hung in the air, silent and yet louder than the GPS voice counting down our destination.

"But . . ." I prompted.

He shook his head. "There's no *but*."

"There's a *but*," I said. "*It's no trouble but . . .*"

"No *but*, babe."

"Yes *but*, handsome."

He sighed and switched on the car's blinker. "It's no trouble *and* I'm happy to do it. How's that?"

"I don't believe you," I said.

It wasn't until he had the car parked and the engine off that he turned to me and said, "No trouble, happy to do it, happy to do anything you ask me." He leaned in and kissed me, and I had to let the matter go. There was a valid chance he hadn't meant *but* at all, and my imagining it was more a result of being in a frame of mind where I had begun to wonder if sweet old Rozelle, my grandfather's secret girlfriend, was growing poison in her garden.

Or more to the point, if not Rozelle—and my gut told me it wasn't—then who?

I waited for Tony to come around and open my door for me then we walked hand in hand the length of the short parking lot and around to the front door of the stained glass shop. As I had become accustomed to do when I was with him, I held back a bit when we neared the door, allowing him to reach it first. But instead of dropping my hand to open the door and wave me inside, he gripped my fingers even tighter and tugged me close. The kiss that followed was no simple matter, no quick touch of the lips to reassure each other we were happy together. This was serious business. This went straight from my head to my toes, with a long, lingering stop in my heart. When he pulled back, the chill of his absence was instant.

"It's no problem," he repeated. "I'm happy to do whatever you need me to because I love you. There." He nodded and reached for the door. "Now we can go inside."

Wow. And there I was worrying about what belladonna leaves looked like. Clearly I was focused in the wrong direction.

I essentially stumbled through the door and into the stained glass shop. Lost in my internal search for "I love you, too," I jumped in surprise at the *blong* of the electronic door chime. A gust of cool air followed behind me and quickly dissipated in the warmth of the shop.

"Look at this place," Tony said. "This is amazing."

I turned to find his gaze on the assortment of stained glass panels hung from the ceiling. Dragonflies on lily pads, hummingbirds and trumpet vines, roses, irises, Celtic knots, and striking geometric designs gave an indication of the variety of design to be found in glass. My gaze lingered on a vertical panel depicting a peacock, its tail feathers folded and flowing like drapes of jeweled silk. It was pieces like that, with blues and greens, teals and aquas, whose beauty helped me stick with the learning process when I first began to work with glass. The idea that someday I might be able to create something so breathtaking was enough to keep me enthused through my days of lopsided butterflies and uneven tulip petals, not to mention the unexpected challenge of cutting and soldering straight lines.

When Tony returned his attention to me, all I could do was smile. "Now you know how I got hooked," I said.

He shook his head, chin lowered beneath a slow smile. "I never would have decided learning to make it myself was a solution," he said. "That's your gift."

"Oh, please," I said, shuffling toward the front corner of the shop, where narrow, vertical wooden cubbies filled with sheets of colored glass lined the walls. "It's not a gift. Grandy would call it Irish stubbornness and I think he's right."

Tony ambled the length of one of the light tables, paralleling my own progress. "Don't sell yourself short, Georgia," he said. "You have a unique bent for finding it in yourself to do things other people would, well, leave to someone else."

I laughed a little, finally finding my balance after his proclamation. Something about being surrounded by glass helped me return to my emotional center. "Also an Irish thing," I said. "Better to do it myself than hire someone. That's how I ended up mowing the lawn every weekend."

"You mowed the lawn because you wouldn't agree to letting me do it." He rested his elbows on the wood frame of the light table and leaned in. "And you wouldn't let me do it because that would have meant I'd end up spending time with your grandfather. You weren't ready for that."

Fingers resting on a sheet of glass I had yet to pull from its cubby, I froze. "That's not—"

"It is true, even if you didn't realize it. And I'm sorry . . ." He paused, took a breath. "Sorry that I forced the issue and insisted on dinner with the family."

I slid a few sheets of glass free then spun and set them on the table. Across the lit tabletop, I met Tony's focused gaze. "Don't be ridiculous. You—"

"Georgia," he said, "I forced it, and I most likely shouldn't have but I've been getting the impression if I wait for you, I'm going to be waiting a long time."

It was a good thing I had already put the glass down. "What—what do you mean?"

The corners of his mouth twitched upward. "You're understandably reluctant to have me spend time with

your family. And you're downright gun-shy when it
comes to talking about anything that's taking place
more than a week in the future."

Something warm, heavy, and sluggish stirred deep
in my gut. Something familiar yet forgotten and unwel-
come. Something like fear. Fear of heartbreak and emptiness. Tony had me pegged. Gun-shy indeed.

I kept my eyes on my task while I separated the sheets
of glass, placing them one by one on the light table. Each
pane was clear, though not all were translucent. Subtle
designs had been incorporated into each, from the gentle
wave in the aptly named water glass to the cross-hatched
randomness of a crackle pattern. I lifted a square of
double glue chip from the stack and set it to the side.

Willing the anxiety to remain in check, I risked facing him. "Look, Tony, I'm sorry I—"

"This is my apology, not yours. As usual," he said
with a slight smile. "And I don't want you feeling guilty
or thinking there's something you've done wrong. I don't
expect you to jump into our relationship without some
sort of trepidation, okay?"

I did a little more slow nodding, trying to wrap my mind
around what he was trying to tell me so quickly following
a declaration of love. A huff marked my surrender. "Okay,
I don't understand," I said.

When I tried to look away, he angled his head to main-
tain eye contact. "I don't want you to think that because
I told you I love you that you have to say it back. Or that
I'm going to start talking moving in together and buying
expensive kitchen knives. I'm okay with waiting for you
to feel ready to . . . move . . . forward."

He kept quiet while I took it all in, while the sensor over the door chimed again and a heavyset gray-haired man wandered into the shop. "What if I make you wait a really long time?" I asked, only half kidding. "What if I never get to the point where—"

Tony lay his hand over mine. The rough skin of his palm, rather than scraping or chafing, seemed to fit like a tongue and groove above my own hand. "You'll get there. I only hope it's with me."

The gray-haired man wandered in our direction, and I straightened and slipped my hand out from beneath Tony's. "Why, um, why are we having this conversation now?" I asked. I backed away from the table. I needed to find a large sheet of plain, clear glass, but didn't want to take my eyes off Tony. He looked so earnest, and not a little bit adorable. "Wouldn't dinner be a better time to discuss these things? You know, when it's just us."

That earned me a sour smirk from the gray-haired man, but I'd been confronted by worse threats.

"Because at dinner," Tony began, "I'm going to ask you if you've given any thought to the idea of me staying in Wenwood and I thought I ought to prepare you for that ahead of time."

My fingers closed on the corner of a sheet of glass, and I learned the hard way that a chip had fallen from the pane and left a sharp edge in its place.

I pulled a hissing breath between my teeth and snatched my hand away from the glass. "Nuts," I said. Then I opened my palm to inspect its potential damage— a foolish move knowing what I already knew about glass and my propensity for cutting myself on the smallest shard. Sure enough, a streak of bright red blood had begun to spread along the pad beneath my pointer finger. A matching streak was forming on the side of my thumb at the knuckle. Just my luck.

Tony rushed around the table. He grabbed my hand and pulled my arm up over my head.

"What are you doing?" I asked, fighting for control of my arm.

"Keep it elevated," he said. He released my arm then patted down his pockets, presumably searching for a tourniquet.

"It's okay," I said. "It's just a couple of cuts." I tried to lower my arm, but Tony took hold of my elbow and forced my appendage aloft.

"I see injuries like this on the site all the time," he said.

"You see injuries from saws and power tools. This is just some jagged glass. Eleanor keeps Band-Aids up by the register."

He produced a rumpled paper napkin with a donut shop logo from his coat pocket and pressed it into my hand. "Put some pressure on it," he said.

He kept his hand firm against mine, wrapped his fingers around mine to keep the pressure. I couldn't stop the smile. Yes, I had a couple of cuts on my hand that were going to be painful for a couple of days based mostly on their locations, but certainly they were not life threatening. Yet there was Tony, leaping into action and taking care of me.

Embarrassing tears burned at the corners of my eyes. It had been a long time since I'd felt like there was someone else looking out for my well-being. You know, someone who wasn't eighty years old and biologically related to me. And the simple fact was, it felt nice. More, it felt right. And that was enough for the moment.

"You know what?" I said.

His eyes cut to mine and creased with worry. "Are you starting to feel light-headed?"

I smiled. "No. The opposite. I think, um." I paused for a breath of courage. "I think it would be good if you stayed."

Wisely, he said nothing, only kept his gaze on mine and let the slight rise of his brows ask the question.

"Yes." I nodded. "I'm sure. No guarantees I'll even like you in three weeks," I teased. "But I think it's worth finding out, don't you?"

14

The moment I popped the metal spring latch on the pet carrier, I knew I'd made a mistake. A big one. Previously stretched along the back of the living room couch like a well-worn rubber band, Friday rolled to her feet and catapulted off the couch with the speed of a cheetah presented with easy prey. Her little paws must have touched the ground as she ran but I never saw the evidence. She was across the room and up the stairs before I even swung open the door of the carrier.

"Nuts," I muttered, and let my chin fall to my chest in momentary defeat. It had been a late one the night before, and having to crawl out of bed even thirty minutes earlier than my usual waking time had felt brutal. I should have been pouring a bracing cup of coffee-to-go. Instead, I was going to have to catch the cat.

With a dramatic sigh that no one was awake to hear, I followed Friday's path through the room and up the steps. As I reached the landing, the sound of her scary sharp claws digging at a wooden door gave away her position.

"Not that bright, are you?" I asked. She was clawing to be let into my room, the room currently occupied by Mom and Ben, as if either one of them were going to let her in.

I bent at the waist, dropped my hands low, and started toward her. My plan was to scoop her up and wrestle her into the carrier. Her plan went better. She ran straight for me, her speed exceeding my reflexes. When my hands came together, all I had hold of was the end of a fluffy white tail. Before my mind processed the fact that I had, in fact, stopped her—though I was bent over with my hair in my eyes and my hands between my calves—she let out a yowl fit to peel the paper off the walls. Afraid of holding on and somehow dislocating her tail, not knowing if that was even possible, I released my grip and she was off again, down the stairs and out of sight.

I breathed out a curse then swiftly slapped my hand over my mouth. Yes, I was an adult. But my mother was on the other side of a closed door and probably asleep. The habits of a lifetime were hard to break.

As I straightened and mentally prepared to continue my pursuit of the cat, the telltale clack-scratch of Fifi pawing at the door sent new frustration through me. Catching the cat wouldn't be any easier with the dog in the mix, but I had woken her and she would have to go outside.

Thinking to avoid Fifi waking Grandy early with her demands for release, I moved to the opposite end of the hall, hand outstretched to open the door.

Before I reached it, the door swung open and Grandy stood in its frame. He tightened the belt of his classic navy blue bathrobe while Fifi bolted from her confines and came at me, body in full waggle.

I bent to rub her velvet-soft head but kept my gaze on Grandy. "Sorry," I stage-whispered. "I didn't mean to wake you."

He made no effort to keep his voice down. "I wanted to catch you before you left," he said, completely ignoring my keep-it-down hand motion. "I knew I could count on Fi to get me up in time. Do I smell coffee?"

Fifi gave me one final shove with her muzzle then barreled down the stairs. "There's fresh coffee," I confirmed. "What's on your mind?"

I had my suspicions as to why he'd set the canine alarm and none of them included Grandy rising early to tackle fallen leaves.

"I want to have a word with you."

I nodded. "I'll take Fifi out and meet you in the kitchen."

"I'll go with you. Less chance of being overheard," he said softly, then led the way down the stairs.

I followed behind, nervous knots forming in my stomach. Anything that shouldn't be overheard couldn't be good.

Grabbing Fifi's leash from its hook and my jacket from where I'd left it over the back of the living room chair, I ran through possible scenarios in my mind. My first thought had been that Grandy wanted an update on my progress in finding Rozelle, but then why the need to take the conversation outdoors? Surely we could have that conversation without using words that would give away what I was up to?

Fifi danced circles around my feet, her back end seemingly leading her front like a particularly furry hula dancer. Her tongue lolled out the side of her mouth, and as much as it sounds crazy, I would have sworn she was smiling.

I snapped her leash in place then waited while Grandy shrugged into his ancient barn jacket.

"You're going out in your slippers?" I asked, tipping my head in the direction of his feet.

"Who are you now? Your mother?" he grumbled. "Let's go."

The willingness to wander outside in one's bathrobe and slippers was a small-town mind-set that I couldn't quite wrap my head around. But the behavior seemed perfectly normal to Grandy and, to be fair, a number of our neighbors, so with Fifi leading the way to the door, we followed Grandy out and down the few porch steps.

The morning air held that clean, dry feel, almost as if Mother Nature herself had drawn in a breath in the face of the oncoming winter. I shivered a little and slipped the loop of the dog's leash over my wrist so I could close my jacket.

"So tell me." He glanced over his shoulder as we walked away from the house, as if Mom or Ben would have run into the living room and peeled back the drapes. "What have you found out? Where is Rozelle?"

Even suspecting the question was coming, having had time—however brief—to prepare an answer, still I was caught opening and closing my mouth, hoping for words.

"You must have learned something." His tone was midway between hopeful and fearful, with maybe a tiny overlay of frustration. "You were gone all day yesterday."

"I have a job, you know," I said, buying time.

"You work mornings."

We turned to stroll along the sidewalk toward the end of the street. Fallen leaves sprinkled the cement and crunched beneath our feet.

"Which is why I went yesterday, after work, to have a look around Rozelle's house."

"Let me guess. She wasn't there."

"I didn't expect her to be," I said over a sigh. "I wanted to get a look at the inside, see if there was any clue to where she might have gone."

He stopped, turned to face me. "You didn't break into her house, did you?"

Fifi, unaware the two humans behind her had stopped, kept right on rolling. The leash pulled taut and my shoulder made instant complaints. "Of course I didn't," I said. "We walked around the outside and looked in the window."

"We? Who's we? Did you drag Carrie into this?"

"She was the getaway driver." I resumed walking. When Grandy rejoined me, I said, "I went with Terry Lister," then went on to explain Terry's background in investigation.

"And were you able to learn anything at all?" Grandy asked.

"From the looks of the kitchen, she'd made a fresh batch of cookies. There were still some cooling on the rack, but on the lower half. So I'm thinking she took the cookies from the top of the rack and maybe brought them to someone."

I peered sideways at Grandy. "Was it you? Was she sneaking you cookies?"

Grandy held up both hands, palms out. "Not me. Why would you think she brought them to someone anyway? She could have eaten them herself or stored them away."

I shook my head. "If she were going to eat them herself, it would only have been a few. At least, I suspect as much. And if she were going to store them, why pack away only half and leave the rest out? The pans were still in the sink. She was taking those cookies somewhere, somewhere . . ." I paused a moment to follow my thoughts.

Somewhere she had to get to in time?

Rozelle had baked perhaps two-dozen cookies, half of which were gone. The mixing bowls were still on the counter, the baking tins in the sink. Someone whose livelihood was baking would logically have the sort of habits that made cleanup a priority. A baker wouldn't leave mixing bowls out to crust over, not unless there was a pressing reason.

"She took her car," I said, mentally dragging myself back to the present. "The police are still looking for it."

A car could be hidden anywhere, from plain sight in a driveway, plates removed, to a garage. Unless someone saw it on the road or spotted it all alone in a parking lot . . . but that was the thing, wasn't it? It would take more than just the police to find Rozelle's car. It would take all of Wenwood.

"The police," Grandy grumbled. "If I thought they'd

be of much help, I wouldn't have asked you to look into matters."

"Would you kindly remember that one of my best friends is a cop? Be nice."

The words had no sooner left my mouth than a Pace County PD squad car turned the corner at the end of the street and shortly zoomed past us. Fifi barked at the leaves the passing vehicle kicked up and blew our way, but she wasn't brave enough to try and catch any. Both Grandy and I, out of some strange-formed habit, looked behind us to see if the car would slow and stop at the house. Oddly I was surprised when the car kept on its way.

"See? Maybe they're looking for Rozelle's car right now."

He gave a snort of disbelief, tucked his hands into his pockets.

"Since you were getting so friendly with her, where do you think she might have gone? Did she ever mention her friends to you? Or family?"

It struck me anew how little I knew about Rozelle's personal life. Until I went snooping around the outside of her house, I'd never even realized she lived alone. I suppose if I had stopped to think about it, I would have concluded as much, but I never gave Rozelle much thought beyond her role in the bakery and her long-standing crush on Grandy. A little seed of guilt threatened to sprout and I squished it down. Small-town living meant I had grown accustomed to keeping up with gossip, but that didn't mean I instantly knew everything about everyone.

"She has a good friend in that assisted-living place in Newbridge," he said. "Dolores, I think she said."

"Any last name?"

"I'm quite certain she has one, but I do not know it."

It was my turn to stop and face him full on. "You asked for my help," I snapped at him. "Why not try being helpful?"

He flinched back as though I'd slapped him. He worked his jaw as though pushing back words he suddenly realized he should rethink. Finally, he nodded. "Quite right," he said. "I'm sorry. It's the tension. It's getting to me. I can't imagine a worse time to have your mother visiting with her latest beau."

I would have giggled at *beau* if I wasn't instantly swamped by sympathy. "Maybe you should spend a little more time out of the house."

"I took time off so I could be in the house, or wherever it is I can be to spend time with my family. It's not every day we can all be together. You might do well to remember that. You didn't come home at all last night," Grandy said when we turned the corner. He kept his gaze fixed firmly ahead, not sparing me a glance.

I lifted my chin and sought my grown-up voice. "I stayed at Tony's," I said.

"I presumed as much."

My breath went shallow as I waited for his next comment. I reminded myself I was, in fact, an adult and as such was capable of making my own decisions. Somehow, though, no matter how hard I focused on that fact, having left my mother asleep in the house while I went for a walk with my grandfather made it tough to shake the feeling of being a misbehaved child.

"I worry, you know," he said.

I glanced up at him. The morning stubble clung to his chin, gray and white whiskers plentiful along his jaw. "I didn't mean to make you worry," I said. "Tony and I were . . . negotiating."

He gave a half snort. "Negotiating. There's a new term for it."

I wasn't sure if the pain in my cheeks was the result of the cold or a blush. Not that Tony and I were even doing anything worth blushing over. Just the thought that my grandfather's mind went there. "We were talking. It got late. That's all."

"And what were you talking about that was so important you couldn't take a moment to call and say you'd be out until morning?"

Fifi stopped abruptly, nose pressed to the dry, dying grass at the sidewalk's edge.

"He's planning to stay in Wenwood." I said it so softly I half expected Grandy to ask me to repeat myself.

"I fail to see how that requires negotiation."

Fifi snuffled her way toward a tree.

"I don't want Tony to stay here be—" But I couldn't finish.

"Because of you," Grandy said for me. "And why not?"

I had no answer for him, any more than I'd had an answer for Tony. I didn't want to be the cause of a mistake, but even that somehow made it feel like I was giving myself far too much importance, as if Tony's choice to stay or go was based solely on me.

Grandy let out a disgruntled huff, and Fifi circled the base of the oak. "You'd prefer he go back to wherever it was he came from?"

"Asheville," I said. "And it's not that. It's if he leaves now, then . . ." I sighed.

"Then he can't break your heart six months from now."

"Sure, if you put it like that, I sound silly."

"You are silly. You truly think if you sent him off tomorrow, you'd be spared some heartache?"

"Well. I—"

"Never took you for a fool, Georgia."

I tugged Fifi back to my side. "What if it doesn't work out? We've only been together a couple of months. That's nothing to change your career plans for."

The muscles of Grandy's jaw rolled as he ground his teeth. "Oh, I wish your mother had left you here for good when you were six. You might have had a shot at growing up understanding that happiness is something you take a chance at and not expect to be a guarantee."

"Hold it. Are you telling me I should have stuck with my asshat fiancé?"

He gave a most Grandy-like harrumph. "I'm saying life is short. And Tony Himmel is a good man. Trust what your heart is telling you."

My discomfort manifested as a laugh. "I don't think my heart has much to say yet."

Grandy made a point of meeting my gaze. "That's because you can't see the look on your face when you think no one is watching, especially him. The moments you let your guard down, Georgia, that's where your truth is."

Fifi chose that moment to leave a particularly odorous clump of doggie extract on the strip of grass between the sidewalk and the road. I suppose it said something about me that I was more eager to clean up poo than I was to face what Grandy was saying. But I had yet to sort through the tumble of the emotions the previous night had left me with. And rushing to get my cat to the vet and returning to look for clues as to where Rozelle might be would have to take priority for the day.

And that was okay. For the time being at least, Tony wasn't going anywhere.

Not a spot was open in the parking lot in front of the veterinarian's office. Of course, there were only four spots to begin with so it wasn't too shocking that they were all occupied. It was, however, frustrating.

Proceeding at a crawl, I drove past the office itself and searched for an open spot along the street. The car behind me wasn't thrilled with my snail-like progress, and was less thrilled with my intention to parallel park. I got an earful of annoyed car horn as the vehicle whooshed around me, and that was the one sound that managed to eclipse the growls of protest coming from the cat carrier.

If someone had told me before I became an owner of one that cats could growl, I doubt I would have believed them. Dogs growled. In fact, Fifi's growl was something to strike fear in the hearts of pseudo-stepfathers and mailmen alike. But once my initial shock at Friday's ability to growl had passed, and I was content she would not suddenly start barking, I learned to ignore the noise and give her a wide berth.

Trapped inside a cat carrier also constituted a wide berth.

Alone on the road at last, I parked the car like a pro—city driving required a very particular skill set—then checked my side-view mirror before opening my door. I waited while an enormous land yacht of a car rolled by and wondered what it was about cars like that one that the older generation found so appealing. Smaller cars were so much more fun to drive than these great big Crown Victorias and Grand Marquises. How old does a person have to be before the fun of driving is gone?

*Grrrmmmooww.*

"Oh, hush now," I told Friday. I climbed out of the car, circled to the passenger side, and hauled out the cat carrier. Of course, the cat insisted on cowering in one corner as we walked the distance back to the vet's office, throwing off the balance of the carrier and making it seem twice as heavy.

On the walk back to the office, gaze trained on the little brick building that was my destination, I was able to see the structure that sprung like an appendage from the back of the office. A shed row extended away from the office proper. In front of its weathered shingle exterior ran a length of fencing a good eight feet high and divided into narrow sections. It reminded me of a horse barn made of chain-link fence, but of course, it was a large dog kennel, and I recalled the vet also offered boarding services. What I could see looked clean and nicely shaded. Not that I could envision ever needing to board either of my pets, I nonetheless was pleased to know I had a good option should the need arise.

Hauling a bulky carrier with a distressed cat inside, I'd worked up a bit of sweat by the time we reached the door to the office, and I was breathing heavily to boot as I skirted around an older man with a black German shepherd waiting outside. He was talking loudly into his cell phone, completely oblivious to my struggle to get the door open.

At last I slipped inside. The entire pet-owning population of Wenwood was there to greet me.

Okay, that's an exaggeration. But there wasn't a seat open for humans, and the floor was crowded with dogs of all sizes—some whining, some panting, one apparently sleeping—and the occasional small animal carrier.

I stepped my way carefully to the counter. The same bleached-blond receptionist stood behind the half wall, and I expected her to ignore my presence as she had in the past. She stunned me by looking straight at me.

"Dr. Bucherati is running behind, Miss—" She squinted down at the clipboard, squinted up at me. "Miss Kelly. She's just finishing up emergency surgery on a Rottweiler who swallowed a ball of twine. You're welcome to wait or reschedule."

I glanced around the room, at the assortment of pets and owners. "I'm only supposed to be dropping off my cat. She's due for a spay today."

She huffed out an audible breath, nostrils widening with the passage of her aggravation. "Have a seat. One of the assistants will be out to collect your cat in a few minutes."

Surely she was kidding about the seat part. Or had she completely blocked the waiting crowd from her awareness?

I shuffled away from the counter, scanned the room for a spot to wait. I knew there was no hope of a seat, but there didn't appear to be anyplace simply to stand either. Outside German shepherd man suddenly made sense—and seemed like the best idea.

I turned back to the blonde. "I'll wait outside, okay?"

She gave me a glare that told me she didn't really care where I waited, and I lugged Friday and her carrier back out through the door.

More *mrrrows* of complaint emanated from the carrier. As I set it down on the sidewalk, I peered within. Friday's big green and gold eyes, wide with distress, peered back at me. She gave another half growl, half meow, never opening her mouth. "You're creepy when you do that," I told her.

Something pushed against my thigh and I sucked in a breath when I looked down to find the black shepherd furiously sniffing at the knee on my slacks. The knee would be right where Fifi's nose reached before I put on my heels. "Um, hi there," I said. The dog exhaled with a *flumph*, while the man holding her leash continued his cell phone conversation. The sniffing recommenced, and I edged backward, away from the dog's range. Just because I'd adopted Fifi didn't mean I was comfortable with other canines. Fifi was harmless. This big black beast could bite my hand off, I just knew it. And I wasn't

entirely sure her cell phone–absorbed owner/handler
would even notice.

I backed away from the reach of the dog's leash, sliding the cat carrier with me as I went, and elected instead
to stand as still as possible, eyes on the dog, just in case.

When the door cracked opened behind me, I nearly
yelped in shock.

"Bliss?" a girl's voice called.

The shepherd turned its attention away from me, ears
pricked, tail wagging.

"Bliss?" the voice repeated.

Cell phone man interrupted his conversation to say,
"Oh. That's us. C'mon, dog."

Bliss? A dog whose jaws could crack a rock in two
was named Bliss? What kind of irony was that?

I was still mulling over what might cause someone
to look at a dog the size of a pony and call it Bliss when
the door opened again.

"Friday?" the girl's voice said this time.

"We're here," I said, reaching for the carrier at my
feet.

I grabbed the handle of the carrier at the same time
I turned for the door. Catching sight of the scrubs-clad
girl leaning out, I slowed my movement. The girl looked
familiar to me. Her dark hair, clear skin, and slight smile
lit some corner of my memory.

"Oh," she said, eyes wide, jaw semi-slack with surprise. "Oh wow, it's you. You're here."

She had a voice that sounded midway between Min-
nie Mouse and Marilyn Monroe, and she made me think
of cookies.

Realization hit. "You're Nicole," I said. "You work for Rozelle. What are you doing here?"

This was a foolish question. With Rozelle's whereabouts unknown, of course the bakery remained closed. Nicole wouldn't be there, would she? But the vet's?

Gaze downcast, she tipped her head in the direction of the waiting room. "My mom works here," she said. "She made me."

"Dr. Bucherati is your mom?"

She started to grin but couldn't seem to bring herself to go through with it. "No. My mom works the front desk. Lee? The blonde?"

"Oh." I was no stranger to being forced (aka guilted) into doing things because my mother insisted on it, but still I had no words of comfort or support.

She nodded at the carrier. "You're dropping your cat off?"

"Yeah." I hefted the carrier a little higher. "It's time for a spay."

Nicole reached to take the carrier from me, her hand trembling a bit. "I'll take her. We're a little backed up, so . . ."

"Your mom said."

She nodded, took hold of the handle on the carrier as I released it. "We'll call you when she's out of surgery and let you know how it went."

Surgery. My stomach clenched. My poor cat, my sweet kitty, was going in for surgery. Anesthesia. Knives. Little kitty heart rate monitors.

I squeezed my eyes shut. "Okay," I said, and turned to leave. "Hey wait."

Nicole paused in her backward progress through the door. Rather than looking at me in patient expectation of what I next might say or ask, she glanced nervously into the building as if she wanted to get away. Then again, she was holding an off-balance cat carrier. I understood the strain.

"When was the last time you saw Rozelle?" I asked.

Again, she looked back into the building. "What difference does it make?"

"I'm worried about her," I said. "Did she ever mention anything to you about, I don't know, any friends she might want to go see or any plans to visit out of town?"

"She wasn't real, you know, chatty, okay?"

"Well, did she give you any idea of when she planned to reopen the bakery? Any sense of whether she would need your help?"

Nicole shifted her stance so she was able to move the carrier inside. "I have to get back to work, okay? We're real busy."

Then she slipped inside, the door closing behind her. I was left on the sidewalk, wondering what it was that Nicole wasn't telling me.

13

"She knows something," I said. One hand holding my cell phone to my ear, I tugged open the top drawer of the filing cabinet in Drew's back office.

"We talked to her," Diana said. "She claims Rozelle never talked about her personal life."

"And you believed her?"

"There's no reason to doubt her," she said. "She's a kid with a part-time job. To her, Rozelle is an ancient old woman who spends her life in the bakery. She probably never had a conversation with Rozelle that wasn't about cookies. What has she got to hide?"

I sighed, pulled out a file labeled ADAMS, and pushed closed the filing cabinet drawer. Moving the phone from my left ear to my right, I said, "I don't know what she's hiding. That's the whole principle behind hiding and secrets and the reason I'm calling you professionals. Isn't this the sort of thing you guys figure out?"

She let out a little huff while in the background electronic phone ringers bleeped and chirped. "I'll look over the notes from the interview again if it will make you happy."

"It would make me ecstatic." I turned and tossed the file gently onto the table at the center of the room.

"You know I'm only doing this because you're my friend," she said.

"I know. And I appreciate it. Any progress on finding Rozelle? Any clues?"

"Georgia, believe it or not, there are parts of my job I can't talk about."

"Does that mean you have clues? Leads?"

"It's an open case."

"That means yes?"

"Before I hang up on you and get back to work," she said with a tone that closed the conversation on clues, "tell me where you and Tony went off to last night."

I paused in my grab for the list of names Drew had scrawled, his appointments for the day. "How did you know I was with Tony last night?"

A few more phones bleeped in the background before she replied, "Small town, Georgia. Really. When are you going to get used to everyone knowing your business?"

Something in her tone made me doubt her words, but I had to be careful with Diana. Her history of anger management issues meant choosing confrontations carefully. "It was dinner and a trip to the glass shop," I said, eyes scanning the list for the next file I had to pull.

"Glass shop, huh? That man's going right for your heart."

"I'll tell you all about it on Thursday," I said, distracted. The next name on the list was Carrie's. How odd.

"With details," Diana said. "And don't hold anything back."

Two steps to my right and I yanked open the R–S file drawer. "How would you know if I was holding anything back?"

"I'd know. I'm a detective, remember?"

"In training," I pointed out. "A detective in training."

"Sure. Rub it in."

"Go look at those interview files, will you?" I flipped past file after file before determining no file had been set up for Carrie. "I have to get back to work."

"I'll give you a call if I find anything."

"Thanks." I clicked off the phone then tossed it gently onto a stack of papers on the table behind me.

I crossed to the door separating the back room from Drew's office and stuck my head out. Drew was alone in the office, head bent over a legal pad, textbook at his elbow. I sidled into the office. "Drew," I said.

He startled, his whole body flinching. "Jeez, Georgia."

"Sorry," I said. "Did you forget I was here again?"

"I was focused on this case." He set down his pen, swiveled his chair so he could face me. "What do you need? And what's all over your pants?"

I glanced down at the offending spot, a clear slick on the black fabric, bits of white clinging to its edges. "Bliss," I said.

"What?"

"Dog slobber. I tried to clean it off with some paper

towel but that only made it worse." I brushed at the spot, knowing full well it wouldn't help but unable to overcome the urge to try.

"I told you that would be a problem when you adopted a bulldog."

"Actually it wasn't Fifi." I crossed to the front of his desk then dropped into one of the button-tuck leather visitor's chairs. "It was one of the other dogs at the vet this morning. I had to drop off Friday for her spay. She seems so small for surgery, though. I hate having to leave her there."

Drew reached for his pen. Using one finger, he rolled the pen back and forth, a sure sign I was losing him. Like Carrie, Drew wasn't much of a cat person.

I had just opened my mouth to ask him how long Carrie had been a client when the sound of the outer door opening reached us. Within moments two very distinct and well-known voices made me sit up straight and turn.

Carrie was the first to reach the doorway that divided the waiting room from Drew's office. "Am I interrupting?" she asked, large hot cup in hand. "Should I wait?"

Drew raised a questioning eyebrow at me. "Something you wanted to discuss first?"

I grinned. "Just wanted to know what time Carrie was expected." Then I narrowed my gaze at her. "And why."

She shuffled into the office. "Drew's going to help me with some legal agreements and contracts and whatnot. I've decided to sell the property."

"Which?" I asked. "The property you co-own with the ex?"

"It's time," she said on a sigh. "I don't want anything tying me to him anymore. I want a clean slate," she managed to say before Terry crossed the threshold behind her.

"Good morning, good morning." He marched directly to the desk and reached out a hand to Drew. "You must be Drew Able. I'm Terry Lister."

Drew stood to shake Terry's hand. "I recognize that name," he said. "You were a private investigator, weren't you? Maybe six, seven years ago?"

"That's right, I was." Terry flashed a broad smile. "Retired now," he said. "But I like to keep my hand in the game when I can."

In unison both men turned to look at me.

I glanced from one to the other. "What?" I asked.

"What are you up to now?" Drew asked.

"Working," I said.

But Terry had his own opinion on the matter. "Georgia's been helping me out with a little investigation."

"Helping *you*?" I asked.

"When Carrie mentioned she was headed this way, I bummed a ride."

Behind him, Carrie met my eye and shrugged. "Sorry," she mouthed.

Terry stood straight, shoulders back, big smile. I wasn't sure if he was proud of begging a lift with Carrie or pleased with himself for laying claim to my investigation.

I nearly shook my head to throw off the idea that I was doing any sort of investigating. I was poking around, that was all. Well, poking around and hoping for a miracle.

Smacking my palms on the arms of the chair, I pushed to my feet. "Fine then." I pointed at Terry then at the door leading into the file-filled back room. "You. That way."

I had to wave my hands a few times, shooing him into the back room, but finally he got the idea and toddled on in. "You," I said to Carrie. "You got tea for yourself but didn't bring me coffee?"

She seemed to shrink a little. "I meant to but I got distracted trying to convince Terry I wasn't coming here."

"Didn't work," I said.

"Didn't work," she agreed.

"All right. I'll go keep him busy while you talk to Drew."

She smiled her thanks and moved to take the visitor's seat.

"Georgia?" Drew said. "Do you have Miss Stanford's file?"

I gave him my best overbright smile, the kind that usually helped him remember I was his accountant-slash-office manager, not his secretary. "Sorry. You'll have to make a new one. I'll just be back here generating some invoices for you."

Pulling the door closed behind me, I fixed Terry with a glare. "Now. What's so important you had Carrie bring you over here?" I lifted my chin to indicate the spindle-back chair tucked up to the table. "Have a seat."

While Terry slid the chair from under the table then settled himself, I gathered together the files I had scattered across the table and, squaring their corners, moved them out of Terry's range of vision.

"You know, at my age, I don't do a whole lot of sleeping," he said.

I nearly asked if he thought sleeping was too much like death, but I held my tongue and waited for him to continue.

"So there I was, watching *The Bob Newhart Show*, when it hits me, I still got a friend in the department. You write down Rozelle's last name, I'll get my buddy to check into her credit card activity. We'll see if she's done any spending."

Grabbing my list of files yet to be pulled, I found the appropriate drawer on the filing cabinet and tugged. "Wouldn't the police already have done that?" I asked.

"If they're worth their salt. Question is did they, and if they did, how do we find out?" He rested his folded hands on the table and leaned forward.

Flipping through the D–F drawer in search of Durnin, using my forefinger to save my place, I kept an eye on Terry. Something in his expression gave the idea of wheels moving knowledge through his brain.

"What?" I asked. "You want me to ask my friend in the police department if Rozelle's been racking up frequent flyer miles on her Visa?"

"You gonna be part of an investigation, you gotta turn over all the stones."

My brow furrowed so hard I was afraid it might remain permanently dented. "Turn? And what . . . Wait. I'm not trying to be part of an investigation here." I pulled the Durnin file and slammed the drawer shut.

"Don't you want to find out who killed that Rayburn fella?" he asked.

"I want to find Rozelle."

He shook a finger at me. "You solve one, you solve the other. You got linked crimes here."

I leaned my hip against the table and let out a long, slow breath. "Rozelle is missing. She could be in danger where she is. She's my priority. David Rayburn isn't going to get any more dead—God forgive me—if I don't spend my time worrying about who did him in. My focus is Rozelle."

Terry took a deep breath, shoulders rising and chest expanding. Eyes locked on mine, he repeated, "You solve one, you solve the other. No way around it."

It took until midmorning before I could finally admit to myself that Terry was probably right. Not that I felt any sudden urge to know who poisoned David Rayburn but that maybe spending a little time learning about him might give me even a clue at a direction to go in my search for Rozelle.

But first things first. When I reasoned enough time had passed since my last call, I picked up my phone and dialed Diana's personal cell.

Diana wasted no time with hello. "Do you have no patience?" she asked. "I told you I'd call you after I looked at the notes."

"It's not that," I said. I yanked open the drawer beneath the coffeemaker and reviewed the single-serve options within. "I have other questions I thought you might help me with."

"Are you finally ready to hear what I think about Tony?"

"No, I— What? What do you mean, what you think about Tony? I thought you liked him." Flustered, I grabbed blindly at a single-serve pod and dropped it into the brew slot on the coffeemaker.

"I like him better than Nolan, that's for sure."

With my finger hovering above the power button, I froze. "What does that mean?"

"Oh, come on," she said. "Like you didn't know the crappiest cop mentor on the planet is not so secretly hoping your relationship with the hunky construction foreman is going to implode."

"Not really," I said. "I've been pretty occupied enjoying that relationship. Are you going to ruin it for me?"

"How could I do that?"

"You want to tell me what you really think about him. Given your profession, I can't imagine you're going to come out with anything positive."

"Have a little faith, will you?"

I gave my mug a cursory rinse before sliding it in place to capture the mystery-flavored brew. At last, I punched the power button. "If it's not something negative, why would you ask if I'm finally ready to hear your opinion?"

"Because you, my friend, are that rare person that needs to be in the right frame of mind to hear positive things about the man she's dating and to handle the encouragement to just let go and get on with it."

I was glad I had already put my easily breakable coffee mug down lest I risk dropping it. And I was annoyed by

the implication I was incapable of accepting encouragement. "What is that supposed to mean? You're not trying
to give me bad women's fiction advice, are you?"

"I'm trying to tell you he's a good guy and you should
just relax and, you know, let yourself be in love." She
slammed shut a drawer, the metallic thunk bringing back
to me memories of years in a crowded office. "My God,
did I just say that? Don't tell anyone I said that. In fact,
let's just pretend I never did. Tell me why you called."

I wanted to pursue Diana's comment about being in
love almost as much as I didn't want to, and yet neither
want mattered. For that moment at least, I had bigger—
or at least other—things to worry about.

"Okay, first question fast question. Rozelle's credit
cards. Any recent transactions? Anything in her history
to give us an idea of where she might have gone?"

"And by 'us,' you mean us the police."

"If it gives me the answer, sure, that's what I mean."

"There's no recent transactions and no prior transactions for helpful things like plane tickets or hotels. Her
last set of purchases was a large order from Bakery Supply Depot," she said, a hint of sadness in her voice.

The same sadness settled around me, as if the emotion
itself were transported along the phone lines. "She was
stocking up to reopen the bakery."

"That's our theory," Diana said.

"And that reinforces the idea that she didn't go anywhere of her own volition?"

"Not entirely. Still going to take time for all this flour
and sugar to arrive. She could have planned to take a little
vacation in the meantime. Take advantage of the fact the

bakery is closed, have a getaway without worrying about who's minding the store or having to close it for the duration."

"Plus she could have used cash for any expenses, even an airline ticket."

Diana chuckled. "You really think she had that kind of cash lying around?"

I thought of Grandy, of the various folds of cash he had stashed in unexpected places around the house. When asked, he told me he'd learned about money from his parents, who had weathered the crash of '29 and never again trusted a bank. He likened his own behavior to their wisdom and the basic common sense of not putting all one's eggs in the same basket. "It's a senior citizen thing," I said. "She would have had cash."

"I don't know, Georgia. We cleaned out my grandmother's house after she passed away and all we found were old clothes and a buttload of lace doilies."

I pulled my new cup of coffee from the tray and carried it from Drew's kitchen to the back room. "All right. So we're back to not knowing whether Rozelle left town by choice or if some sort of mishap has befallen her."

"For the record, I'm working on the mishap approach."

I sat down in the chair Terry had finally vacated when Carrie left. Propping one elbow on the table, I rested my head against my hand. "How about David Rayburn? What have you guys learned about him?"

"Well, he's not my case," Diana said. An exhale and a clatter made me picture her rolling back her chair and getting to her feet. "And I . . . don't see Webb around so I can't ask him."

"Don't you talk to one another at all? Over coffee or—"

"You say donuts and I'm hanging up."

"I was going to say or during a meeting. Give me a little credit."

"Webb and I don't spend a lot of time *chatting*," she said. "But, um . . ."

"What?"

"This sort of sucks."

I knew, then, what she was going to say, but she said it anyway.

"You want to know what Webb knows about Rayburn's death your best bet is to talk to Nolan."

16

The tail end of the lunch hour meant the tables and counter at the luncheonette were crowded with patrons whose meals were finished and whose checks were waiting to be paid. Tom was in his usual spot, nursing a cup of coffee and grappling with the crossword. I spent a few moments talking with him, confirming he and Terry had no plans for the later afternoon. When at last a table opened, I snapped it up without waiting for the dishes to be bused.

Sipping an ice water with lemon and waiting for my lunchtime appointment to arrive, I pulled out my phone and dialed the number for the vet.

I listened to the phone ring on the other end and reviewed the calculations in my head. Friday had been in their care for over five hours. If the surgery took less than half an hour, as I'd been told it would, then my cat must be recovering, right?

The woman who finally picked up the call sounded like answering the phone was the ultimate inconvenience. When I told her I was checking up on my cat and gave my name, she told me to wait while she checked and put me on hold.

While I listened to the local soft rock station playing on the vet's phone hold, in walked the man I was meeting for lunch.

He dropped his notebook on the table before he slid into the booth. "Georgia," he said.

I tapped the "End Call" icon on my phone and set the device facedown on the table. "Thanks for meeting me, Detective."

"I could hardly resist the curiosity," he said. "And I've asked you to call me by my name."

"I know." I lifted a shoulder. "But this is sort of an official kind of meeting. I thought I'd keep it professional."

"Are you going to try and sell me a stained glass night-light?"

"Not my business," I said. "Yours."

He blew a noisy breath through his nose. "That much I guessed when you called."

A pair of menus landed on the end of the table. Grace pulled an order pad from her apron pocket. "Something to drink while you decide, Detective?"

"Coffee," he said, and he lifted one of the menus to hand back. "That will be all."

"Georgia?" Grace said. "Coffee?"

"I'll stick with the water," I said. I peered at Detective Nolan as I eased the remaining menu closer to me.

"I'll get the coffee."

When Grace moved on to the next table, I opened the menu as though I intended to search for something to order, but I looked at Nolan. "Did Diana happen to mention why I wanted to talk to you?"

"Davis is in the house today," he said. "She's on paperwork. I haven't seen her."

"Let me see if I have this. I'm supposed to call you Chris instead of Detective Nolan but you're going to continue to refer to Diana as Davis?"

One side of his mouth rose in a quick grin. "It's a professional thing."

"Fine," I said. "You said you guessed it was business when I called." In the library of suppressed memories, the recollection of him inviting me to dinner stirred. Sitting opposite him, just the two of us alone—in essence—since that night, I began to wonder . . .

"So why don't you tell me what you've discovered about your missing friend, and I'll tell you what we've discovered, if I can."

I gave a half laugh. "What makes you think I've discovered anything?" Or that Diana hadn't already shared what the police know, for that matter?

"Really?" he asked. "You're going to try pretending you haven't been conducting your own personal investigation?"

I sighed. "You're right. Okay. You're right about that, but that's not what I want to talk to you about."

Grace strode to the table, plunked down a porcelain

cup—empty. She held a carafe of coffee above the cup and glared at Nolan. "You want coffee?"

The detective glanced at her. "Please."

"How bad do you want this coffee?"

"Excuse me?"

"I'm not pouring this coffee until you tell me what you're doing to find my friend," she said.

He looked to her with what I knew to be his most sincere expression. "We're doing everything we can."

Grace huffed. "That's what my niece keeps saying."

"I don't think I could tell you anything that Da— Diana hasn't already," he said around a grimace.

"That's what I was afraid of." She poured his coffee then, displeasure turning down the corners of her mouth. "What are you having, Georgia?"

"Oh." I shook my head, rattling the marbles in my brain, and lifted the menu. "I haven't looked, I—"

Nolan laid his fingers against the top of the menu and gently pushed down. "Would you mind? Could you not order until after I leave?"

"Are you serious? I asked you to meet me for lunch. I haven't eaten."

"Please. I'd appreciate it."

"I'm hungry," I said.

"Georgia."

Grace huffed, turned away. "I'll be back."

"Okay, seriously," I said. "What is the problem with me eating? I assure you I have top-notch table manners. I never even slurp my soup."

"It's a personal issue." He lifted the coffee cup straight

from the end of the table to his lips and took a gulp that had to be painfully hot.

"Of course it is, but what is it?"

He shook his head. "Personal."

That little memory in the back of my head popped up to ask what the man intended when he invited me to dinner. Would there have even been a meal involved?

But a surprising realization rolled through my mind. It didn't matter what might have been. And it didn't matter what Nolan's reasons were behind his food avoidance. They were his personal issues. I didn't need to know them.

Of course, I was still hungry.

"All right, since I need information and I'm starving, let's make this quick. What's going on with the investigation into David Rayburn's murder?"

"Death." He shook his head. "Not my case."

"According to Di— Davis, it's Webb's case and you and Webb are good friends." For all I knew, they hung around not eating together. "You're going to tell me you two cops have never discussed the case?"

Sighing, he sat back. "What do you need to know?"

"What's your theory? I mean, what is the police department's theory on why Rayburn was, um, possibly murdered?" I took several gulps of ice water. Maybe it would keep my stomach from collapsing in on itself from hunger. "Is there anything in his life, his history? Any enemies, debts?"

"Rayburn was an insurance rep for an outfit out of Connecticut. Traveled a lot, but his family have been in the county for, I don't know, four or five generations. Folks we've spoken to say he'd never admit it but it looked like he was angling for a future in local politics."

I nodded, showing I was following along. "And you think that would explain why he was involved with the group opposed to the promenade?"

"He was at the head of the group. He was in charge," Nolan said. "So I'd say, yeah, that's a fair bet."

"Wait. So you think it was just posturing? Some staged crusade to raise his popularity with the residents?"

"Raise his popularity, I doubt it. Raise his profile? That's where my money is."

"Why would you doubt the popularity angle?"

He lifted a shoulder. "Not a whole lot of folks opposed to the promenade."

This was news to me. The surprise clearly showed on my face, prompting Nolan to explain.

"You have a stretch of empty land, along the river no less, that no one's making any use of. There's no view because it's all flat, and the houses that were there predate standard insulation and central heating. Development there is a step in the right direction. You'd almost have to be crazy to oppose it."

"Or looking for personal visibility."

He nodded and pointed at me, a wordless way of showing I was catching on.

"Okay, but if that's all true, why would anyone kill—I mean—allegedly kill Rayburn? What's to gain? For that matter, what was to gain by Rayburn's protests anyway? The promenade was a done deal. The developers would be the most likely to want to silence Rayburn, but the ink was already dry on the building agreement. They had no need to keep Rayburn quiet."

"Sums it right up," Nolan said. "You can't have murder without motive and Webb can't find one."

"Then why is it still an open case? It is open, isn't it?"

He gave a sad sort of smile. "An otherwise healthy man dies suddenly after eating a specially made pastry. The coroner might have ruled the death as unexpected but most likely natural causes. Then the baker disappeared. That changed everything."

"If Rozelle hadn't vanished, Rayburn's death would have been—"

"Tragic and unexpected but in the end not suspicious." He took another deep drink of his coffee. "By the way, what did you think of him?"

"Who? Rayburn? I never met him."

"I meant our coroner."

There was no sense pretending, not with Nolan. "How did you know I met the coroner?"

He smiled, big, broad, and more than a little wolfish. "Not a lot gets by me."


"Why do I have to be the dumb one?" Terry asked. I'd lost count of the number of times he had asked this question in different variations, making me wonder if perhaps he was pulling my leg. Wouldn't it be just like a kidder to keep forgetting the answer to a question like that? But as we crossed the parking lot from my car to the glassed-in entrance of The Regency Assisted Living Complex, I got the sense there was something more going on than a poor attempt at humor or a case of rampant forgetfulness.

"Why are you so against this?" I asked. "You said this was a good plan. Why the change?"

Terry shuffled along next to me, his pace slowing with each step. "It is a good plan. It was better when you were going to get Pete to come with you."

I, too, would have liked to have Grandy along but he apparently took my advice to heart and decided to get out of the house. There was no answer when I had phoned. I turned to Terry as a backup. Still . . . "Why is it better with Pete? You're the one with experience pretending to be someone you're not, Hank."

"I have to go in there and pretend I'm looking for an old friend but can't remember her last name," he said. "They're going to mistake me for a resident. They're going to think I'm an Alzheimer's patient who wandered off."

"They're not." I slipped my arm through his, matched his reluctant pace. "They're going to believe you're my great-uncle Hank and I brought you to visit your old friend Dolores. Do you think you're the first person who's no good with names? I assure you, you are not. And I'm not talking about residents either."

I kept a constant stream of chatter going, gently tugging him along through the sliding doors, through the glass-enclosed lobby, past the ring of wheelchairs gathered in front of a big-screen television, and to the horseshoe-shaped reception desk.

"Hi there." I rested one elbow on the reception desk and held tight to Terry's arm. "Do you think you can help us?"

The short-haired brunette behind the counter peered up at me over the rims of her half glasses. "What do you need, hon?"

"My great-uncle Hank here," I said. Hey, if Terry could go around making up aliases without warning, so could I. "He's just on his way back down to Florida for the winter and wanted to stop in and say hello to an old friend."

The woman nodded and tugged a keyboard closer to her. "Uh-huh. Name?"

"Well, that's the problem," I said. "His friend's name is Dolores—they were neighbors back in the day—but he, uh"—I leaned into the counter, moving that much closer to the receptionist, and whispered loudly—"he can't remember her last name." I gave her my best innocent smile, threw in a half shrug for good measure. "Of course, I told him that shouldn't be a problem. I mean, how many women named Dolores could be living here, right?"

She tap-tapped away on the keyboard then tipped her head back so she was viewing the monitor through the bottom half of her glasses. "Uh, we have three."

I felt my jaw lower as my brows rose. "Oh. Oh. Okay. Three."

She grabbed a notepad from some hidden shelf. "I'll write them down."

"Thanks," I said. I grinned at Terry, hoping the grin looked more confident than I felt. Three women named Dolores. What were the odds?

"This is where Dolores is?" he nearly shouted.

It took me a moment to pick up his cue. "Yes, Uncle Hank. We'll see Dolores."

"Well, what are we standing around for?" he demanded.

"Hold your horses there, Pop," the receptionist said. She passed over the piece of paper on which she had written three names with a different number beside each. Sliding a log book from its spot beyond the computer monitor to directly in front of me, she said, "Just sign in for me. The elevators are past the television and to the right."

Terry picked up the list of names while I used the worst handwriting ever to write our fake names in the visitors' log.

Placing the pen back in the book's gutter, I thanked the receptionist again then made a show of turning Terry toward the elevators.

When I reasoned we were both out of eyeshot and earshot of the receptionist, I let go of Terry's arm and shrugged out of my jacket. "Okay, what is with the heat in here? Dang." It wasn't the kind of heat that made you sweat, not right away. It was the sort of heat that slowly suffocated you, dried the life out of you. The kind where any sweat that might gather on the surface of your skin instantly evaporated.

"Just wait. You'll be old one day, too." Terry punched the elevator "Up" button. "And you'll be looking for a house in Florida."

Rapid mental arithmetic allowed me to extrapolate his meaning. The older you get, the colder you get. And I was going to spend a winter in Grandy's house. Suddenly unpacking all my sweaters, wool socks, and fleece pull-overs seemed a waste of time.

We rode the elevator first to the fourth floor, where

Dolores Number One had never heard of Rozelle Schurz and nearly broke my nose slamming the door in my face. One floor down and at the opposite end of a long hallway, Dolores Number Two peered at me through the gap created by a safety chain between door and jamb.

"Who are you?" she asked.

"Um, hi, Dolores," I said. "We're friends of Rozelle Schurz's and we're looking—"

The door slammed shut.

I was, at least, prepared this time and had kept my distance from potential injury. Sighing, I turned to Terry. "Third time's the charm," I said. "Where next?"

But the clatter of the safety chain dropping announced the imminent reopening of the door.

No more than an inch shorter than I was, Dolores Number Two had short, rich red hair combed in neat waves and the smooth skin of someone who had spent their outdoor life beneath a sun hat.

"Is Rozie all right? Did something happen?" she asked.

I glanced to Terry; he swept a hand upward in a manner indicating the answer was up to me. "That's what we wanted to talk to you about," I said. I laid a hand against my heart. "I'm Georgia Kelly. I'm Pete Keene's granddaughter. Has Rozelle—"

Dolores's face lit. "You're Pete's granddaughter." She swung wide the door and stepped back to wave us inside. "Come in, come in. Oh, Rozie's told me how Pete hardly stops talking about you."

She seemed to suddenly catch sight of Terry. "Who's that?"

Prepared to make the introductions, I ended up

stepping back as Terry moved forward, smile on his face, twinkle in his eye, hand outstretched. "Terence Lister. Please call me Terry." When Dolores rested her fingers against his palm, he lifted her hand as though to kiss it, but he stopped just short and gave a half bow. "It's lovely to meet you."

Why, the charming devil.

Dolores very nearly giggled as Terry released her hand. Smile slowly fading, she closed the door and invited us to sit.

"Now then," she said. Tucking the tails of her pale pink cardigan under her, she lowered herself into a gold-and-cream-striped arm chair that sat at right angles to the gold-and-green couch on which Terry and I settled. "Tell me what happened to Rozie. Is she all right? She's not . . ."

Again I glanced to Terry, not out of any sort of deference to his age or his supposed wisdom, but because for a moment I lost my nerve. I had not an inkling how to tell this woman that her friend was missing.

Terry proved to be no help whatsoever.

Letting out a breath, I slipped my fingers behind my knees and leaned forward. "The thing of it is, no one's seen or heard from Rozelle since Saturday morning." I waited, eyes on Dolores, to be sure she wouldn't go into any sort of shock or distress. But she sat calmly. Only the shifting of her eyes belied the worry within. "We were wondering if the last time you saw her she mentioned anything about taking a trip or maybe going to visit her sister or . . ."

Dolores slowly shook her head. "She was here Friday," she said. "We go out to dinner. The early-bird special."

She gave a soft laugh. "More so Rozie doesn't have to drive back home in the dark."

"Completely understandable," Terry said. "It's tough driving at night."

"Did she maybe talk about any plans for the weekend?" I asked.

With a little grimace, she said, "What are the police doing? Are they looking for her? Why aren't they here talking to me?"

I shook my head. "I don't know why they haven't, um, gotten here yet. But they are looking, I can assure you of that."

Dolores put her elbow on the armrest of her chair. Chin resting on her hand, she slumped over a little, as though she had suffered a sharp pain to the gut. She shook her head, gaze fixed on a random spot on the carpet. "She said . . . she said she was going to go home and . . . and call Pete because he worried about her driving and wanted to know she'd gotten back safe."

"He calls it worry but it's really because he likes to give orders." I smiled, trying to bring her mood a little lighter. I imagined she'd made the call or Grandy would have mentioned if she hadn't.

"She planned to go to the luncheonette in the morning and make fresh biscuits."

"Oh, those biscuits." Terry touched the tips of his fingers to his lips. "Delicious."

"But she didn't mention anything other than that. She did say she was disappointed she wouldn't be seeing Pete, that his daughter is visiting?"

I nodded.

Dolores twisted around, straightening her spine while continuing to lean her elbow on the arm rest. "What about Rozie's sister? Does she know? Has anyone spoken to her?"

"I haven't," I said. "I wouldn't know how to contact her."

"That's something that really is best left to the police," Terry said gently. "Her sister will have questions only the police can answer. But maybe you can be part of that talk."

Quiet gripped the room as we each followed our own thoughts.

"Dolores," I said, keeping my voice quiet, matching the hush in the room. "It looked to me like Rozelle had made cookies on Saturday and took half of them . . . somewhere. Would you have any idea if that was possible? Was she in the habit of bringing anyone cookies or pastries?"

Dolores pulled in a shaky breath. She gave me a quivering smile. "She used to bring those cookies here and I had to ask her to stop. I could go through a whole dozen in one sitting."

I smiled in sympathy. "You ladies have any other friends here Rozelle might visit? Anyone still living in the neighborhood?"

She gave a half laugh. "No, just us diehards. The rest were wimps like her sister who couldn't stand the cold. I doubt Rozelle drove off to Florida just to deliver cookies."

With Terry's help, the conversation turned to more general topics. We chatted awhile longer, talking of the upcoming season, of life in an assisted-living facility, and the benefits of having a pet.

Reminded once again that I had not heard from the vet, I slipped my phone free of my purse under the guise of checking the time when in reality I was checking to see if I had missed the call. I hadn't. Nonetheless, the time proved alarming. "Goodness," I said, dropping the phone back in my bag, "we've taken up quite a bit of your time. We should be getting back."

I stood from the couch, eager to escape the room so I could call and check on Friday. "I can't thank you enough, Dolores," I said as we ambled toward the door. "You've been a big help."

"I don't see it quite that way," she said.

"Nonsense," Terry put in. "It was very kind of you to invite us into your home and answer our questions."

"Well, it's always nice to have a visitor. The days around here can be a little empty."

Getting the uncomfortable feeling I was in danger of preventing some important flirting, I hustled a little faster for the door.

"You must have a hundred friends to fill your day with," Terry said.

"Oh, if only that were so," she said, only the slightest hint of sadness weighing her words. "But everyone's so busy these days, trying to fit in so many things. Sometimes a quiet visit among friends gets pushed to the bottom of the list."

I steeled myself and dug in my purse for my car keys. Staying for a good long visit would be a kind thing to do, but I was one of those people trying to fit a million things into her day. And one of them was finding Rozelle.

"Maybe you'd like to come for a visit another time?" Dolores suggested.

"Well now, that—"

"Oh, wait now. Hold on," Dolores said. "I remember now."

I turned my back to the door, fingers clutching my key ring.

"Rozie did say something. She said she was worried about the girl who works for her. She was going to call and see if she was all right. You should try talking to her."

"To who?" I asked. "Nicole?"

"That's the name," Dolores said. "Nicole. Yes."

I shook my head. "Nicole said she hadn't heard from Rozelle since the shop closed."

Dolores raised both neatly drawn-in brows. "I tell everyone I have no use for a man in my life," she said. "Saying something doesn't make it true." Then she winked at Terry and I hurried out the door.

On our way down the hall to the elevator, I dialed the vet's office. On the other end of the line, the phone rang, rang, rang. No one picked up.

I wanted the truth from Nicole and I wanted my cat.

And nothing was going to stop me.

17

On second thought, there was a chance someone might try to stop me. The obvious approach was to stack the deck in my favor.

I dropped Terry back at Tom's house, thanked him for his help and his company, then flat-out lied and told him I was going home to put my feet up and plan for tomorrow. I hadn't reached the corner before I punched the Bluetooth button on the dashboard and commanded the car to call Diana.

"Why do you keep calling me? I told you I would call you when I had information. I just got backed up doing—"

"Paperwork, I know. Nolan told me. That's not why I'm calling," I said. I stopped the car at the street corner, having to do a little extra thinking to figure out the best route to pursue. "What are you doing right now? Are you busy?"

"I'm in the car with Nolan," she said. "We might have a lead on Rozelle's car."

Good thing I was stopped since I hit the brake harder in my excitement. "That's fantastic. Where?"

"Over in Saint Mark's," she said.

In the background, Nolan said, "Who are you talking to? This is police business, not town gossip."

"I don't gossip," she said, her muffled voice indicating she was holding the speaker away, as if I couldn't hear her anyway. "It's Georgia."

Nolan mumbled something that might have been profanity.

"Hey," I said. "Did the person who called about the car happen to mention if there was a plate of cookies in it?"

"I don't know and I'm not asking because that is seriously bizarre," Diana said. "Do you have something sane I can help you with?"

"I wanted someone to come with me to help pick up Friday at the vet," I said. With Nolan in the car, there was a chance he could overhear everything I was saying. I didn't exactly want him to know the extent of my plan.

"Well, I have police business to do, after which I'm sure I'll have to fill out a couple of dozen forms for Nolan."

There was more mumbling that no doubt involved profanity.

I didn't want to get in the middle of what was becoming a slightly strained work marriage. "All right, no worries."

"Why don't you call Carrie?"

"Carrie barely tolerates Friday."

"I can barely tolerate a lot of people but somehow I get through it," Diana said.

I chuckled, thanked her, and hit the receiver button on the dashboard to end the call.

I could call Carrie; that much was true. It was also true that Carrie and Friday were not best buds, mainly because Carrie disliked cats . . . a lot. Odds of Friday being the only cat at the vet's office were not in Carrie's favor.

Flicking on the indicator light, I pulled the car forward and into a right-hand turn. I'd have to go to the vet's office by myself. If they refused to give me my cat, I could always threaten to call my lawyer, or the police, or whatever it would take to make them see it my way.

I navigated the twists and turns away from Tom's house and opted to take the few back roads I knew to get to the center of town. Or more accurately, the few back roads I didn't really know. It took me a good fifteen minutes to realize I'd made a wrong turn somewhere and had traveled resolutely in the wrong direction.

Mentally kicking myself, I took my smart phone out of my bag and punched in the address for Carrie's store—because frankly I didn't know the exact address of the vet but I would have no problem getting there once I was on Grand Street.

Back on the road chosen by my GPS to get me to my destination, I switched on the headlights against the setting sun and thought fleetingly of calling Tony. But what could I tell him? I was going to pick up my cat from the vet. Did I really want to share with him the minutiae of my life? Was that where our relationship was? I tried to do a gut check, that thing everyone always says is the best way to make a tough decision, to be quiet and focus on your dilemma and listen to your gut. But my gut was currently busy churning over whether or not my cat was okay, over whether or not the car Diana was on her way to look at was indeed Rozelle's, and whether or not locating the car would lead to locating Rozelle. And mercy, I hoped she was all right.

With all those things on my mind, how could I expect my gut to accurately answer my concern about Tony? How could I trust that the little glowing sense of *yes* was correct?

Pushing the thoughts out of my head, I flipped the radio station over to the evening baseball game. I'd never been much of a fan, but living with Grandy was having its effect on me. Plus it was nice to be able to chat with him in the morning about last night's game. And maybe it would take my mind off all the other thoughts swirling through my head. A distraction.

By the time the coach finally pulled the pitcher who was giving away runs like it was Christmas, I had reached Grand Street. I drove its length and then some, closing in on the veterinarian's office. Meanwhile, my GPS, disturbed that I had bypassed what it thought was my destination, had begun insisting I turn left at every corner. The poor program wanted to recalculate my route in the worst way.

When I reached the vet's office, I was surprised to

find the parking lot empty and the windows dark. Closed? Had they closed for the day? Had the staff failed to set the phones to forward to the answering service? Or had someone like Lee seen my number pop up on caller ID and decided not to pick up?

I pulled the car over to the side of the road just past the building and let the engine idle while I tried to pull myself back from the brink of paranoia. No one was ignoring my calls. They had no reason to, did they? I forced myself to swallow back the belief in an anti-Georgia conspiracy. That left me with two strong emotions. First, a slowly building but nonetheless powerful fury that no one had called about Friday, no one had given me a report of how she'd handled her surgery, when I could come pick her up, just . . . anything. Second, anxiety-coated heartache. I wanted to see my cat. I wanted to know she was okay. It was all right, I told myself, if she needed to stay overnight because of whatever reason—maybe her surgery had taken place late and she was still groggy, maybe they hadn't gotten to the surgery at all and they were going to do her spay first thing in the morning so they decided to keep her overnight instead of making me come pick her up only to bring her back first thing in the morning. Many things were possible, but I had only one response to any of them: I wanted to see my cat.

I switched off the engine and flicked off the lights.

I wanted to see my cat. But the building was closed.

But I knew, because I'd seen them this morning, that there were dog runs and kennels out the back. I hadn't spotted any dogs, though. Maybe there were none. And maybe when there aren't any dogs being boarded, the fence gates weren't secure.

Maybe I really needed psychological help because even I couldn't believe what I was contemplating, and I was the one doing the contemplating.

I pulled the keys free of the ignition.

I was wearing black pants—with dog slobber on them—and my navy jacket had a hood that would cover my hair. You know, provided I felt the need to be sneaky, provided I was even serious about doing what I was considering.

I zipped up my jacket, pulled up my hood, and opened the car door.

The interior light illuminated the car and I felt like I had just sent up a flare. I practically dived out of the car, keys in hand, and slammed shut the door.

Okay, I was out of the car.

I got out of the road and stood on the sidewalk, eyes on the building, heart pounding.

One car rolled past, not going fast but not slowing down either.

I took a deep breath. Theorizing that skulking around might attract attention, I stood straight and set out, walking purposefully toward the building.

Taking a quick left a few feet before I reached the parking lot, I plunged into the carpet of fallen leaves and stray twigs littering the side of the building. Sticks stabbed at my ankles as I walked, and I both wished a motion sensor light would come on to illuminate my path and prayed no light would come on to announce my presence.

A car whooshed along the road, and I fought the urge to turn and look. I had to keep my dark-covered back to the road. I didn't really think walking around the outside of a veterinarian's office at night wearing dark clothing was a crime, but I didn't feel like having to explain myself to anyone. And guaranteed, within minutes, that "anyone" would be Detective Nolan.

I duck-walked a few feet in order to pass beneath the low-hanging branches of a tree that was already bare, and when again I could stand straight, I had reached the chain-link fencing of the dog run.

I followed its length back and away from the road, scanning the links for any spot where I might sneak inside. Turning the corner at the far end of the fence, I caught sight of a dimly lit window at the back of the vet's office. Did they leave a night-light on for the animals? The light certainly didn't seem enough to see much by. Still, I stopped and watched, tried to be patient while I stared at the window, watching for some sign of movement.

The light held steady while my toes grew colder.

Pulling in a breath of courage, I resumed my path, running my hands over the fencing, looking for a latch, a handle, anything that might give me access. I reached the cement blocking, the indoor side of the large-dog kennel, without finding a point of access to the area.

Straight ahead, though, at the back of the building, another window glowed dimly.

Night-lights, my mind insisted. The inside of the building featured night-lights. Dim, constant, night-lights.

And the beauty of them was, they might not shed much light, but it was enough for me to be able to spot the gap in the window, the gap that meant the window was partly open.

I took another deep breath, thought of Friday—her fluffy white fur, the smudge of gray at the top of her head, her sweet little purr and the peculiar chirping noise I never knew a cat could make. The poor little thing was all alone, recovering from surgery—maybe. What if she thought I had abandoned her? What if she thought I didn't love her?

Well. I'd done stupid crazy things before. What was one more?

Returning to the idea of moving with purpose, I practically stomped my way to the back of the building and up to the window.

The sill lined up with my chest. I reasoned it wouldn't be easy to use the window to gain access to the building, but it wouldn't be impossible.

Both palms against the lower edge of the window, I tried to ease the window up.

It didn't budge.

I put a little more muscle behind my effort and still the window wouldn't give. A little more muscle, and still nothing. I was beginning to get an idea of why the thing had been left open. I was beginning to suspect the damn thing was stuck.

Gritting my teeth, I took a breath, bent my knees, kept

my body rigid then slowly straightened, using the leverage of my body to force the sash to rise. Sweat popped on my brow and the wood of the window dug into my palms as I pushed. Pushed. The heels of my shoes sank into the ground, my jaw ached from gritting my teeth, and still I pushed.

At last, the window shuddered upward—a little, a little, all the way.

"I really need to get more exercise," I murmured.

Brushing my palms against each other to rub away the sting of the wood, I turned to face the window. All I needed to do now was hoist myself up over the sill and into the building. Piece of cake, right?

I laughed at my delusions of strength then clamped my hand over my mouth.

There was no way this was going to be a quick and easy entry. This was going to be hard and potentially painful. But I wanted to see my cat.

I rested my hands against the windowsill and tried to straighten my arms. My muscles shivered, twitched, and ached, and I'd only managed to lift myself off the ground by inches. Seeking the wall with my toes, I pitched myself forward, head and shoulders through the open window.

My feet scrabbled against the brick. I huffed and grunted, pressed and pushed and tugged and made any movement I could think of that might help me through the window. I whimpered, felt the sting of frustrated tears bite at my eyes. Then I felt my hips rest against the sill.

I was half in the building and half out, hanging from an open window like the incompetent thief in a bad buddy cop comedy. I knew, as I hung there, things were about to get even uglier.

One final push-pull and I tumbled through the window. Head first, shoulder catching the edge of heaven-knew-what that clattered and sent a hail of unknown objects to thump against the floor, I landed sideways on the floor, hip and elbow striking the tiling with enough force to make me gasp in pain.

Profanity followed as I curled into a momentary fetal position. "There must be a method to this," I said to myself. "Maybe acrobat training or something."

Slowly, I unfolded myself and sat up.

From the darkness of night to the semi-light of the room, my eyes adjusted rapidly, and I saw far more than the arc of the night-light plugged into the wall beneath the window should allow.

The night-light was clear glass with a small white bulb. Shame, really. There were so many lovely stained glass patterns for night-lights and yet the vet had gone with boring clear.

As I prepared to stand, pressing my hands to the floor so I could push myself up, I knocked the side of my hand against a lightweight object. I turned, looked at the clutter of individually packaged items. Reasoning they must be what I had knocked into with my shoulder, I lifted one of the little packages and brought it to the light. The size and feel of the item inside the paper made me think of a ball-point pen. Given my location, I amended my assessment to syringe, and I nodded as I accepted my medication theory. Indeed. What I held was a package

labeled ATROPINE, 1 SYRINGE, and some further information printed in a lighter tone, too faint to read.

I reached to set it back atop the steel table I thought it
may have fallen from. It wasn't until I had gathered the
other half a dozen or so boxes I had also knocked over
that the memory struck me.

Atropine. The coroner's office. Lucky Hendricks had
mentioned atropine as one of the poisons that were almost impossible to detect. And yet here was the substance, just lying around a veterinarian's office where
anyone could . . .

I froze.

No. Not just anyone. Only people who had access to
the private areas of the vet's office—or who had tumbled
in through a window—could put their hands on this substance. And of those people who had legitimate access,
one face came clearly to mind. The face of the same
person who had access to the stockroom at the bakery.

Nicole.


Unsurprisingly, my less-than-stealthy entry into the
building set a couple of yapper-type dogs into alert
mode. They may not have been protecting their home, may
not have seen an unauthorized person wandering around,
but they knew the noise I made was wrong and therefore
worthy of much high-pitched barking.

That was good news for me. It meant I could follow
the sound out of the exam room I'd landed in and find
the small animal kennels. On my way to find Friday, I

could call Diana and let her know what I'd found. She might be surprised to hear I'd talked with the coroner about poisons—and I'd have to confess to it and apologize, maybe over a glass of wine—but she was with Nolan, and according to him, he knew everything about what I'd been up to anyway.

I got to my feet and took the few steps to the door. Reaching into the pocket of my jacket, I closed my hand around my car keys. Rats. Reaching into the other pocket, I closed my hand around . . . nothing. Not even lint. Twin rats. My phone was in the cup holder of my car, acting as a GPS device.

This shouldn't have been a challenge. There were phones throughout the office. Of course, I didn't actually know Diana's number, or Nolan's for that matter. I stored those numbers in my contacts, obviating the need for memorizing them. But, I could call 911 and ask for a patch through to the precinct.

Thinking that was my best option, I lifted the receiver on the phone by the door. The numbers on the panel obligingly lit. By their glow, a strip of paper to the left became visible. It had names like RM 1, RM 2, SURGERY, RECPT. Great. A networked phone system. A little red light beside RM 2 informed me of where I was. But how did I get an outside line? Did I need one?

I punched in 911. Waited.

No further sound came from the phone.

But somewhere in the building a door slammed.

My heart leapt to my throat; my stomach sank to my knees. The odds of that door being slammed by wind, free roaming dogs, or ghosts were slim to none. I was not alone.

I sucked in a breath intended to calm me. I reasoned I might still be all right. I may not have been the only one creeping around a closed, dark veterinarian's office under cover of night, but that didn't mean the other creeper knew about me, right?

Slowly, as quietly as possible, I set the receiver back in its place. The lights winked out. And from my knees, my stomach sent a wave of dread and nausea to the rest of me.

The little red light beside RM 2 told me where I was. And told anyone else in the building the very same thing.

I loved my cat. Before that day I think I never understood the depth of my affection for her. She was sweet to have around, especially when her little warm body curled against my feet at night. She was fun to play with and made me laugh at the way she teased Fifi. I loved her a bunch and more. But I had to get the hell out of the vet's office.

Breath gone shallow, I turned around and tiptoed back to the window.

Climbing in had been one thing, and it had been hard work for a reason. From the outside, the window was slightly higher off the ground than it was from the inside. Deep foundation? Storage cellar? Didn't matter. What mattered was that rather than the window ledge being level with my chest as it was on the outside, it was now level with my navel.

I rested my hands on the sill and stuck my head out. Before my motion was complete, I knew that would be the wrong approach. It equated to diving out the window head first, which made the action a whole lot like a frying pan vs. fire choice. I would have to reverse my climb.

I pulled head and shoulders back into the room then tried to hike my leg up onto the window ledge. My hamstring shrieked in protest. The side of my shoe hit the wood. I wriggled my foot, trying to ease my leg farther up and over. My hip lodged a complaint. And the lights came on in the room.

Startled, I lost my focus on the window. My foot dropped back to the floor, and I turned, blinking against the light, hoping to face a nighttime vet tech, hoping to have explaining to do, explaining that would result in a call to the cops—a win for me either way. Lee stood in the doorway, fury writ deep on her face.

"Where do you think you're going?" she growled.

"Um. My cat," I said. "I just wanted to see my cat. You never called. I wanted to see if she was okay."

"I called your house," she said, not a hint of kindness in her voice, not a note of nice. "I left a message."

"Oh. Okay. I'll just, um—" It hit me anew that I was alone, really alone. Sure I'd had my brushes with trouble in the past, but someone had always been with me. This time, it was only me.

"You'll stay right where you are," she snarled.

I put my back to the window. "You should call the police," I said. "Have them, uh, have them come arrest me for trespassing."

She tipped her head to the left, ear over her shoulder. "Not yet," she said.

Fear felt like it opened up a hole in my belly. There was a strange sense of emptiness there, as though all the blood in my body was racing for one extremity or another.

"I should have listened to Nicole." She took a step toward me. "She warned me you were clever. Said Rozelle was always talking about how *clever* you are."

"Where is Rozelle?" I asked, all the while thinking, *Please say you don't know, please say you don't know.*

She tugged forward the handbag draped over her shoulder. Without so much as a glance, she reached inside and withdrew a slim paper package, another of its like falling to the floor. "That's no concern of yours," she said. Her voice had gone quiet, almost hollow. The overt anger that had been there when she first turned on the lights seemed to have receded. But this new tone raised goose-flesh on my skin.

She peeled the package open the way you would an elastic bandage, exposed the syringe within.

My mouth went dry and yet I swallowed hard. What was up with that? Frantic thoughts bombarded my brain, none of them making any sense, given the severity of the moment. How could I care at a time like that, that I might have forgotten to lock the car? What did it matter that I still had the hood up on my jacket and I was beginning to sweat? And why was Lee walking around with syringes in her purse anyway?

"Look," I said, backing hard against the window ledge. My fingers found the sill and I clutched it tightly. "Just

Jennifer McAndrews

tell me how my cat is and I'll go. We can forget this ever happened."

"Your cat?" She dropped the paper wrapping. It fluttered to the floor, the top layer curled backward but facing upright. "Don't worry about it."

There was something written on the paper, but I couldn't make it out without giving it my full attention. And I needed to keep that attention on the woman with the syringe.

"This was meant for Rozelle. But I'll make an exception for you. After I give you this tiny little injection, I'll make sure your cat is waiting for you in the afterlife. You just hold still."

Like that was going to happen. After she threatened both me and Friday.

She tugged the small plastic safety cap off the syringe and tossed it away. It hit the floor in the same moment she took her first step toward me.

Exam table to my right, cabinets to my left, I had limited choices for escape. I couldn't get around the demented woman walking toward me wielding a syringe of who knew what. But I wasn't keen on throwing myself out the window either.

She took another step, and I went with the only plan I could devise.

Hands gripping the windowsill, I rocked my weight backward then kicked up and out with both legs. I wanted to catch her in the chest, knock her back against the wall. One foot rose higher than the other; only that foot connected. The judder of impact, my foot against her midsection, traveled up my leg and to my hip. I knew I'd hit her hard. But not hard enough to move her far. A half step, no more.

She bared her teeth, jaw clenched, hesitated.

I considered diving out the window. If I did it right, I might hurt a shoulder or an arm. I wasn't likely to hit my head, and there was an excellent chance I'd be able to get up and run away. But I'd have to be faster than Lee.

She spread her arms and came toward me again. Again I kicked out at her, one leg lower not making contact. The other leg grazed her front—she'd not gotten as close as she had before—and as gravity and lack of muscle brought it back down, Lee took hold of my ankle and yanked.

Ripped off balance, I fell. My fingers slipped from the sill and both my elbows smacked against it as I went down.

Lee didn't let go until my lower spine hit the ground with a stab of blinding pain.

I yelled, an incoherent shriek of pain.

She fell on top of my foot, her knee pinning my lower leg to the floor.

I did my best to sit up, reach for her, try to keep her from—

"Aaaah!" I screamed anew as the needle slipped effortlessly through the thin fabric of my dress slacks and sank into my flesh. Searing hot pain exploded in my calf, and I cried out again then proceeded right on to a continuous shout of expletives and tears.

She jumped off me, pushed the hair that had fallen from its bun out of her eyes.

"Not so clever now are your six horses," she seemed to say.

My vision squeezed sideways . . . or the room did. I blinked. Slowly. Her face elongated, chin falling to mid-chest like a fun-house mirror. The fading of functional brain cells warned me what I was seeing wasn't real, but the terror began to rise within me all the same.

"Water is cat." I thought she grumbled. And then she spun away from me, spinning and spinning and spinning.

A group of men appeared in the doorway. Hundreds of them. All wearing the same coat. Shouting. Pointing fingers. Shining lights and yelling, *Freeze! Freeze! Freeze!* The echo went on forever.

My head hit the floor. My eyes closed.

I was so tired . . .

18

I always thought that when you wake up in a hospital, the first thing you're aware of are the bright lights overhead followed by the sound of a heart monitor comfortingly bleeping away at a steady pace. I have every confidence I got this idea from television.

In reality the first thing I was aware of was an increasing discomfort on the back of my hand. Wiggling my fingers only made it worse. And when I opened my eyes, all I saw, in order, was a honeycombed white blanket that I knew didn't belong to me, a white board on a yellow wall, and ceiling tiles that looked like they had coffee stains on them.

I lifted my head, lifted my hand, trying to see what the problem was. An IV. That indeed was a problem.

"There she is," someone said. The voice. I knew the voice. Grandy.

"I'll get a nurse," someone else whispered.

And then Grandy was standing beside me, one hand on a bed rail I had failed to notice, the other resting heavily on my shoulder. "How do you feel?" he asked.

"I think I feel like you look," I said. Dark circles ringed his eyes, he had wrinkles I'd swear I'd never seen before, and he was visibly in need of a shave.

"Thank God you're all right."

I wanted to touch him, to reassure him. I tried to lift my arm, the one that didn't have a needle stuck into it, but it was heavier than it should have been and . . . why couldn't I bend it?

"Careful," Grandy said. "You've got a little fracture there."

"*What?*" I gritted my teeth, girded my loins, and hoisted my arm into the air. A plaster cast reached from mid upper arm to mid forearm.

"Do you remember hitting your elbow at all?" he asked.

"Um." I had to think, needed to piece back together the last memories I had.

When they came back in a rush, I decided the heck with the pain in my hand. I smacked the mattress repeatedly. "I want to sit up. Help me sit up. Does this head lift? Make . . ."

Grandy was already untangling the control box from the bed rail. A moment later the upper half of the bed began to rise and that made me happy right up until the pain at the base of my spine asserted itself. I gasped, and Grandy dropped the control box.

"Why does that hurt?" I whimpered.

"You broke your ass," Grandy said.

I chuckled. "I didn't know that was a thing."

"The nurse will explain. There's a series of bones. Well. They'll tell you."

"Grandy," I said, lifting my head again. It was the only way I could really communicate urgency. "Rozelle. Is she okay? Did the police find—"

His smile was blissfully content. "She's fine. She's down the hall, sound asleep."

"She's here in the hospital?"

"The doctors just want to keep an eye on her. She was a little dehydrated but otherwise fine."

"The police found her? Where was she?"

"In Lee's house. In the basement," he said. He went on to explain how Lee and Nicole had kept her there, arguing over whether they should let her go and turn themselves in or dose her with the same drug they'd given to David Rayburn. Atropine. Just like Lucky had suggested, and readily available in the veterinarian's medicine closet.

"But . . . " I squinted, trying to put thoughts into words. "But why did they drug David in the first place?"

He shook his head. "If I understand it right, Lee wanted to put a permanent end to any opposition to the promenade. She had some notion she could get a job there, get herself out of debt, and put her daughter through college. She saw David Rayburn as getting in the way."

When he put it that way, I almost felt sorry for her. Almost. "What about Rozelle though?

"You know how Rozelle is." He smiled fondly. "She wanted to do something nice for Nicole because the poor kid was out of work, too. So Rozie baked her some cookies, and when she dropped them by the house, Nicole confessed everything her mother put her up to. Of course, Lee couldn't let Rozelle leave after that."

I followed along, worry and relief for Rozelle chasing circles through my mind, until my thoughts wandered back to my own troubles. There was one thing—well, probably a lot more than that but one primary thing—I didn't remember at all. "The police found Rozelle," I said. "But who found me? How . . . The last thing I remember was Lee talking gibberish."

Grandy nodded. "That would be the anesthesia she'd managed to get into you, right before the police arrived to save the day."

It hurt to furrow my brow. "But how did the police know?"

"Because," Diana said, striding into the room with a nurse on her heels. "We were watching you. Did you honestly not notice? We've been following you for days."

"You've been following me?"

"Not just me. We took turns. All of us. Nolan figured you'd stumble on to some important information sooner or later and you'd lead us to Rayburn's killer or Rozelle's kidnapper if we gave you enough space. So he gave the order and we followed."

As she spoke, the nurse wheeled a portable blood

pressure machine into place then slapped a cuff on my somewhat free arm.

"And so they broke into the vet's office? They . . ." I had climbed in through the window. How did they get in?

Diana leaned over the bed, grin on her face. "The front door was open, you dummy. It seems Lee planned on making a quick getaway after she helped herself to a few syringes of sedatives. While she was stuffing her purse, you went and climbed in a window. And the door was open the whole time."

I was remotely aware of painkillers dulling my nerve endings, and yet I had the instant sensation of feeling every muscle and bone in my body ache at the thought of clambering through that window. "And you're never going to let me live that down, are you?"

"Not a chance."

"Pressure's good," the nurse said. She released whatever control allowed the cuff to relax its grip on my arm and I felt a dull sense of blood returning to its normal flow. "How are you feeling?"

I told her I was feeling confused, beat up, and hungry.

"I'll see if we can get some food up for you. You've got a hairline fracture in your elbow and you've cracked your tailbone, so I'd avoid hard chairs for a while if I were you. The crazy woman you tangled with injected you with a pretty heavy anesthetic. It's going to take a couple of days for your system to really clear it, so you're spending the night with us here and the doctor will see you in the morning. Questions?"

I ran her request through my brain. Did I have any questions?

"You comfortable? Doctor left a scrip for a painkiller if you need one after your last wears off."

"Question," I said.

She raised her brows, expression welcoming my question.

"Is my cat okay?" I asked.

"Questions I can answer," the nurse clarified.

"Friday's fine. I spoke with Dr. Bucherati. After she got past the shock of finding out her receptionist was an alleged killer, she said the surgery was uneventful and all you have to do is make sure the fur ball doesn't go hanging off any chandeliers for a while," Diana said. She smirked at the nurse before looking back to me. "Your stepfather has her."

Oh, good grief. "He's not my stepfather," I said as the nurse murmured a "be right back" and headed out of the room.

"Your mother's husband."

"Ben. Fine. He'll have to do. I'd hate to ask Carrie to have to take her."

"Well, she couldn't anyway. She's down in the coffee shop waiting with your mom."

Dread dragged through my belly. "Mom's going to try and get Carrie on her side to convince me to move out of Wenwood the minute I'm released."

Grandy caught a curl of my hair between thumb and forefinger and tugged, the same as he had when I was young. "You stay as long as you like. Leave your mother to me."

Tears pricked the corners of my eyes. I was in the

hospital; my friends and family were there with me. And I could stay with Grandy indefinitely. Maybe it was the anesthesia aftereffect, maybe it was the pain and discomfort, maybe I had some lack of sleep going, but I was on the verge of becoming a puddle of mush.

"Did you call Carrie?" Grandy asked.

Diana shook her head. "Not yet. I thought I'd give Tony a head start."

"Tony?" I said. "He's . . . he's not here, is he?"

Diana gave me one of her oddly rare smiles. "That loser's been in the chapel for the past half hour. He swears he wasn't asleep but—"

"I wasn't asleep," Tony said.

Because all at once he was there, in the room, pushing past Diana, taking my hand in his as he slipped past Grandy to stand next to the head of the bed. He leaned over the railing and pressed a long, fervent kiss against my forehead before pulling back and locking his gaze on mine. "You okay?" he asked softly.

Ignoring the discomfort of the IV hanging from my hand, I pressed my palm against his cheek. "You're here. You're staying. I'll be fine."

Well, I could have done without the cast that was going to limit my stained glass work for the next several weeks, and heaven knew the broken tailbones were going to pose a problem with Grandy's antique and hard-as-stone furnishing, but Rozelle was safe, Friday was okay, I would heal, and most of all, best of all, I may have been a lot of things, but alone wasn't one of them.

## Also Available

# Jennifer McAndrews

## *Ill-Gotten Panes*
### A Stained-Glass Mystery

After a banking scandal loses Georgia her job and fiancé, she decides that a change of scenery will help piece her life back together. But escaping to her grandfather's house in the old-fashioned, brick-making Hudson River hamlet of Wenwood, New York, turns out to be less relaxing than she expects. Not only is the close-knit community on edge about their beloved brickworks being turned into a marina to draw in tourists, one of those most opposed to the project winds up dead—cracked over the head with a famous Wenwood brick.

Georgia wouldn't be broken up over the news except for the fact that the main suspect is the deceased's biggest adversary—her grandfather. Now, to remove the stain from her grandy's record, Georgia will have to figure out who in town was willing to kill to keep the renovation project alive, before someone else is permanently cut out of the picture...

Also in the Series
*Death Under Glass*
*A Shattering Crime*

Available wherever books are sold or
at penguin.com